Match Game

Brittany Arreguin

Cover designed by Kelsey Bowman @myblogisgreat

Editing done by:

Developmental Edits: Sarah Ward

Line and Copy Edits: Laura @hummingbird.editing

Proofreading: Cassidy Hudspeth

Formatting designed by Brittany Arreguin via Atticus

Content Warnings

This book has the following content warnings that may not be suitable for all readers: racism, sexism, physical violence, on-page sex, mental illness (anxiety, depression), alcoholism, and injury in detail.

To all the boys who have fueled my love for video games over the years, thank you for letting mediocre me play with y'all.
And to everyone who just wants to be Player 1.

Dicktionary

The following chapters include on page sexual content:

tent:

Chapter 17

Chapter 19

Chapter 28

1

Lydia

AT FIRST SNIFF, THE room reeks of cologne, making my nostrils burn.

I get it, college boys sweat and they want to mask it. But a lot of conflicting smells have made their way through the cracks in my door and are distracting me from the task at hand.

I should be complaining less. I signed the offer letter to be my alma mater's first Director of Esports, a role that anyone would assume would have lots of testosterone in the job description.

Hard to believe that ten years ago, I roamed this campus bright-eyed and excited to be independent, even if my parents were less than ten miles away. The vivid memories of being at the club fair, my eager eyes taking in the rows of tables on the lawn, not knowing where to start, happily overwhelmed that there were so many options for extracurriculars; are still ingrained in my mind to this day.

As a new student, I was drawn to the Esports Club immediately. On their table sat a computer monitor showing video game footage from some of their most popular games. One of them was this co-op game called *Hero Seek*. It was a favorite of mine because you could level up NPCs, or non-playable characters, that would defend your "point" while also finding fun legendary weapons along the way. A bit of hide and seek, and a bit of last man standing, but you never fully won until you successfully found what point was captured, and they were secretly hidden on the vast map.

I never called myself a "pro gamer." I played *Hero Seek* enough to reach level 100 each season, but there was never a time when I thought I could play in a tournament and do well enough to bring home a prize. The first *Hero Seek* World Championship was televised on the same channel that later aired a big college football game. I watched from my laptop in my college dorm room as elite teams duked it out for a chance at hundreds of thousands of dollars. Not to mention all the sponsorship opportunities that would skyrocket their net worth into the millions. But after growing up playing video games with my brother in his bedroom late enough that my parents had to pry the controllers from our hands and practically fight us to go to sleep, you could say I enjoyed gaming.

I remember walking up to the table to see three guys standing behind it, all of whom gave me a quick glance before continuing their conversation, happy to avoid speaking with me. *This is a club fair, guys! You're supposed to sell your club.* I peered down at their interest form and noticed it was full of names and emails of different male students, some of whom put their names down and stood around to make conversation with some of the club members. I thought maybe they didn't need to worry about talking to me due to all of the interest in their club. Maybe they didn't want a girl to add to that mix, which is why I folded my arms across my chest and cleared my throat to get their attention.

"Um, hi," one of the members, wearing an "LGU ESports Club" shirt, said. He not-so-subtly rolled his eyes at his fellow members when they nudged him forward to speak to me. "Welcome to LGU ESports Club. Just making sure you're aware of what table you're at."

"Yeah, believe it or not, I can read," I responded bluntly, gesturing to their tablecloth that had their logo screen printed in big, colorful letters. "I like to play video games."

He raised a brow. "Alright, cool, what games?"

"*Hero Seek.*"

His eyes widened. What did he think I was going to say? "No, what is this video game you speak of?" As if I would battle my social anxiety to approach a group of strangers and not overthink every single detail.

"Oh. What's your favorite character?"

"Esser," I replied confidently.

He perked up as if starting to slightly come around to a woman being at his club's meetings. "Huh, cool. Me too."

I softened up a bit. "Yeah? Do you normally play Support?"

"Yeah," he nodded. "I don't like being Offense. It's for some-one who likes to be in charge, and I want to bolster our defenses while someone else much better at aiming and shooting, can do better at Offense. We have a few good *Hero Seek* players here. It's not our most popular game, but the group of people who play, myself included, are a fun bunch."

"Okay, good to know, thanks." I felt a little better that it seemed like I could fit in with this group of people that shared my interests, and hopefully weren't too snooty when it came to skill set.

I talked a little more to this guy, who later introduced him-self to me as Blake Potter, VP of Marketing. After putting my name and email down, he let me know their first informational meeting was happening in a week and that he hoped he'd see me there.

That encounter spun into some of the best memories from my undergrad life. I ended up going to that meeting, and the one after that, and so on. In my last year, I was voted as the club's first female VP of Recruitment, and the club's gender ratio grew exponentially because I tried to convince other girls and non-binary people I shared classes with to join if they had any interest in playing video games of any kind.

That part of my history probably sealed the deal in being offered the position of Los Gatos University's first Director of Esports. But, in my reminiscing of the good ol' days of college esports, I receive the rude awakening that nothing really remains as it was.

My first few weeks had been busy. Before the school year started, I needed to have a recruitment game plan. The Esports Club was a great place to start, but the club had grown tenfold since I was a member in college. And we needed to fill six spots per sport. So, we held auditions to weed out the highly skilled players. I'm lucky that my brother, Landon, is a fourth-year student at LGU, and also involved with the Esports Club. He feeds me intel on who's good enough to be on the team, and because I can say he's helping me, it makes those who are on the outside looking in not have as critical of a stare.

Well, almost everyone.

When Jared, one of the coaches we hired, waltzes into the cologne-infested room with a stench of Axe to the millionth power he's got on himself, his face down and his brows slanted, I'm ready to shrink back and disappear through the wall.

Jared is one of those men I worried about when I was a student: the sexist know-it-alls who do not respect decisions or the people who make those decisions. No matter how good a woman will be at a video game, Jared doesn't care because he thinks the gaming world is only suitable for men. Men rule them all. And he refuses to acknowledge that I am technically his direct report. Sure, he can make decisions on strategy for gameplay all he wants, but he critiques me for making "dumb business decisions," and that's where I get fed up.

"We need to talk."

Really? No "Hey Lydia, can we talk?" Is it truly a need? There are a lot of wants in the world, less so needs, and us talking doesn't need to happen. If I could need anything, it's to get the hell away from here.

"Hello to you too. What do we need to talk about?"

"The monitors you bought are not curved."

I blink back at him.

"You know," he says, a little more irritable this time, "the twenty monitors we have in the game room? They're basic as fuck."

"Sheesh, watch your language," I mutter. "I'm sorry? You want us to get new monitors after we just bought these ones about a month ago?"

He groans. "Yes. And they're not great. You can get a curved monitor with a better resolution for not that much more."

"But it does cost more. And when you're talking about twenty monitors, we don't have that money in our budget to up and buy completely new monitors."

"Well, these monitors do not make the game look good. And I am bringing it up to Dr. Jones that our gaming performance will be inhibited greatly if we keep using these."

And add even more work for me if I need to figure out a fundraiser plan, which Dr. Jones will insist on if he agrees that we need to upgrade our monitors to boost our performance.

"Okay." When he gets Dr. Jones involved, there's no use fighting it. I'm stuck with having to heed everyone's demands. "I'll start thinking of a fundraiser plan."

"Great. No charity tournaments, please. The team isn't ready to play in front of an audience yet."

I wish I had a roll of duct tape that I could just rip a piece off and use it to cover his mouth. I can guarantee that the team didn't tell him any of that. He's speaking on their behalf because he doesn't want to be embarrassed if our team loses on our turf.

"Noted." At this point, I wish I could shrivel up into a ball and hide in the darkness so people and their unrealistic expectations are out of sight, out of mind. "That it?"

"For now," he shrugs. "I'm sure there's some other things that I'm blanking on right now."

"Well, feel free to send them in an email and I can take a look." And so I don't have to listen to your snooty voice berate me for how I'm not doing my job properly.

"Great." He gets up from the seat across my desk and walks out of my office. As he's making his way out of the room, I hear him shout Landon's name as they cross paths, and Landon gives a fake "Heeeey man" that I know he does on purpose to people he can't stand to tease them into thinking he's their "bro" or something.

"Jared came to see you?" he asks as approaches. He sets down a paper to-go box on my desk. I give it a puzzled look.

"Pasta," he says. "You didn't come down, so I assumed you'd be holed up in your office."

"Thank you." I take the box and open it. Landon and I meet weekly to eat lunch together. I'm surprised that my younger brother would rather dedicate a day a week to eat with me, versus his friends, but it also gives us a chance to talk about esports. "Yeah, he did. Some shit about curved monitors."

"He's an asshole," Landon notes. "It makes me upset that he's actually a good player and knows how to coach decently, or I'd get his ass out of here."

"Yeah. I wish I could fire him. But Dr. Jones cares more about the team being good than anything else. I'm just here to make sure we're getting funding and people to notice us."

"A lot of people are excited," Landon quips. He's trying to say that with a hint of airiness in his voice like there shouldn't be anything I have to worry about. A snap of my fingers, and we'll get to where my boss, Dr. Jones, the VP of Student Life, can look at everything and nod silently to himself.

"Students," I counter. It's awesome that we'll have no problem getting students to attend the events. But students don't have as much money as alumni, whom Dr. Jones wants me to find a way to woo into donating money so we can participate in tournaments, buy uniforms, and now, apparently, these curved monitors.

"I need to get the people who have a lot of money excited, too. Because if we're going to be replacing our monitors with curved ones, that's going to cost us a whopping..." I type "curved gaming monitor" into the search bar and the first one that comes up is going to run us nearly two hundred dollars. Multiply that by twenty, add tax and shipping, and I'm starting to feel beads of sweat on my forehead. "Five thousand dollars?!"

"Yeah, esports isn't cheap, unfortunately."

"No, it isn't." And I have only a finite amount of time to fundraise for a sport that people don't even believe is one. I have to do what I can to prove that esports is worth fighting for, and if I don't, I'll be kissing this dream job goodbye.

2

Griffin

THE CONTRACT FOR "BECOMING a professional hockey play-er" should have included a clause that detailed, "If [Player] has a strong skill set that may earn him a few trips to the All-Star game and worldwide recognition for said strong skill set, they will be subject to incessant internet fame in the form of direct messages, comments, and the occasional marriage proposal." It probably wouldn't have stopped me from signing a contract, but I could've trained myself to navigate this newfound fame as the NHL's current "heartthrob."

I blame all those hockey romance books. I've never read one myself, and to be honest, I'm a little weary to pick one up, but the moment those kinds of books made it onto bookshelves, everyone started making content around "cute hockey players" and someone on the Stingrays social media posted, "We heard you wanted to see cute hockey players?" with a picture of me arriving to the rink in a teal suit and gray tie.

It didn't help that some of my teammates added their comments to the photos.

> what a babe @griffinmarkey

> I'd tap that!!

> you got me pucking around for more @griffinmarkey *wink wink*

Look, I get it. We're a team, but we're also a business, and businesses need to make money. Social media helps a lot with that. I'm happy that I get to do a job that I love, and after nearly ten seasons with San Jose, I've been battered and bruised and I've adored every moment of it. Some players stay for less than a season before they get traded to another team and are forced to make a home in three different places over two years. This is my home, and I don't want to leave it.

I just wish that people would stop fawning over me like I'm a sex symbol. I'm here to play hockey and try to win enough games for us to make it to the playoffs and win a Stanley Cup.

I drive up to the arena ahead of our last preseason game and park my car next to those of a few other players in our designated parking area. In my peripheral, I can already see a few photographers waiting to snap photos of us for social media. Today, I've got my sunglasses on because I don't want my face to be pictured, and after grabbing my bag and pushing the lock button on my car, I walk towards our locker room with my gaze straight on. I hear their shutters click rapidly so they can get the perfect action shot. They want me to smile and look like I enjoy this, but my to-do list includes playing some hockey, and that's it.

I step into our locker room and place the sunglasses in my suit jacket pocket. Once they're secured, I stumble, almost landing face-first on a bench as Ross tackles me from behind.

"Well, well, well, if it isn't the NHL's Sexiest Man Alive!" He gives me a wink when I regain my footing and turn around to face him.

I give him the stink eye. "That's not a real thing, is it?"

"Oh yeah, it is. You're all over the web, bud."

Ross is probably the most social out of all of us in our close-knit circle of players who have been with the team since we got drafted. People who leave comments telling him he's hot don't phase him. He thrives on it. He tries to force me to embrace it, too, because somehow, I get all the accolades for being the sexiest man in the NHL, however the hell they measure that.

"What do they say?" I ask. A part of me can't help but be curious, even if I try to avoid social media to protect my mental health.

"Someone was reading a hockey romance, and they're like if I could cast the main character in this book, I would have to pick Griffin Markey. He's got this suaveness to him that makes me feral."

I recoil. "Someone actually described it that way? Feral? What are they, a cat?"

"It's something they say in romance novels. You know, to describe being attracted to someone."

No, I don't. My teammates should know that it's been a long time since I was attracted to someone. Maybe that's partly why I get placed on the "Sexiest Man in the NHL" list. Because I've spent my entire pro career being a bachelor. The last time I dated was in college. Meanwhile, some players who got drafted at the same time as we did, talk about raising children, and I, nearing thirty-three, think about my life's trajectory and how it's gone in a completely different direction.

"That's weird. People are weird," I tell Ross. "Let me ask you. Chris Evans, Ryan Gosling, Michael B. Jordan—do you think they like being called sexy?"

"I'm sure they love it," Ross argues. "People pay attention to them, and then they get all this money for whatever movie they star in." He starts putting his gear on, and I do the same.

"Look, man, I know where you're coming from. It's weird. For complete strangers to fantasize about you when they don't even know who you are. But you're an athlete. And hockey doesn't see the money like basketball or football does. These hockey books come out, and it's like people who have never thought about a sport before start paying attention. All you need now is a billionaire music star to start dating you, and then you'll really take off."

I chuckle. "No, thank you. If I'm going to date, which I'm not planning on for a while anyway, I'm going to be with some-one who meets me and doesn't care about who I am or what my status is. Dare I say, I'd much rather have them not know a lick about hockey. Then, at least, I can teach them."

"That sounds nice. If you encounter the heir to the Wizards of the Coast empire, let me know. That's who I want to be getting to know and hopefully getting my hands on all the rare trading cards."

Ross, myself, and another player, Micah, are all in a group that plays various trading card games once a week. We've been doing this since we were kids, and it's ironic that we've known each other for so long and found out we like the same stuff later in life. When people think about athletes, they don't necessarily think about them having nerdy hobbies, but I'm not a typical athlete, even if I might have the looks of a "sexy one."

I start lacing up my skates, the final step of assembling my uniform. "Oh, I forgot to mention, Drea set up a call with me to talk to that rep from *Hero Seek* to see if we can work out a sponsorship. Apparently, they're doing some ice expansion on their map, and on the rare chance I do post online, someone caught wind that I posted about playing *Hero Seek* on my story. Now they want me to be their spokesperson." I'm very selective when my agent comes to me with sponsored deals, but *Hero Seek* is undoubtedly my favorite video game. As part of my sponsorship, I'm guaranteed a lot of money, both in real life and in the form of in-game currency, so I said yes in a heartbeat. Give me all that lifetime battle pass.

"Hey, that's awesome!" Ross says. "Get those sponsored deals. And *Hero Seek*? I loved that game. I actually should look into getting back into it. Hey, you wanna play tonight?"

"Sure." I shrug. "Why not? I wasn't planning on going any- where else tonight."

"Yeah, some of the rookies wanted to go to a club later and asked if I would like to tag along. I flat-out told them that I don't mess with my bedtime anymore. And after a game? Don't they want to like...reflect? Show up bright and early for the next practice, eager to do better? The kids nowadays, man. They're little party animals."

I start laughing. The good ol' days. Once I was drafted, all my time was spent diving headfirst into my performance. I had fun in college, throwing ragers as a means to warm up in the New York winter. But these rookies aren't going to get better if they're partying the night away instead of evaluating their performances after a game. Especially if the next morning, they show up with a raging hangover.

Then again, with how many hours I clock on *Hero Seek*, I think I might be coming back a bit fatigued myself.

"I don't know, Ross; you're talking to the man who reached level 175 on *Destin* and single-handedly defeated their capture team with the Support down."

"God, you're such a nerd," Ross laughs. "I love it, but I'm realizing how addicted you are to this game."

"Who's addicted?" Our fellow nerd, Micah, chimes in. He occasionally plays online with us, but he is also wildly into his

D&D campaign, so he never has time to play video games with us.

"Griff," Ross says. "Did he tell you? He got approached for a deal with *Hero Seek* to be their new expansion pack spokesperson."

"Dude, no way! I loved that game as a kid. People are still playing it, huh?"

"Yeah, I think a lot of people play it," I chime in.

"I didn't know. I've been so detached from which video games are popular now. New shit's coming out, like, every day. No one talks about *Hero Seek* anymore, now that it's what? Almost ten years old?"

"Well, it won't be anymore now that Griffin's the ambassador," Ross says.

I wince at the realization that my face is truly going to be plastered on *Hero Seek* marketing all over the world. Everyone is going to see my face, smiling, with my name and "*Hero Seek* Ambassador" captioned under it. What if they require me to post about it all the time online? Am I going to feel even more overwhelmed with having to showcase a private part of my life in the public eye? That's the exact opposite of what I want: people to see me and comment with assumptions about me because I'm a nerd who just wants to play a video game every once in a while.

"You know what? I don't know if I want to be the ambassador for *Hero Seek*. That is a lot of people who will have eyes on me. I already don't like all the attention. This is just asking for more."

"What?" Ross yelps and bolts up from next to me on the bench. "Dude, this is such a cool opportunity. They could have asked anyone – a streamer, a pro gamer. Dare I say, an influencer. But they reached out to you! Won't you feel like you made a mistake if you see someone on all that promotion?"

Maybe. I might regret it, but life will move on. Someone else out there will benefit from it. Someone who loves the spotlight and doesn't mind getting more of it. I'm trying to get less.

"I mean, my life will be the same. I'll wake up, go to practice, and play games. Life will be as it is now."

"But life can be better," Micah notes. "You'll have a bunch of free *Hero Seek* shit. Maybe even a free computer setup to play as much *Hero Seek* as you want. And it'll bring in like, a ton of publicity for the Stingrays. We're already looked over in terms of popularity. No one thinks a team from San Jose, California, is going to win the Stanley Cup. Come on, man. Do it for the team."

I narrow my eyes at him. "I hate you."

But Micah is right. We haven't been a stellar team for a long time. While I've made my mark as a good hockey player, enough to be selected on the All-Star team, we've ended the last few seasons almost in last place, and this year, we may have that chance to turn it around. On game nights, the arena is full of fans who, thankfully, stick with us through it all and fill up seats in the arena. But we've started to see more pockets of empty seats, which breaks my heart. I wish they could be full and amplify the room with cheers.

"So, are you gonna do it?" Ross asks.

I peer down at my jersey, the teal blue color, and the weirdly cute but menacing stingray patched across my chest. This could be great exposure for the team, even if it feels like the scariest thing I've done in a long time. "Eh, we'll see. I still feel uneasy about everything. I don't know how you both can have hundreds of thousands of followers who like and comment and tag you in posts and not think that's completely creepy."

"It's not like they know where I live," Ross shrugs. "And if they do, they don't bother me. Also, out of the three of us, I'm definitely the one who's on their way out."

"You?! Are you thinking of retiring?"

We were all part of the same draft class ten years ago. And every year, when we somehow make it through without severe injuries so that we can do it all over again, we make a pact that if we go down, we're going to all go down together.

"Maybe? We've all been playing for a decade as of this season. Do you know how much my mother is hounding me for grandchildren?"

"No." But I can be glad my parents don't.

"Well, she is, and I've tried to tell her that it's not happening until after I retire at this point, and she's just begging me to stop playing. That, and my parents are getting old, and I don't spend nearly as much time with them as I should, even though they live like, thirty miles away."

"Tell you what," Ross nudges me. "We'll make a deal. After the game tonight, when we go home and play *Hero Seek*, we're going to play a 1v1 match. If I win, you have to take the sponsorship with *Hero Seek*. If you win, you can choose to do whatever you want. I hope that you'll change your mind and take the job, but if you decide not to, I won't stop you. But you have to agree that if I win, you will agree to do the sponsorship. You can't back down." He holds out his hand. "Agreed?"

I ponder the thought while looking at Ross's outstretched hand. At this point, if I don't take the bet, then I'm being a coward. I haven't played *Hero Seek* in a long time, but I think I can beat Ross. My defense still holds up strong, and the minions can do all the heavy lifting. I guess the worst that can happen is that I'll be subjected to more attention, and Ross will gloat that he's better at *Hero Seek* than I am, but I like a challenge. It's motivated me long enough to do a good job in hockey. Now, it's time to apply it to another facet of my life.

"Okay." I shake his hand. "You're on."

In our first preseason game against Colorado, we win in overtime. It feels good to be back in the arena, hearing fans cheer for me after I do something big or small. I skate onto the ice, cheers. I keep control of the puck, cheers. I don't score any goals, but I get an assist, and I feel pretty good after the game, even if I can't stop thinking about how every move I make is sexualized by fans.

After some final comments from Coach on our performance, I get back into the car and drive home. There are a few fans who are smart enough to know where our exit road is, and as I'm about to head out, I hear my name being yelled and see signs of things along the lines of "I Heart Griffin," which I try not to make eye contact with because I don't want to be reminded of the fame I don't want.

I reach my house in the southern part of San Jose, a two-story home that sits in a development of recently built homes. After unlocking the door, I put my bag down near the entrance, and my feline friend, Leslie, comes prancing from the kitchen to greet me. I'm not at home enough to get a dog, but I wanted a companion for the days when I was feeling lonely. Leslie is an adopted adult cat I got last year from a shelter, and she, like her namesake, Leslie Knope, is both eager and energetic. It's a good thing I got this house for her to explore because she gets quite the workout from jumping up and down the stairs.

"Hey, Les." I reach down to pet her. "Did you miss me? We won today, isn't that exciting?"

I head over to the kitchen to grab her a pouch of broth as a treat and decide to treat myself to a beer. I may get on the rookies for partying it up, but I *do* like to unwind with a nice cold one.

As I'm about to boot up the computer, I get a text from Ross.

Ross: Hey man, guess who roped me into a drink @ the club? Anyway I'm just going to be drinking this one and then I'll head home. But it'll be like an hour.

"Typical Ross," I tell Leslie while she's lapping up the savory broth I put in her bowl. "Always getting roped into something. Well, I guess this works for me. I can get some practice in."

I head up to my office and turn on the computer. It takes a while for it to do its thing and load up *Hero Seek*, but once I'm in, I'm greeted with the familiar medieval-looking logo and a pan-over of a forest-like map with castles that serve as home bases and little minions that roam around.

I don't feel like playing alone, so I decide to find a random duo player in the lobby. Quickly, the game tells me I've been paired up with someone with the username "DiddyLiddy." I chuckle when I read their name back in my head.

"DiddyLiddy, funny."

I message them to introduce myself.

> PianoPuck18: Hey DiddyLiddy! Love the name. It's fun to say ten times fast.

> DiddyLiddy: Thanks PianoPuck18! Pi-anos and pucks, huh? What's up with that?

> PianoPuck18: Grew up playing piano and hockey.

DiddyLiddy: That's a cool combo! Music & sports. Renaissance Man. Sorry, I shouldn't assume. Person!

PianoPuck18: You're correct. Yes, I think I am a Renaissance Man of sorts. I play less piano now, but I still enjoy it. Any special meaning behind your name?

DiddyLiddy: Nothing special other than it rhymes. My parents' nickname for me growing up was Liddy.

PianoPuck18: That's cool. So, you play Hero Seek a lot?

DiddyLiddy: Not as much as I used to. With the adult job and all that.

PianoPuck18: Ah yes, the good ol' adult job. That's why I don't play much, either. But I'm excited to get back into it. Just promise me you won't get too upset if I fuck it up for us.

DiddyLiddy: Absolutely not. I have seen some toxic people in this game, and I wouldn't do that to another person. I'll cheer you on for all your accomplishments. Yay!! You didn't trip over that stick!!

PianoPuck18: lol thanks. Oh, I forgot to ask. Support or Offense?

DiddyLiddy: Support, if that's okay. My main's Esser.

PianoPuck18: Works for me. I play Offense usually anyway. My main's Alliana.

DiddyLiddy: Ah, the sharpshooter Angel. Good choice. Well, good luck to us, right?

PianoPuck18: Yup!

I wonder if I should ask Liddy to turn on voice chat. I know she's a complete stranger, but I'll do a lot better if I can speak commands or instructions to someone instead of typing. I don't know what it is, but something about Liddy feels really inviting. I don't know anything about her except her username rhymes in a fun way, but she seems funny and chill. The odds of me ever meeting her are what? In the billions? Why not just ask?

PianoPuck18: Hey, weird question. Do you mind if we used VC? I think it'll be better for us to tell each other commands if we can speak instead of using the chat.

DiddyLiddy: Sure, why not? Let's do it.

I take a deep breath and press the "Join Party Voice Chat" button.

"Hey," I say. "How's it going?"

3

Lydia

♥ 🎮 ⬮

"Uh, it's fine. Good." I stammer. I'm reeling over how smooth and silky PianoPuck18's voice is. It makes my insides tingle in a sensual way that I've never experienced before. I clench in my chair at how much of this is affecting me right now. *You don't even know his real name, Lydia. What if he's a serial killer?*

"Do you have your character ready?"

"Yeah, as ready as I'll ever be," I laugh. "Just warning you, I don't play as much as I used to. My rank this season is abysmal. Work has been extra stressful this past month, and, to be honest, I only logged on today because I was so fed up with work that I needed to play."

Typically, I play with Kristian, but when I asked her to play last minute, I got turned down because she was on a date. The only reason I even logged on was that I needed to get my mind off of Jared and how he made me feel like absolute trash. To not think about how badly I'm doing my job. The thought occurred to play solo, but I don't love it because I don't have a strong grip on Offense. I guess deciding to play co-op worked out because PianoPuck has been nice to me so far. He already reassured me that he wouldn't be toxic because of my performance. I'll still feel bad if I make a mistake and cost us the game, but it seems like he's in a similar situation as me: playing just for fun, just to get our minds off things.

"That's okay. I am not someone who is going to be yelling at the computer if we lose. I just enjoy the game."

PianoPuck selects his go-to player, Alliana, and we both hit the "ready up" button. The game loads for a beat, and we are teleported to the Forbidden Woods.

"Tough map to start with," PianoPuck notes.

"Yeah." The Forbidden Woods is graded as a "Super Hard" map among the randomly selected ones in the game. Besides the defenses that each player brings with them to fortify their base, the map is splattered with in-game NPCs that are randomly deployed to scare the players as they make it to the other team's area. And they're strong. I would feel so ashamed if I died to a freaking NPC instead of a player on the opposing team.

"I hate those little goblins that spawn randomly on this map. They move so quickly that it's hard to kill them. And they multiply? Like, give us a break!"

"Right?" PianoPuck chuckles. His deep laugh is sensual, sounding smooth, almost butter-like in my headphones. I inhale a sharp breath, picturing a face. Maybe he's gruff like Pedro

Pascal. And then the sparks go off in my nerves, starting from my fingers down my spine and ending up down there, where heat begins to pool. From what? A freaking laugh?

"We'll be okay though. You have level 25 minions. And a level 10 rifle? Are you sure you haven't played this game in a while?"

"Okay, to be fair, I did play for five hours straight one day and compromised my sleep schedule, but would you believe me if I told you that I used to regularly get Level 200 every season? And those minions were like Level 55."

"Shit," he says. "That is really impressive. When was that?"

"I was part of the Esports Club in college. So, as part of being in the club, we'd participate in tournaments with other schools. We weren't, like, winning championships every single time, but we did get one tournament win, and we each took home, like, five hundred dollars, which was the best thing that could've happened to me as a broke college student."

"That's really cool," he says as we reach our first wave of demon goblins.

"Shit," he mutters. His character is shooting arrows as fast as they can reload, and it's taking a few arrows to obliterate each one. "These goblins are not making it easy."

"Here." I try to deploy some more of my minions when they're ready. I hit one of the keys so they could use one of their special powers to do more damage. "That...should...do the trick," I say, feverishly clicking my mouse to send each one to his rescue.

They successfully obliterate the goblins, and we sigh in relief.

"Good job," he says. "Those minions of yours really helped me out there."

"I'm glad." I feel my face start to get warm. I know that he's not complimenting me directly, but I feel proud of myself. I don't know the last time that happened. With all the people wanting to tell me I'm not doing the right thing at work, this small thing means so much.

"I kind of wish I participated in some sort of esports club in college. But I feel like it was so new that people didn't really know how big it would become. Like, did you know people are being recruited on scholarship to play esports?"

I want to be like, "Of course I do!" because it's something I'm actively working towards. But if I tell him that I work in esports, will he think the same way as the other men I work with think? I'm starting to get comfortable with this guy, even if I barely know anything about him, and I don't want that to sour if he shares that "esports is a man's world and women don't belong" bullshit mindset.

So instead, I softly utter a "yes" and try to act all nonplussed about the idea. "Maybe that would've gotten me to actually work hard on something if it meant I could get a scholarship for it. I like the idea, though. Give some more money to esports and less to those stuck-up, self-entitled athletes."

He lets out a forced laugh, and I wonder if I struck a nerve. Was he an athlete in college? Shit, I might've soured this myself.

"Sorry," I blurt. "That might have been offensive. I don't know if you were an athlete in college. I was just talking about the athletes at my school. You probably went to a different school than I did, so you probably weren't a self-entitled athlete. I mean, you definitely don't radiate those vibes—"

"Liddy," he says, stopping me, and my eyes widen, staring at the screen. No one calls me that anymore, and when I hear it coming from his mouth, it makes my heart beat faster. "It's okay. I'm not offended. I was an athlete in college and definitely fooled around a little bit because I thought I was the king of the university. But I'm happy if money gets put into esports if it means that there are more chances for people to show off their skills to an audience, same as any other athlete would."

"Okay," I sigh, relieved. "I don't think you could ever be a mean person. If you used to be, well, you've definitely changed for the better."

"Thank you," he says. "My job requires me to be in front of people a lot, which can be really touchy for someone who's grown up being an introverted gamer his whole life. So I try to stay in people's good graces whenever I'm talking because...if I don't, then it'll be tough to bounce back professionally."

"That sounds rough," I tell him. "But I get it." What's the harm in telling him anyway? Especially now that I accidentally offended him by shitting on athletes, which he was in college. "My job is actually in collegiate esports. I'm the director of a brand new esports league back at my alma mater, and I love it, but my colleagues want wins. In big tournaments. And I have to put on a happy face about everything because it's such a foreign concept to these older people who are alumni that we're trying to get money from. They ask questions like, 'Is this really a sport?' and say things like, 'Kids shouldn't be spending so much time on their computers.' I wish I could throw a computer at their face." I mutter, gripping my mouse so hard it almost breaks in half.

He chuckles. "But you can't because..."

"Then they're never going to give money to our program. And I'd probably lose my job."

"Well, that's really cool. Being the first director, that is," he says. "You mentioned that you started playing tonight because your job was stressful. Was there something specific that was going on that triggered the stress?"

I feel a warmth flood over me, like invisible arms wrapping around my torso. All because someone's kind enough to ask how I'm feeling. It's wild how much hearing someone's voice is pushing all the red flags out of my mind. So what if I don't know what he looks like or if he lives in another country? I'm ready to spill my life story to this guy.

"There's one esports coach who might have a shot at bringing us a title, but God, he is so entitled. He always condescends to me for everything I do. He does not believe that I can do my job well. Maybe because I'm a woman. Maybe because I'm not a pro player. He's never said. But he doesn't want to accept that I've directed a team before and know what needs to be done operationally. He doesn't see me in meetings with these alumni and the freaking president to make people aware of who we are. It's a lot of give for very little take."

"I'm sorry to hear that," he says before yelling that there's a minion from the opposing team sprinting right towards us.

"Die minion!" He screams, and I laugh to myself.

"Do you want help?"

"No," he says through gritted teeth. "I am...a big...strong angel. I don't need no support. This time, at least. I think we're approaching their base."

I hover my mouse to zoom out the map in the corner of the game. We're more than halfway through the map. The other team has tried to get forward, but they keep getting stopped by the barrier I've made that has a griffin defending it and successfully killing them and so they've had to keep starting back at the beginning each time.

"We're close," I tell him. "And they keep getting caught up by the griffin I put near our small tower. They're not even close to our home tower."

"Gotta love those griffins," he says. "I don't see any other minions. I'm guessing we're safe, but I think they might have fortified their home tower more, which makes getting there a piece of cake."

"Well, I still have a lot of heals. So I think we'll be fine." I reassure him. Anything can happen, like we might completely fall prey to their strong defense, but when I taste victory on my lips, I feel a rush where my senses become heightened, and I feel almost invincible.

"You can't beat me fuckers!" I shout into my monitor like these computer-generated monsters can actually understand and hear my attempt at a menacing voice.

"I think we will be, too," PianoPuck replies to my earlier comment. "I haven't played this game a lot, let alone with someone I don't know, but I'm having a fun time."

"I am, too." I'm having so much fun that I want to play with him again. I don't want to go to sleep without knowing more about the man than just his username.

We approach the opposing team's other tower, and I start to survey the area. As I had predicted, the entire area is fortified with strong Level 10 minions. We're not in range yet for them to come attack us, so it gives us a moment to think about our game plan.

"Okay, we made it. What do you think we should do?"

"Do you think we should split up?" He asks.

I gasp and cover my mouth. I don't want to think about leaving his side, even though this is just a game, and I barely know him. It aches for a moment; I've been having such a good time with this man without even knowing what he looks like or how he acts in real life. I'd even go on a date with him based on this interaction alone. But maybe he's nice in the game and a jerk in real life. This is all truly just a simulation, and I want to stay in the bubble so I don't need to face the reality that we'll probably never meet in person.

"Uh, I don't know," I say, hoping to mask my reaction.

"Maybe it'll be better if we do? I can try and storm the tower, and you can take care of the minions. Of course, if you need help, then let me know and I'll come and give you a hand. The last thing I want to do is leave you hanging."

"Sure," I croak. The ticking clock stares me in the face, and the excitement I'm trying to feel because we're so close to winning is conflicting with the sadness that we're so close to not playing with one another anymore.

"You got this," he tells me. "I believe in you!"

"Thanks," I tell him. That belief might just be enough to get me through these pesky minions.

We split up, and I start moving forward, towards the swarm of minions. I try not to get overwhelmed because there are so many of them. My tactic is to go slowly, killing each of them one by one and taking breaks to heal if I need to, but I can't let them crowd me. If I try to take a little health off each of them, one at a time, then they'll all simultaneously die.

I start taking one, two, three down, and I feel good about my progress. I don't need to heal up because these minions are more on the weak side.

"Hey, Liddy," PianoPuck calls for me over the mic. "I need your help around the tower. The other team is here and they've got some strong weapons. I can't do this on my own. I'm starting to lose health."

"Okay, I'm coming right now. Hang on." I break away from the minions and rush to the tower, where I see PianoPuck shooting arrows, fighting for his life against the two characters on the opposing team. He's got a shield around him that is temporarily doing its job, but his health bar is at about 50%.

"Shit," I mutter. The players themselves are arguably the toughest part of the match we've faced tonight. Their Offense is a rifle shooter named Artemis, who is shooting bullets a mile a minute, and their Support is dropping bombs around us. I'm spending more time avoiding them than I should be.

"I have my ultimate. If we can get them together, it'll do a lot of damage. Have you used yours yet?"

"No," he tells me. "But it seems like now is as good a time as any to use it."

"We just need to get them in one place, or else it's not going to work. Do you think you can lure them to us?"

"Well, considering they want to kill us, I don't think getting them in one spot together is going to be a problem."

"I just want to make sure!" I tell him. "Victory is so close, I can taste it." I wonder if his lips taste as sweet as the victory we're about to have. "We've come so far. We can't blow it now."

"You're right. Alright, I'm heading near them. My shield's down and everything. I don't know if they can tell that we're trying to lure them over, but they are coming towards me. Now, get over here, and we can use our alt. Hurry, the Artemis one is about to reload."

I rush over and countdown for us to deploy our ultimate move. Once I yell, "One!" I press the key and together, our powers successfully drain their health. All that PianoPuck needs to do is shoot a few arrows, and we successfully get the other team down so that I can run over to their tower and shoot it down.

The "Victory" banner lights up on the screen, and I squeal in delight.

"Oh my god, we did it! We did it! We won!"

"Mostly thanks to you," he notes when our stats come up, and it shows that I made a whopping ten out of thirteen kills. "You basically carried us the entire game."

"Oh." I feel bad that I had done so much of the work. I mean, he played, too, but I definitely took charge of a few of those monsters. Maybe I should have shared more of the work instead of hogging it all to myself.

"Sorry," I add. "I didn't mean to hog all the kills. Hopefully, you'll still get a lot of XP to help you level up?"

"Hey, why are you apologizing? You did an amazing job. You should be proud of how good you did."

"I just feel bad that I might've not allowed you to level up and get some more XP. I just want you to feel like you had fun."

His voice is light. "This is the most fun I've had playing a game in a long time. So, thank you."

Alright, here it goes. We're going to do a scary thing, and we're going to ask if he wants to play again. It's not a date. It's simply making plans to play games. As two...platonic people that play games together.

"Thank you," I tell him. "I had a lot of fun too. I'd love to do this again. Would you mind if we shared each other's Discords? So we can chat and plan another time to play?"

"Uhhh..."

Shit, I went too far. "Sorry, I know it's a lot to ask. But I don't want this to be a one-and-done kind of gameplay."

"No, no. Me neither. I just, I have a busy schedule. So, my chances to play can be pretty slim. But it seems I might be free this...Saturday? If you are?"

I respond so fast. "I am. Same time?"

"Yeah, that sounds good. My Discord username is the same as here. I'll talk to you later?"

"Sounds good. Have a good night, Puck."

"Puck?"

"You know, like your name. And the character from Midsummer Night's Dream. If you know your Shakespeare."

"Barely. But yeah, I kind of remember Puck. I like that. Night, Liddy."

He logs off from voice chat, and I look at my phone. It's way past my bedtime, but I'm too giddy to go to sleep. I feel like I'm in grade school again, like those times when you get a valentine from a crush, even though they're forced to give it to everyone in the class. It's a small thing, but it puts a grin on my face. I've made plans to meet someone, even if it's just online and through voice chat. A minuscule thing that is making me fall into a deep hole, and I'm scared I won't be able to find a way out.

4

Griffin

"AHEM, EARTH TO GRIFFIN," Micah says while waving a hand in front of my face. "What's up with you? You keep turning over the puck!"

"Sorry," I respond, blinking rapidly to try and escape the daze I've found myself stuck in. It's just practice, but that's not an excuse. While I should be fixating on controlling the puck, a voice causes my mind to wander elsewhere. A sweet, soft voice that's repeating sweet nothings over and over again.

T-minus two days until I'll be playing with Liddy again. Besides her being amazing at *Hero Seek* and getting us to a victory that I don't even think Ross could have helped me achieve, she seems super down-to-earth and easy to talk to. Her voice, slightly high-pitched and bubbly, was music to my ears.

While my head fills with giddy thoughts about spending my night playing with her, I also realize that everything that we do has to remain online, which is difficult when I know that if I met her in real life, I'd absolutely enjoy every minute I got to spend with her. But we're from different worlds. She's an esports director somewhere, living a somewhat normal life. If she gets roped into the grandeur of celebrity life that comes with dating me, I would never forgive myself for getting her into something that she didn't know about because we met in a nontraditional way. All online, all without seeing each other's faces. It kind of feels like a spin on "Love is Blind," except we were battling monsters at the same time.

We do a few more drills, and I end practice more exhausted than usual. The team quickly skates off the ice, and I try to blend in with them, avoiding any eye contact with Coach, who I know is going to tell me my performance sucks in three, two, one...

"Markey!" he yells after me. I twirl around and act like I'm surprised at hearing him call out to me.

"Yes? What's up, Coach?"

"What's up?" he mocks my tone. "What do you think is up, Markey? You played like absolute shit today."

I bite my lip. "I'm sorry, Coach. A lot's going through my mind right now."

"Like what?"

My mouth forms a straight line. I've never really beefed with Coach. I mean, for the past ten years, I think he's done a pretty decent job of coaching the team. He gives us pointers on how to work with one another, and he doesn't get too hard on us when we have those bad days. His mentality is, "Keep trying hard, and we'll get them next time." But he's not too enthused with me and my lackluster performance today.

"Just...stuff going through my head. I don't know how to explain it."

He pinches the bridge of his nose and keeps his eyes shut. "Look, Markey. I know we all have hard days, and I'm not saying your feelings aren't valid, but we have a game tomorrow against LA that I want us to win. We'll only be that much closer to playoff contention if we do. And you're our All-Star. Your team needs you to make those goals so we have something to celebrate tomorrow."

"Yes, Coach," I sigh. Despite the internal monsters that I've been battling, I try to have a "team-first" attitude when it comes to work. It would be selfish of me to mope around all the time, focus solely on the challenges in my own life, and expect others to be dancing through life while experiencing the same thing.

"You're a good player, Markey. And captain. These rookies look up to you. Show them that love of hockey you had when you first signed on to play for me."

"Sure thing, Coach." I will myself to smile. Picture it: the young, eager Griffin Markey had just moved to California from New Jersey at the ripe age of twenty-two and was over the moon that he got drafted to play for an NHL team. I could have gone in two different directions in college as a performing arts major-slash-athlete. I could have enjoyed my time playing college sports and then chosen to spend my adult life as a normal person. Which, I guess, with my major, would have been tricky anyway. I was a great piano player in college and initially set my sights on playing in a Broadway orchestra. But that kind of went along the wayside when my coach in college told me that teams were very interested in me. I was one of the top shooters in the NCAA, and while not every NHL player comes from a college team, scouts had their eye on me as early as my second year. I think about how I haven't touched a piano to play my own music since my senior recital. People don't look at me and think about my musical gifts; all they really think about is my hockey performance. I step back into the locker room, where my teammates are packing up their things before they leave. Tonight's our games night, so Micah and I are heading to Ross's to play card games and possibly other things if one of us can convince the others. Micah always tries to get us on a "mini-campaign," but those always end up lasting eight hours.

"Hey," Micah says, looking over into my locker from his. "You were talking to Coach?"

"Yeah," I say, taking off my gear to put away. My body always feels so free after removing all the layers of protective armor that we have to put on.

"Did he bring up your lackluster performance today?"

I groan. "Is it really that big of a crime for me to have *one* bad day?" Micah rolls his eyes at my dramatics.

"Yes, he said I was off my game and wanted to get to the bottom of why my head wasn't in it."

"Did you tell him anything?"

I shake my head. "I mean, I just said I had a lot on my mind. What, am I supposed to say, 'Hey Coach! Have you heard of this thing called anxiety? Well, I get it sometimes, womp womp! Guess my performance at practice is going to suck today.' No, I didn't tell him because he'll tell me that I need to get over it and focus on the game."

"Oh. Sorry, man. I know it's been a tough few days for you. I didn't mean to yell at you at practice today."

"It's fine." I know he didn't do it to cause harm. Micah never shows any outward feelings, so I don't really know what makes him angry or anxious. Besides his infatuation with role-playing games, I don't really know anything else about his life. I think he likes it that way. Wish I knew how to do the same.

"I, uh, am not the greatest with therapy or giving advice, but you know you can tell us when something is bothering you. Ross can give you his whole spiel about therapy and all that while I'll nod like I agree."

I laugh and reach to give Micah a pat on the shoulder. It's rare in sports to find three players who have remained a part of the same team for so long. Maybe it's fate, which means that we have to stick together and that I should be telling my friends what's going on in my life, but I can't even make sense of it myself. I sure as hell don't know how to talk about it with them.

"Thanks, man. I'll tell you when I can. There's just...a lot going on."

"You're still coming to games night, right? That might help cheer you up."

"Yeah, I wouldn't miss it. Do you need me to bring any-thing? Drinks? Snacks?"

"I don't think so? Ross already has so much stocked in that damn fridge of his."

"I have what?" Ross chimes in. He's got his bag slung over his shoulder, already rearing to go.

"A stocked fridge for games night, right?"

"Pfft, of course I do. It's like you don't even know me. And I got something special planned tonight. When y'all see it, your minds are going to be blown."

"Sure, man," I tell him, feigning excitement. "Well, we bet-ter get a move on then to see what this special surprise is."

"Uhhh, gimme like ten minutes to get ahead of y'all. I gotta get the oven hot." Ross turns around and starts speed-walking out of the locker room and to his car.

"Watch the surprise be frozen pizza," Micah says.

"Hey, I'm not going to say no to some frozen pizzas."

We finish packing up, and I figure I might as well shower before heading over. I could shower at home, but I live a bit farther from Ross, so I head for the locker room showers and take my change of clothes with me.

I'm about to undress when my phone vibrates with a no-tification. I check where it's coming from, and to my surprise, it's a Discord notification.

DiddyLiddy: Finished a few games and my minions are Level 15! And I started training a few tanks that I think will be huge assists.

I chuckle softly to myself. I love how excited she's become about playing. It makes me want to abandon everything and play with her tonight instead. I don't back out from games nights though, and any excuse I could give to the guys will be BS because they literally saw me seconds ago.

> PianoPuck18: Nice, tanks! What'd you snag? Forest golems?

> DiddyLiddy: Yes! These things are HUGE. One step and SQUASHED.

> PianoPuck18: lol can't wait to see them in action.

> DiddyLiddy: About 48 hours to go! Not that I'm counting or anything...

> PianoPuck18: I like that you are :)

I look around, crossing my fingers that no one is going to be coming into the locker room, and sigh in relief when all I can hear is the whirring of the bathroom fan. I try to imagine Liddy's sweet, high-pitched voice in my head as I read over her texts, adding energy when she says, "SQUASHED." I wish I could keep my fingers glued to my phone for once instead of being social so I can play the game of "dreaming what Liddy's expressions" are while I read over her texts.

I argue with myself that if we finish up at Ross's by ten, I could save myself a little bit of time to talk to her. Maybe get one game in. It's not what we had scheduled, but I can't wait to hear her voice again.

> PianoPuck18: Random q, I got a thing until 10 PM. Think you'd want to play a quick game when I get back? Maybe around 10:30?

> PianoPuck18: sorry I shouldn't assume. I'm in PST. might be a bit late if you're in another time zone.

> DiddyLiddy: oh! I'm in PST too. And I'm free. I can log on at 10:30 to play.

> PianoPuck18: Sounds good I will give you a call then.

> DiddyLiddy: yay can't wait! :)

I quickly wash my hair and body under the hot shower, taking care of the hard-on that I developed from a measly text conversation with Liddy before bolting over to Ross's. Whatever we do tonight has an end time, and once the clock strikes ten, I am making my way home and booting up *Hero Seek*.

I drive as fast as I can while still trying to be safe in the San Jose traffic. I park in Ross's driveway and sprint out of the car, opening his door since he keeps it unlocked for us.

"Hey, I'm here!"

"In the kitchen!" Ross yells.

I see Ross's dog Reaper, and give him a few cuddles before walking over to the kitchen. Micah and Ross are sitting around his kitchen island, drinking cans of craft beer while they watch episodes of *Shuffle Up and Play!*

"Did you make a pit stop at home?" Micah asked. "I thought we left the locker room at the same time."

"I took a shower at the arena. I needed some freshening up."

"You could have used my shower," Ross notes. "Micah took a quick one here. You know I have the fancy rain shower head that comes down from the ceiling. Way better than those basic showers they have at the arena."

"I just wanted to get it over with," I tell them. I exclude the other part about getting off to a person I only know by username and an icon of a cartoon minion because I'm already judging myself, so I don't need anyone else to do the same thing.

"Fair," Ross says. "Oh! I didn't tell you what the surprise was, Griff."

"Let me guess, frozen pizzas?"

Ross's jaw drops as he pulls out the cooked pizza from the oven. "How'd you know?"

I roll my eyes. Ross may have a lot of money, probably enough to hire a live-in chef, but his diet consists of comfort foods you can heat in the oven. Like pizza in the form of a bagel or a roll. "Because I know you and what kind of things bring you joy, aka multiple types of frozen pizzas. I'm not complaining, obviously."

"Good," he says, laying it out on the table. "Because there're four different kinds to choose from."

"But there's only three of us," Micah says.

"Whatever you don't eat, you can take home. Duh. Now, eat up! Today's game of choice is going to be a long one."

I gulp. "Wait. What do you mean? What'd you pick, Monopoly?"

"Maybe...what's it to you? Do you have somewhere to be tonight?" His eyes narrow at me, and I feel the large kitchen shrinking in on us.

"Yeah," I nod. "Dammit. Okay, well, at like, ten thirty which is late anyway, when we have to be up at practice at eight in the morning! Can we do Monopoly another day?"

"Woah, woah, woah, back up, Griffin Yamamoto Markey. That's right, I used the full name. Where do you need to be at ten thirty?"

"Home!" I countered. "Because it's important to be well rested, considering we play on Friday."

"Fair, but I smell bullshit," Ross says. "You've never dipped out early from games night before or told us we need to be on a time crunch. So fess up. What's really going on?"

Ughhhh. I hate that feeling you get in the pit of your stomach when you feel like you should be trusting your friends and spilling your life's happenings to them, but they're utterly cringeworthy.

"I started playing *Hero Seek* again."

"That's great, man. So you're thinking about taking that sponsorship deal?"

"Maybe," I shrug. "I still feel unsure about being in the spotlight in that capacity, but I've really enjoyed playing again."

"That's awesome. Well, I guess that's valid reasoning to dip out early."

Phew. That went better than I thought it would. I didn't even need to mention Liddy, and my friends don't even suspect a thing.

"So, are you playing with like, a friend or something?" Ross asks.

I start stuttering. The room suddenly feels dark, except for a spotlight cast on me.

"Um..." Just lie and move on, Griffin. Ross and Micah's eyes widen at me and a loud gasp from Ross echoes in the room.

"Holy shit, you do!" Ross points an accusatory finger at me. "You traitor!"

"What the fuck? No, I'm not a traitor!"

"Well, you're definitely keeping a secret from us. Why do you need to be home at a certain time? Unless you're playing with someone. Who's your new secret friend, Griffin?"

I bury my head on the marble countertop and slump towards the ground. I want to snap my fingers and turn invisible right now. My face is beet red and not from the glow I get from drinking.

"Oh my god, is it a woman? Is Griffin talking to someone online?"

Both guys raise their eyebrows in curiosity, and when the silence equates to an affirmative, Ross yelps like he's discovered a cure for the common cold.

"You...Oh my god. Griffin's in love!"

"I am not in love," I stammer.

"Your blushing tomato face says otherwise," Micah says.

"No one asked for your observation," I note. "And I don't even know the woman. For all I know, we could be like, not made for each other at all. We both just got matched up on *Hero Seek* and started playing on the same team. Then we exchanged Discords and started sending messages to each other, and I was supposed to wait to play with her on Saturday, but she messaged me that she was upgrading some things, and I thought I could just jump on tonight and play for a little bit. Sue me."

"Oh, he's in deep," Ross says, flashing me a wink.

"Yeah, he is."

"I'll admit, but only because you two are my friends, that I kind of like her. I think we'd be good friends. Hell, I consider her a friend now. But I can't have any romantic feelings for her. It'd be like falling in love with the equivalent of a Karen from Spongebob. Someone I only know through chatting on a computer."

"That's...a weird comparison," Micah replies. "But I guess that's a good way of putting it. Do you know where she lives? What if she's nearby?"

"It's never really come up in conversation." And if I asked, it would really radiate creepy stalker vibes and ruin this whole dynamic. "All I know is that her screen name is DiddyLiddy because her nickname is Liddy. I don't know what her actual name is. Lid-di-a? Lydia? Huh, maybe. Well that, and she's also works in collegiate esports and lives in the same time zone as us."

"Woah, collegiate esports! That's pretty cool. Is she a pro-gamer?"

I shake my head. "I don't think so. I think she does more of the business side of it. Like she said, she talks to alumni and tries to convince them to donate to the program. That, and she also has this coach that's a sexist asshole that's been making her job a living hell. That's why she started playing. Because life at work got to be really stressful, so she needed to unwind one day and got on *Hero Seek*."

"Well, for someone you just met on the internet, it sounds like you know a lot about her. How much does she know about you?"

"Just my screen name. And it's going to stay that way. Probably forever."

"Wait, so you don't want to meet her in real life?"

"I do." More than anything, I want to put a face to the name, to see her smile in front of me, and actually spend time talking without also thinking about killing minions online. But us meeting, even if casual at first, might lead to a lot of public attention, and I don't want to subject anyone to a spotlight they aren't prepared for. "But I don't want us to meet for the first time and cause a media storm."

"So what if you two get to know each other, and then she wants to meet you in real life? What are you going to do? Just be like, 'Eh, sorry, I'm actually just not that into you?' That'd be a pretty jerk move, G"

I groan. I really don't want to lead her on. Maybe the only thing to do is create some distance? It will make me a certifiable jerk, but I'm going to hope that she never brings it up, and we can just continue to live in this bubble. By playing games and having a fun time.

Because we can definitely live in a bubble that's never going to break, right?

5

Lydia

I NEVER THOUGHT THAT seeing a little bubble in the corner of my screen turn green would give me so much joy, but it truly is the only good part of my day.

I was a reclusive hermit for the majority of the day today after giving up and admitting that the only way I can get my colleagues to like me is if I adhere to their demands. I've never heard of an actor telling the director how they should act in a scene. And yet, it's always another case of the men in my professional circle thinking they can tell me what to do.

I almost leapt so hard that my chair fell over when PianoPuck told me he wanted to play earlier than our scheduled time. That has to mean that he enjoys spending time with me, right? The gesture propels me to that feeling when you're young and in love for the first time. Even the smallest gestures make a huge impact. And yet, there's so much "eh, but is it?" that keeps shielding that whimsical feeling.

It would be strange for me to explain to my friends what I'm going through. Like, how do you tell someone that you're "talking" to a boy, but all the talking is done through voice chat and instant messages? It's like the days of my youth, when people would flirt on AIM or do that name/gender/age thing in private chat rooms.

My screen lights up with an incoming call, and I almost fall out of my seat again when I see it's PianoPuck and his little icon of a hockey player wearing a Stingrays jersey playing a piano. Huh, is he a Stingrays fan? How am I just noticing that? I'm not one, but Landon will go to a few games during the season with his friends. The thought that Puck might be even more local than I thought makes me more anxious. Is that something that you ask someone? "Hey, I noticed you're a Stingrays fan. We might be neighbors. Let's go out on a date!" No, that's taking it a step too far this early on. I want to make sure that feels what I feel before I start initiating questions about dates.

I click the "Accept" button.

"Hey," I say excitedly.

"Hey. I'm a little early, hope that's okay. My previous event finished earlier than usual, and I saw you were online, so..."

"It's fine," I tell him. "I'm glad you're here. What was the other event you were coming from?"

"I do a board game night with some friends every week. We switch off who gets to pick the game and today, my friend originally wanted to play Monopoly, but I shut down that idea really quickly. I did not have the time to spend it losing friendships and building hotels."

"That may as well be reserved for an all-nighter. What did you end up playing instead?"

"We played some *Mario Party*. Fifteen turns, took us a little over an hour. And I won."

"Wow," I grin. "Nice job. Well, I hope you're ready to kick some *Hero Seek* butt."

"Absolutely."

We boot up the game and get paired with our opponents. The loading screen appears with the map selected: The Frosted Expanse, which is the first new map they've created in over a year. They've been teasing the campaign with "Coming Soon" messages and teasers on their social media saying, "Your Favorite Man on Ice is Ready to Take on The Expanse!" indicating that whoever their mystery ambassador is really enjoys being on the ice. Maybe it's a hockey player. I wonder if PianoPuck would know him.

"Have you seen the teaser they've been playing about this map?"

"Uh...no. I...haven't. What have they been teasing?"

"They're hinting that the ambassador for this campaign is like a hockey player or figure skater. They're headlining with 'Your Favorite Man on Ice is Ready to Take on The Expanse!'. I saw your profile picture was of a guy in a hockey jersey playing a piano, so I assumed you were a fan. Stingrays, right?"

"Uh, yeah. It's supposed to be a Stingrays jersey. Do you watch hockey?"

"No, not really. My brother goes to a few Stingrays games during the season. I live in the area, so it was all around me growing up. But I don't really know much about hockey. Maybe you can teach me how the game works, though, since you know how to play?"

"Yeah, sure. I can do that." His response sounds rushed and not as enthusiastic as I was hoping he'd be. Did I say something wrong? Maybe he had a traumatic experience playing hockey, so he doesn't like talking about it. I don't know why he'd still be such a fan of a team, though.

"You don't have to," I say to try and ease him up. "I'm sorry, if I struck a chord by talking about hockey. You just don't seem as enthusiastic all of a sudden after I brought it up."

"No, no. It's okay," he reassures me. "I don't mean to be all sad. You're right. I kind of have a love/hate relationship with hockey. I wish I could go into more detail than that, but I just want to protect you and enjoy this good part of my life, which right now includes you."

"I..." I'm speechless. I don't know what to say. Is that the indicator that he might be feeling something more than just platonic feelings? Is this an instance where I follow my heart and see what happens? I mean, it's not the time for a love declaration, but maybe, if that picture of him in a Stingrays jersey is any indication, he's closer to me than I could have ever imagined.

"Are you near San Jose by chance? You know, because you're a Stingrays fan."

A moment passes, and he responds. "Yeah, I'm near the area. Are you?"

"Yeah!" I say gleefully. Oh my goodness, I was not expecting him to be near the area. That makes this a lot easier then. If he likes talking to me online, then he should be excited that we can meet somewhere in real life. See each other face to face!

I take a deep breath in and exhale audibly through my mouth. Here goes nothing.

"That's so cool. What are the odds?" I chuckle. "Um, so listen. I really like talking to you, and I really enjoy playing games with you. And since you're nearby, I wanted to know if you'd like to get coffee? Or dinner?"

The sound of screaming minions and rifles shooting in the background could not be more annoying at a time like this, where his lack of response is making me feel like I just did something completely wrong.

"I...I'm sorry, Liddy, but I don't think that's a good idea."

Oh.

Oh god.

Oh god, no.

"Oh. I'm sorr—"

"It's not your fault!" He rushes out. "Shit, can these guys simmer for just a second? It's not you at all, trust me. I...if my life were less complicated, then I would say yes. A million times, yes. But I can't have you getting roped into my messy life. It's not you, it's me!" He forces out a light-hearted chuckle. "I'm so sorry if I led you on."

Messy life? What could he mean by saying something so vague? "I...You're not married, are you? Like, this isn't a 'we're legally married but separated' kind of thing?"

"No. No, I'm not married. Or dating anyone. I haven't been in a relationship since college."

My lips begin to form a straight line. "Got it. It's just complicated."

Complicated. What a blanket word to basically say he's just not that into you. I start to feel a deep heaviness in my chest. Being let down sucks, and I'm frustrated with myself that I was reading the signs all wrong.

"Complicated," I repeat. I'm starting to hate the word. I think I'd rather have him tell me he doesn't like me that way.

"Liddy. Lydia, which I think is your name...I'm really sorry."

Hearing my actual name causes my eyes to start watering. I can't even hear his voice anymore without becoming an emotional wreck.

"It's fine," I say before my words become garbled amongst the tears.

"It's not you," he pleads. "I...have a lot of shit going on, and I don't want anyone to get roped into it. I...I don't want to lead you on."

"Yeah," I whisper. Whatever reasoning he has, I want to respect it. Whatever he means by complicated. Maybe he's still trying to get over an ex. Maybe he has a child. Maybe. Maybe. Maybe. "I understand."

I don't want to think about the what-ifs anymore. They led me to think I had a shot in the first place, and now I'm wishing I could take it all back.

"I'm...sorry. I think I just need to log off for the night." Suddenly, playing video games doesn't sound like the most fun thing in the world anymore.

I don't even let anyone kill me before I press "Quit" on the menu. My cheeks are wet, and I turn off my computer as quickly as I can and scurry to lie down in bed. He tries to call me again on Discord, but I reject it.

Work the next day is a struggle. And that's putting it gently. I've ultimately given up on everything. On trying to fight back at the people who talk back to me, on love, on trying to be excited about gaming anymore. Every time I think about video games, I just think about PianoPuck and the good thing we had before he ultimately crushed it to smithereens.

I head down to the cafeteria to meet Landon for lunch, and I don't even smile when he jogs up to meet me.

"Hey, woah. What's wrong? Why are you so sad?""

"I don't want to talk about it," I grumble.

"Hey, come on." He grabs my arm and leans in closer to me. "Are you crying?"

I sniffle, turning my head away from him. I hate that I get emotional so easily. I feel embarrassed doing this with students passing us in both directions.

"No," I say, wiping my eyes.

"Liddy," he says.

And then I lose it. Gut-wrenching sobs escape my body, and I grip onto him for dear life. Sorry in advance for the snot that's going to be on your sweatshirt, Landon.

"Hey, it's okay." He rubs my back in a circular motion. "Let's go sit down."

He guides me to a secluded booth in the far corner of the dining hall, and I plant my face down on the table.

"What's going on?" he asks. "Is it Jared? If so, I'm going to kill him for making you feel like this."

"No," I mutter. "Not this time."

"Then what's wrong?"

"I don't want to talk about it. You're going to think it's dumb."

"I promise I won't. I don't think that anything you do is dumb. Or could be dumb."

"No, Landon. This one is different. I'm a fool for even taking a risk on something like this. And now it's going to haunt me for the rest of my life."

"I promise I'm not going to judge you," Landon says.

"Fine." I lean back in the cushioned seat and take a deep breath. "Buckle up."

I go on to tell him everything, and it's actually very therapeutic to finally get it all off my chest. All the secret feelings I've been holding onto. I tell him how I got paired up with PianoPuck randomly online. How we won that first *Hero Seek* game and felt the absolute rush from winning, along with a few *other* feelings. I admitted that I felt like PianoPuck led me on, but also realized that he could simply be a friendly person. That's where I become the fool. And now, I'm a jumbled-up sack of feelings that really doesn't know where to go because things are, again, complicated.

"You were interested in someone you got matched with on *Hero Seek*?"

"That's all you got from this?" I wail.

"No, no, I'm sorry." He reaches his arm around me, and I rest my head on his shoulder. We're not *physical touch* people at all, but I'll admit, this is nice. "That really sucks, Lydia. I can't believe he said all that stuff and still turned you down. And he lives in San Jose?

"Well, he said he lived in the area. That's the only reason I asked in the first place. Now I'm thinking I would have been better off if I didn't know that the colors of a Stingrays jersey are grey and teal."

"I think I'm partly to blame for that one," Landon notes. "I do enjoy a Stingrays game once in a while. But if I bump into this PianoPuck18 at a Stingrays game, I'm going to give him a piece of my mind."

"Well, lucky for both of us, I don't even know his name or what he looks like."

"I guess he got off lucky with that one." He hands me a napkin so I can wipe the snot off my face. "Feeling better?"

I nod. Everything still sucks right now, but it feels slightly better that I was able to express my feelings aloud. I don't really have much of an appetite, so I watch Landon eat lunch while I sip on a smoothie. I listen to him talk about how well his life is going—a lot better than mine—and feel a little bit lighter to hear so much joy as he talks. He soon finishes up and heads to class, while I return to the cave that is my office.

I start packing my bag to head home for the day when Landon waltzes into my office with a grin all over his face. A wide grin that makes me think he's up to something.

"Landon? What are you doing here?"

"Wanted to ask if you're doing anything tomorrow." He's rocking back and forth on his heels.

I wish. "No. I'm not busy tomorrow. Why?"

"Okay, before I tell you, I just want to preface this by saying I love you, and I'm just doing this to take your mind off things, even if it seems like I'm not. You'll see why."

"Landon," I look at him skeptically. "What are you trying to do?"

"So Alyssa and I have tickets to the Stingrays game tomorrow, and I..."

"No." I already know where this is going, and I have no idea how this is supposed to make me feel better.

"You didn't even let me finish!"

"Why do you think going to a Stingrays game is going to make me feel better?"

I don't even attend hockey games of my own free will, and then I meet a former college hockey player who could have taught me the ins and outs of hockey, but look where that ended up. Did he really think that if he said yes to teaching me how hockey works, I couldn't restrain myself from developing feelings towards him? Or he just thought that I would be okay with the bubble we existed in – a fantasy where we can simply play games and not let our real lives get in the way.

Well, news flash: bubbles pop.

"Because there's someone that I want to invite that I think you'd really like."

I roll my eyes and lean back into my office chair. Oh great, now Landon's response to my heartbreak is to set me up on a date.

"Landon, I don't think now is a good time at all to be thinking about dating. Remember my most recent heartbreak that I *just* told you about?"

"Okay, yeah, but do you know what's different about this? I know him. And I think you do, too. He's a good guy. Likes to play video games too, when he can. And I think he'd be a good fit for you."

"Okay, who?"

"My coding professor. Dr. Brosamer?"

I gasp. Oh god. I was not expecting it to be one of Landon's professors. Actually, I was expecting him to be like, "someone in my class," and then I'd have to remind him that while age gaps are more acceptable the older you get, my thirty-year-old self doesn't want to be going on dates with someone who recently finished undergrad. Or is just navigating legal drinking for the first time?

"Dr. Brosamer?"

"Yeah. You know him, right? Tall, kind of reddish brown hair. He's got three chili peppers on RateMyProfessor."

"Well, I didn't know that."

"He's like the bachelor professor of the Engineering school. He's…in his thirties. I don't think much older than you. He's only been at LGU for a year, but he's such a good teacher. He's patient with the students and so damn eloquent. Like, I didn't think that you could make coding sound sexy, but he does!"

"Did you tell him that?"

"No." Landon makes a "psh" sound. "But I did tell him that I have a beautiful, nice, very hard-working sister who is single and would love to meet new people. And I would just like to note that he has seen photos of you and concurs."

"Does he?"

"Yes," Landon says. "You're not ugly. You don't think you are, right?"

"I mean…" I don't tell myself that I'm beautiful every time I look in the mirror. And I'm not model material. I have spots of acne on my face. And I was too sad to shower last night. I sniff. I wonder if I smell.

"Well, you aren't," Landon argues. "And he's excited about tomorrow. I think you'll have a good time. And despite your preconceived notions about hockey, it's a fun sport to watch. There's fighting."

"Fine," I relent. "I'll go to your double date hockey game with someone I've never met."

An unsettling feeling boils in my stomach. A blind date. I have to trust my brother because it seems like he wants to do this for my own good. To try and make me feel better. I have to give him credit for trying. Landon used to have a heart of stone. I would have to bribe him to get him to abandon whatever video game he was playing to hang out with me. Maybe I can thank his girlfriend for softening that heart of his, one that is looking out for me and trying to think of ways to make me feel better.

"I can't believe I'm trusting you with setting me up on a date."

"I would like to think I know a thing or two in the dating department. I am in a committed relationship, after all."

"Yep," I nod. "That is something that you have over me. Who knew you would be so knowledgeable in software engineering *and* in love?"

"Not me. But there are those people out there who do love a man that can carry a payload."

"God," I chuckle and roll my eyes. "You're such a nerd."

"Runs in the family," he winks. "I'll meet you here tomorrow to take you to the arena. Be ready by five."

"Alright. I hope you know what you're doing!" I shout after him.

"I don't, but I can at least say I'm trying!"

And it looks like I'm going to have to try and get myself done up for a date. When it's been years since I've even been on one. At least it's a double date...with my brother and his girlfriend. I slump back in my chair. Hopefully, this date will help me get over what happened with Puck, an experience I would love to forget ever happened. Especially the part where I got rejected and had my feelings hurt.

Oh god, what have I gotten myself into?

6

Lydia

As I begin wrapping up for the day, I hear Landon talking to someone on the other side of my office door.

"Have you been to our esports computer room before?"

"No, I haven't. This is awesome."

"Yeah, it's been a work in progress, but Lydia's been doing a great job of making it all come together."

I gasp quietly and start stuffing my laptop and other papers quickly in my bag. A little bit of notice would have been nice, Landon! Should I freshen up? Do I look like a mess right now?

I ruffle through my bag. I know I have some blotting papers in here somewhere to at least do their job with my oil-ridden face.

"Hey," Landon pops in. "Are you ready?"

"Huh? Oh yeah." I jump a little bit, all frazzled. "Yep. Ready to go!" I make a sweeping motion with a thumbs up and immediately want to cringe at my awkward response. Great first impression, Lydia.

"Awesome. Lydia, this is Dr. Brosamer. Dr. Brosamer, this is my older sister, Lydia. Also, the Director of Esports here at LGU. The first Director of Esports, I would like to add."

"Mark." He holds out his hand, and I shake it. "Great to meet you, Lydia. Uh, Landon's been telling me a lot about you."

"Oh, that's great." I blush. Seeing Dr. Brosamer, or Mark, in person, I can definitely see why he has a chili pepper rating on RateMyProfessor. His hair is voluminous and swept back, and he has a muscular build that really does great things for that button-down shirt he's wearing. I see a hint of a well-trimmed beard covering the bottom half of his face. I didn't think I'd like beardy facial features, but he's growing it out well.

"Well, we talk a lot about video games in our spare time, and he always mentions how you're the school's *first* Director of Esports, which is awesome. You've definitely got the dream job of teenage me right here. What made you want to go into esports?"

"I used to be a part of the Esports Club here when I was a student. And even after I graduated, it was a big part of my life. I watched all the major tournaments when they came around, and one day, I decided to take a chance and use my sales and marketing experience and applied to be the first Esports Director here. There are good days, and there are stressful days, but I can definitely say I'm living the dream."

"Lydia's great at her job," Landon notes. "She's already gotten almost fifty thousand in alumni donations to get this program to where it is."

"Eh," I shrug. "I just want the team to be successful."

"God, stop being so humble," Landon says. "Some people refuse to believe she's good at this, so I need to hype her up sometimes."

Mark laughs, and it's oddly reminiscent of a particular hearty, full belly laugh that I'm trying to remove from my brain as we speak.

"Hey, the same thing happened to me when I started out. You'll have students who really love your teaching style and some who will just not agree with it."

"Oh really? Are there students who don't like you?"

"I mean, I'm sure they tolerate me, but yeah, they aren't huge fans of mine. Maybe because I am kind of hard on grading, and I give a lot of homework. But that's how you're going to learn. And coding is a lot of learning by doing."

"Ah, that makes sense."

Landon chimes in. "So, should we leave? I want to make sure we have enough time to grab food and drinks before the game starts."

"Yeah," I say. "Let's start making our way out."

We walk out from the student union to the parking lot, where Landon's car, more specifically, our old trusty Toyota Camry that my dad bought when we were kids, is parked.

"You sure you don't want me to drive?" I ask Landon. I know we're not far from the arena, but sometimes I wonder when Ol' Reliable will inevitably break down completely.

"No," he says. "You're supposed to be my guest. Besides, Ol' Reliable is doing just fine. I just got a new transmission put in last month."

"You did? How much was that?"

"More than a college student should be spending. But Dad helped. Besides, I can't afford a new car right now. I don't work full-time like you do."

"But...never mind." It might just be better if I let him figure things like this out on his own. But if we break down on the freeway, I'm not hesitating with the I told you so.

Mark and I hop in the back seat while Landon and his girlfriend, Alyssa, sit in front. The car is mostly clean, save for a few receipts scattered around the floor. Landon turns the key in the ignition and starts her up. We start making our way to the arena and thankfully, despite the slight bumper-to-bumper we face getting into San Jose, we make it in relatively good time.

When we turn and enter the parking lot, we're already stopped behind a line of cars trying to get in. It's decently full already, with fans in their hockey jerseys making their way into the arena. I realize, looking at my entourage, that I'm the only person who isn't wearing any Stingrays fan gear. I'm not even wearing any Stingrays colors. Unless you count my black blouse.

We scan our tickets and get a sheet of temporary tattoos that say "Stingrays Gamers!" on it. Huh, I didn't even think about sports teams having esports programs.

"Landon!" I shout for him as he's walking towards our section. "Did you know about this?" I flash the sheet in front of him.

"Oh. Yeah, that's part of the reason why I wanted you to come."

"What's the Stingrays Gamers?"

"It's this program that a few leagues are doing, where they play competitive video games. So, the Stingrays have a team that plays hockey online against other NHL teams."

"Wait, that's really cool!" I didn't even know something like this existed. I guess you can take any competitive game and make a league from it. "Do you know who runs the program for the Stingrays?"

"No, but I'm sure they'll mention something about it between periods. Or they might have a table for advertising it."

"I'll have to check it out then."

We take our seats, and I am amazed by how close we are to the ice. I don't ask how much Landon may have forked over for this to happen, but once I sit down, I'm propelled to a different zone, feeling a little lighter once I see players stretching and doing shooting drills on the ice. My eyes fixate on how easily they're skating back and forth in their uniform.

I take a sip of the seltzer I bought, hoping I can take my mind off things and focus on having a good time.

"Hey, y'all. It's Griffin Markey and I'm here to welcome you all to Stingrays Gamer Night here at SAP Center."

I almost choke on bubbles. Why does that voice sound so familiar? I look up at the jumbo screen to see one of the Stingrays players, Griffin Markey, talk about his gaming experience.

"Growing up, video games were such a huge part of my life. I remember the first console I got when I was a kid. I would play games like *Mario* and *Zelda* for hours on end. And now, I really like to play this game called *Hero Seek*."

No. No no no no no no.

It CAN'T be.

"Which is why I'm excited to tell you all that I'm partnering with *Hero Seek* for their new Winter Expedition release! All Stingrays fans attending tonight will receive a code to unlock a special new minion, the Abominable! To redeem, use the code SEEKSTINGRAYS, and you'll be able to unlock your new minion today! Go Stingrays!"

"Motherfucker!" I yell.

Mark jolts. "Is everything okay?"

Shoot, I just realized I said that out loud.

"Uh...yeah," I stammer. "I just...am so excited about the new minion, but did they really need to do an abominable." I let out a hearty chuckle. "I mean, why couldn't it have been like a reindeer?"

"Uh, yeah, I guess so. Although I think an abominable is going to be really cool. Don't you? That's gonna look badass with the new map."

I turn my head to face him. "Wait, do you play *Hero Seek*?"

He shrugs. "Here and there. I haven't played in a while. But since Griffin Markey just announced he's the new ambassador, I'm definitely going to pick it back up this season. He's one of my favorite hockey players."

"Oh." Apparently, he's a shady son of a bitch too. I know that voice. I've heard it for hours on end. I've smiled at the sound of it ringing in my headphones. Shit, and to realize that I might have been falling for a...hockey player?

"Um, I need to ask Landon something really quick. Up on the concourse. Landon!"

He leans over and raises his eyebrow at me. "What's up?"

"I need to talk to you. On the concourse. In private. Like...now."

"Now? But the game is about to begin! Can it wait until the end of the first period?"

I groan. "When is that going to be?"

"Maybe like a half hour? I don't know? Depends on penalties!"

I bury my face in my lap. "Ugh. Fine. But as soon as the period ends."

Unable to hold in my shock, I pull out my phone and text him.

Lydia Goh: hey, u remember the guy i was talking to on hero seek? ya know THE ONE that turned me down?

Landon Goh: yah what about it? do you see him here???

Lydia Goh: yeah. I think it's Griffin Markey.

The three dots indicating that Landon is still typing remain on the screen, and Landon leans over again with his mouth agape.

"What?!" he mouths. His eyes quickly shift back to his phone.

Landon Goh: Really? No way

I shake my head. I know it's hard to believe, but I think I would recognize that voice anywhere. Before I can formulate my response, the announcer's voice booms over the arena.

"Get ready, Stingrays fans, to welcome your San Jose Stingrays!"

The arena goes dark, and a Stingrays mascot glides onto the ice as fire shoots up from the posts around the arena.

"Number 18, Griffin Markey!"

The crowd roars, including Mark, who jumps out of his seat and claps wildly. Landon, who is a little more chilled out than his usual fanfare, eyes me and mouths, "Are you okay?" I shake my head slightly. Certifiably, no. I am not okay.

We stand for the national anthem, and Landon beckons his head to the aisle, asking if I want to get out of here immediately.

I nod furiously and excuse myself.

Mark gently taps my arm. "Is everything okay?"

"Yeah. It will be. Don't worry about me. Landon and I… just need to talk about something." I feel bad because he looks genuinely concerned. I am not saying that he doesn't have a chance, and that I immediately don't like him because I can see with my own eyes that PianoPuck18 is actually Griffin Markey, All-Star hockey player, very good-looking and making my heart go thump, thump, thump. He doesn't even know I'm here, and I'm not under the delusion that he'll look up at the stands and know it's me. Amidst the noise of eager fans cheering and shouting, the clink of the puck dropping, I can't stop sucking in breaths or the tears streaming down my face. Again, the wrong place to be crying for the second time this week. We get to the top and scurry over to a spot near the restrooms where there is less foot traffic. Landon doesn't say anything but wraps his arms around me and rubs circles on my back.

"It's okay," he tells me. "Let it out."

"I just can't believe it. Of all the people that live in the South Bay, hell, that live in the Bay Area—hundreds of thousands of people—it just had to be him!"

A gorgeous, dimple-faced, stubbly player who is one of the top scorers of the NHL and has played in the All-Star team twice.

"I can't believe I looked up to that man." Landon shakes his head while resting it atop mine. "Besides being the new ambassador of *Hero Seek*, he's also one of the faces of API Heritage Month in the NHL."

I didn't even realize he was Mixed. That's an even bigger blow to people like us, who gets so excited when Mixed Asians are represented in sports and the media.

"I didn't know he's Mixed."

"Yeah, he's half Japanese. There's only, like, ten players of Asian descent active in the NHL right now."

"I'm sorry," I tell him. "I feel bad that it's someone you look up to."

"What? You shouldn't be feeling bad. You did nothing wrong. He's the one who turned you down." Landon says that last part with a little more bite, which makes me jump a bit.

"Landon, it's okay. I can see now that he might have had good reason for rejecting me. I mean, come on. A famous hockey player? I'm sure he has a lot of people watching his every move."

"Still, I wish he told you who he was instead of keeping things vague with an 'it's complicated.'"

I feel slightly guilty for getting Landon so angry over this, so I try to calm myself down so he can simmer as well.

"I'll get over it, Landon. I don't want you to get upset about this." When Landon gets a temper, it can easily get explosive. "I feel more at ease now that I know who he is. That's good, right?"

"Yeah, I guess," he mutters. "I'm still mad. But...I'll try calming down. Since you said so."

I smile. "Good. Come on, let's go watch some guys beat each other up. Hey, maybe Griffin will get into a fight with someone on the other team. That'd be fun to watch, right?"

He nods. I pat him on the back and lead him back to our seats.

"Everything okay?" Mark asks upon our return. Before I open my mouth to respond, a siren blares throughout the stadium and everyone's cheering. For what?

"Stingrays goal! By Number 18, Griffin Markey!"

Of course.

"Yup!" I shout over the roar of the crowd's screams for the golden boy, who's pumping his fist in the air and chest-bumping his teammates.

We sit through the remainder of the game and I try to set any distractions that I might have aside to focus on Mark. I genuinely feel bad that he's trying so hard to make conversation and explain to me how hockey works, but my eyes and mind continue to fixate on Number 18, who has scored three goals and assisted with two more, making this a blowout of a game. Yay for Stingrays fans and the team, boo for my bruised heart and ego.

The game ends with a Stingrays win, and we make our way out of the arena with the other fans. Mark and I start heading towards Landon's car, who calls out to us to stop walking.

"Why? Your car is this way."

"We're not going to my car yet."

Weird. "Did you forget something in the arena?"

"No. Just follow me."

Landon leads the pack around the arena to a gated waiting area where fans holding signs and pieces of paper, likely to be autographed, are patient and eager for who's coming out of that door.

"Oh no. Landon, what are you doing?"

Players begin exiting to sign autographs, and I lock eyes with Griffin. He doesn't know who I am yet. But this is the closest we've physically been to one another, and I start to feel my heart beating faster.

Griffin passes, and an excited Mark waves at him.

"Mr. Markey, you did such a good job tonight! Can I get a photo?"

"Yeah, sure," Griffin says, and Mark politely asks me if I can take a photo of him. My hands are shaking as I try to grip the phone and shoot the picture.

"Your hands are shaking a lot," Mark says.

"Sorry, just...cold."

"Her hands are shaking because you fucking rejected my sister!" Landon shouts.

"Landon," his girlfriend scolds.

"I'm sorry, what are you talking about?" Griffin asks.

"I can't believe I fucking looked up to your scumbag ass! You're a disgrace to hockey and a disgrace to the API community."

I want to shrink away right now. Do I think Griffin is a scumbag? No, but he isn't really on my nice list right now. I get that Landon wants to defend me and tell Griffin that what he did affected me negatively, but this is not the way to do it. His inebriation mixed with anger is upsetting and, frankly, embarrassing. I try and mouth apologies to everyone who's staring at us right now over Landon's uncalled-for outbursts.

"Landon, please," I beg. "You're being more dramatic about this than you should be."

"Wait," he turns to me. "Your...voice. You sound like..." He points to me. "Lydia?"

I silently nod and give him a sheepish wave. "Hi."

7
Griffin

What are the odds?

Truly, someone must be fucking with me.

In front of me is none other than Lydia...whatever her last name is. DiddyLiddy. The same woman I have spent all night thinking about. Losing sleep over. Feeling like absolute shit over how I turned her down.

She's beautiful. With her long, brown hair styled in waves. A slight hint of makeup adorns her face, a black blouse that helps brighten her slightly tanned skin, and jeans that hug her hips so well. God, how I've imagined touching those curves and now I'm seeing it in front of me. I had a slight picture in her head of what she might look like, but seeing what she actually looks like takes my breath away.

"You...you're here. How did you find me?"

"I...I didn't," she whispers. "I had no idea who you were until tonight."

"I..." I don't know how to react. "Can we talk?"

"She's not going anywhere near you," the man shouting expletives at me says. "Not after the shit you put her through."

I have to assume, based on how similar they look, that this is her brother. Explains the vitriol.

"Hey," I hold my hands up. "I'm not trying to pull any funny business. I just want to talk."

"Too late for that," he says.

"Landon," her voice is more stern now. She walks up to me so we're inches apart. The only thing that separates us is the barrier put up to separate fans from players. "I think I know how to speak for myself."

She peers into my dark eyes and furrows her brow at me. "You wanna talk? Guildhouse, tonight. Right after you're done here."

I sigh. I can't argue with that. If that's how she wants to meet, then I will risk being alone in public to do so. I could just say that I made my decision to let her go, but now, as I see her face-to-face, all of that changes.

"Lydia," her brother starts.

She holds up her finger to shush him. "This is my life and my decision. I'm allowed to chase after what I want, and right now, I just want answers."

"Okay," he says, tilting his head down.

"Thanks," she says. "Let's go."

She turns her back and starts walking towards the parking lot without a goodbye. I stay still, waiting to see her disappear from my view, still in shock that I can see her with my own eyes. That she's no longer just a voice I can hear through a speaker.

I quickly get through the remainder of the fans who have waited for an autograph. They've probably witnessed what just happened and I'll be on the cover of some trending topic online, but there's no escaping it. It would have been worse if I completely ignored it and pretended that I didn't know Lydia or she didn't exist. I think I could have gotten her brother arrested for trying to mangle me.

I try to grin and bear it with the fans who are excited to see me, and I feel bad that I was smiling at seeing Lydia but these fans barely mean anything to me. I'm thankful for them, but I also want to go back into the arena and hide.

I head back inside once I reach my mental capacity and need to be alone again. I sit on the bench facing my locker and pull out my phone. It's creepy to look up people that you have slight feelings for, but I need to know if there are any photos of Lydia out there so I can see her face again, not angry and not when it's dark outside.

I type in "Lydia Director Esports" in the search bar. I should've thought about doing this sooner. The first search result comes up with an article titled, "Meet Los Gatos University's First Director of Esports Gaming Lydia Goh."

I click on it and read through the article published by Los Gatos University, which I believe is a small private university not far from here.

"Lydia Goh, '13, has been named LGU's first Director of Esports Gaming. Goh, who was Vice President of Recruitment at LGU's Esports Club when enrolled as a student, brings a wealth of knowledge in Sales, Business Operations, and competitive Esports as an online gaming influencer and commentator.

"I'm excited to be building the first competitive Esports League at LGU," says Goh. "Video games have been a consistently good part of my life, and I'm excited to see it grow at my alma mater."

There's a photo of her smiling, wearing a grey jumpsuit. She looks happy, and I ache a little, wishing that she'd look at me like that, but my rejection ruined that.

"Heeey," Micah and Ross walk in and take a seat on either side of me. "Uh, we heard what happened."

"Oh," I respond while keeping my eyes focused on my phone screen. "Yeah. That happened tonight."

"Out of all the people that could have been here tonight, it just had to be your...ex-crush? Still crush?"

I don't know what to think of her anymore. No, I'm constantly thinking about her and nervous about what she might want from me when we talk later tonight. "I think I still like her, but I won't force her to like me back. We're seeing each other later. Not as a date," I caveat. "I just asked if we could talk, and she agreed."

"What are you going to talk to her about?" Ross asks.

I didn't have a script all drummed up yet. Hell, I was happy that she agreed to speak to me at all after what I put her through, compounded with the shock of seeing me everywhere tonight. On Gamers Night, ironically.

I shake my head. "I don't know yet. I want to apologize, of course. And then we'll see how much she'll let me say after that."

"Are you gonna ask her out?"

My head turns sharply at Micah, and I raise my eyebrows at him. "Do you really think that's a good idea? I mean, I already said I didn't want to go out with her because it'd complicate things. Is it going to be much better now that we've met?"

"I don't know, maybe? The internet's already made it a thing, might as well roll with it."

"What the fuck?!" I grab Ross's phone. "What are they saying?"

I read aloud the trending headline: "NHL All-Star Griffin Markey seen talking intimately with mystery woman."

Damn. The whole reason I didn't move forward with this thing with Lydia was that I didn't want to draw more attention to myself and to someone associated with me.

I scrub my face rapidly with my hands. It's too late now to deflect or deny. I'll just need to explain to Lydia what's going on and why I said what I did—to try and make sure she doesn't suffer the brunt of the media attention.

"Great," I wail. "This is exactly what I was afraid of."

Ross takes a closer look at the photo on the phone. "I mean, it's a dark photo. You can barely make out what her face looks like."

But the problem is, I can notice everything. The brown eyes that are looking straight into mine. The plump lips of her open mouth. The way her hair drapes down her back and the curves that come into full view. While the rest of the world is dark, she shines.

"I guess we'll just have to see what she says," I admit. "I'm meeting her at Guildhouse. You know that bar that has the computer station where you can play games?"

"Oh yeah," Micah nods. "I've always wanted to go there."

"Me too. I was always weary, though, because of fans. Although, it seems like if there's anyone that we shouldn't be worried about, it's fans who are just like us. The nerdy, game-loving fans who kick our asses at the same games we love to play."

Still, I put on a beanie and a hoodie and hope that I can get through tonight without fan interruptions. I pack my things into my car trunk and begin the drive to Guildhouse. It's a short drive: from one point of downtown to another, and I find street parking with it being late out.

I head inside the bar and see it's decently full, with people mingling on couches and at the computer stations. The space is much larger than what you'd expect, looking at it from the outside. There's a projector screen with gameplay footage and string lights canvassing the ceilings in a zig-zag pattern.

I spot Lydia sitting down at one of the high-top tables, sipping on a cocktail of some sort. She's changed clothes and is now wearing an LGU crewneck hoodie with some leggings that are definitely testing my urge to not stare down at her well-sculpted legs.

"Hey," I say.

Her response is a soft smile, not turning up to look at me from her drink. "Hi."

"How are you?" I wince at how forced and bland that sounded. Like I already know the answer to how she's doing.

"Alright," she shrugs. "Honestly, there's just a lot on my mind right now."

"Same." After a beat, listening to the sound of teens shouting at the computer area, Lydia excuses herself awkwardly to get a drink.

"Can I get you something?"

I gesture in the direction of the cocktail I ordered for myself immediately when I arrived at the bar. While they had a large menu of curated cocktails, I needed something strong, yet tasty. An Old Fashioned fit the bill well.

"I'm good," I tell her, raising my glass up slightly. "Grabbed something as soon as I got here."

Lydia nods and steps away to order at the bar on the other side of the space. She returns with a burnt yellow drink in a highball glass garnished with a pineapple slice.

"What'd you get?" I ask.

She eyes it closely. "This Red Bull cocktail, which maybe isn't the best idea right now, but I don't think I'll be getting much sleep anyway."

"Ditto." I give my glass a sheepish raise and motion to clink our glasses together. "Cheers to a restless night, and I guess the universe really showing us that we're meant to meet?"

She lets out a soft giggle. "Yeah, cheers." She takes a sip of her drink.

"Wow, that is sweet. It's good, but...whew. I forget the last time I had an energy drink. Oh well, I don't have to work tomorrow. Do you? Well, you actually have kind of a non-traditional job, so I'm not entirely sure."

"I have practice. Then we have an away game in Vancouver, so we'll be traveling that night. While I probably should be getting sleep, I doubt I will."

"Got it," she nods. "Yeah, the last few days have been... a whirlwind, to say the least."

I take a sip of my drink and nod to agree. Vancouver is currently at the top of our division, and I am trying to figure out a game plan, one that will get us the win, but my mind is entirely focused on Lydia's face, staring off into the distance.

"Yeah," I sigh. "That's mostly my fault."

"Yeah." She doesn't even hesitate. "But now I can give you the benefit of the doubt. I mean, I did not think that I was talking to a superstar hockey player."

"Yeah, so you can kind of see why it's complicated."

"Yeah..." She makes a pouty face and stares into her drink. "But is it?"

I choke on my sip and start coughing. "Wait, what?" She shrugs, and I'm starting to feel nervous about what kind of idea she has up her sleeve now that I notice her cheeky smile.

"You didn't want to go out with me because why? You're scared of the spotlight?"

"Um..."

"And you didn't want anyone who might be seen with you to also be the subject of everyone's attention?"

My eyes start to widen. "How..."

She gives me a stern expression. "Look, Griffin. What you did to me hurt. And I can give you the benefit of the doubt and say you did it because you're a big hockey player, and you want to keep me safe from the spotlight. But you didn't even ask me if I was afraid of the spotlight."

I mean, fair. But...why would she want the attention? She seems like the kind of person who doesn't like to be involved in drama, and that's exactly what I don't want to give her because my life is full of it!

"Are you afraid of the spotlight?" I ask.

"Not really," she shrugs. "I have to talk to strangers all the time. And I have to learn how to publicize myself and what I'm working on. So, I'm thinking it could be good practice."

"Wait..." I am somehow fearful of what that little brain of hers is thinking. "What are you proposing?"

"I think we should fake date."

I stare at her blankly for a second while the background of music and people exclaiming over whatever game they're playing fill my ears. This is definitely not the direction that I was hoping our conversation was going to go. I can't even remember if I got around to apologizing, which was the script that I was reciting along in my car on the drive here.

"Fake date?"

"Yeah," she nods. "It benefits both of us. You're trying to help yourself be more comfortable about being in the spotlight to get more brand deals, and I need someone I can latch onto to help my colleagues and donors respect me."

"How would fake dating do that?"

"Fans are a sucker for a celebrity romance. You're going to get so much attention for having a whirlwind romance. And icing on the cake? We can tell people that we met on *Hero Seek*. Can you imagine the attention that it would draw to the game? Everyone will flock to it like it's the hot new dating app."

But there's still one confusing part that I am trying to understand, and I don't know why it has to be this way. Admittedly, her idea is a really good one. It'll drive more fans to games and *Hero Seek*, which I know is trying to bolster its competitive gaming front to be in the likes of the big three. And Lydia benefits greatly from this, because being with me will help more of her students and peers respect her.

"Why fake, though?" I thought we had feelings for one another, and I might argue that we still do. Does she not anymore?

"Because I think this just needs to be an experiment. If it works, great, but after what you did, I'm not really interested in dating anyone for real."

Okay, sure. Maybe she's on to something. And maybe I'm not, either. She does make a good point about how this will be in our best interests. Mine for getting people excited about *Hero Seek* and hers to get attention towards her school's esports program.

"Yeah, I suppose that wouldn't be in either of our best interests."

"Then let's try it. Until the end of the hockey season. Which is when...February?"

"April."

She leans back her her stool. "Ah. Well, I guess that's not too bad. Six months, give or take? That's a good time frame to work with."

"Okay." This is weird. I didn't think I'd date, but I sure as hell wasn't expecting to fake date. How do you fake your feelings for someone while still having your mind think you really like them? Separating that is going to be hard, and I don't know if I'll be able to ignore the very real feelings I have for Lydia and fake the rest.

She holds her hand out. "Okay." My hand envelopes hers as we shake on it. Her small hand, cold from holding her drink, feels safe in mine, and I'm already having trouble reminding myself that this needs to be fake.

"So, uh, what's step one, fake girlfriend?"

She looks around the bar, fixing her gaze on the LAN stations over to the left of us.

"Do you wanna play a game?"

My head turns up. "Actually, yes. I'd really enjoy that."

We walk over to a pair of computers.

"What are you thinking?" I ask. "Wanna play *Hero Seek*?"

"Nah, that feels like it's too much strategy for me right now. Also, something to know about me is that one drink is enough to make me feel some kind of way. Let's play *Mario Kart*."

Huh, I think that might be the perfect game. It requires little strategy and just offers good vibes.

"Um, sure. *Mario Kart* works."

"Did you used to play as a kid?" Lydia says, returning with a console and a few controllers to can hook up to the computer.

I nod. "Not much, but I had a Nintendo 64 as a kid."

"That's...wait. How old are you?"

"Thirty-two."

"Huh, is it weird I thought you were in your late twenties? I didn't know how old you were when we played *Hero Seek*, but I was kind of afraid you'd be like, my brother's age. Sorry about him earlier. He just wants to be a good brother but he kind of has a temper. He's been taking care of me since, you know, what happened."

"Yeah. I'm kind of old to be in the NHL. I'm one of four players on my team that are over thirty. A lot of my teammates are fresh out of college. Or a few high schools."

I forget that my body is starting to deteriorate a little every day, and I have to hope that I won't run into some kind of career-ending injury that will throw off the trajectory I've set for myself.

"But yeah, I mean, I wasn't mad at your brother. I wasn't going to get him arrested or anything. He had every right to be upset." I take a seat in the comfortable gamer chairs and scroll through games on the console until I find the one I'm looking for. "So, are you guys close?"

The intro music for the game starts up and I'm in awe at how crisp the picture looks. For someone whose last memory of this franchise was a 64-bit game where every face and body had edges to it, this is a beautiful sight to see.

We each choose our character, and Lydia sets up the match for us: four courses, and at least forty to choose from with the expansion pack included. I'm tempted to just choose a course that I'm familiar with, like the iconic Yoshi Valley, but instead, I choose a new one from the game.

"Yeah, we're kind of close," Lydia says. "We are pretty far apart in age, so growing up, it was hard to get along. I always wanted to do things that allowed us to be best friends because I was jealous of all my girlfriends at the time who had tight bonds with their sisters, but you know how boys are. They get older, and they don't want to be the kid that plays with his sister. But now he's older, and he goes to the same college that I work at, and also graduated from, so it's impossible to escape one another. We get lunch once a week. I bitch about the mean people in esports that he also knows because he's a part of the club. And uh, yeah. He kind of surprised me, too. With that whole spat. Mostly because I didn't know that he cared about me that much to stand up for me like that. How about you? Do you have any siblings?"

"Yeah. Two older brothers. Neither play hockey. One of my brothers works on Wall Street, and the other one is a conductor on Broadway."

"Holy shit," she says. I don't know if it was from my family confession or the red shell that I just threw at her. "Fucker."

I laugh. That one was from the red shell.

"Sorry, not sorry," I cackle.

"Okay, but your family sounds really successful though. Your parents must be proud."

I shrug. They might be, I'm sure they are, but I kind of got cast aside because I live the farthest away from my family. I thought that I would get more love because of the distance like my parents telling me that they want to come visit for a week and see me play, but they never want to leave their home. Well, no, they'll always go into the city to see Graham and Gordon, but they're never "free enough" to fly to California to see me.

"If they are, then they don't tell me. The only time I see them is if I'm in New York or New Jersey for a game."

"I'm sorry," she tells me. "That's not very fun then."

"Yeah. Tough part about having brothers: it always felt like a competition with one another."

Although we're all in very separate industries, any time we are able to have a family gathering, it feels like it's just a debate on who can one-up the other with their accomplishments. When I was selected to the All-Star team, my family barely celebrated because, at the same time, Graham's company had a huge spike in their stock price, and Gordon got selected to be conductor for the revival of *Sweeney Todd*. Maybe that's where my desire to stay away from the spotlight stemmed because I never felt like I had the chance to be in the spotlight in the first place.

I cross the finish line, and the flashing "1st" lights up the screen.

"Hey," she elbows me. "Looks like you won something!"

I smile at her. "Yeah, looks like it." I might've won in other ways, too, but I'm going to have to fight the urge to keep whatever this is fake if that's what Lydia wants. And I'm starting to believe that might not be so easy to do.

8

Lydia

I DON'T KNOW HOW I thought I could succeed in having a public relationship with a celebrity.

Although it's a fake public relationship, I still feel completely overwhelmed that someone was able to find out who I am, and now my name is on every major news outlet and social media site as "Griffin Markey's Newest Mystery Girl."

"Sources have confirmed that the woman Griffin Markey was seen talking closely with at last Thursday's game against Los Angeles is Los Gatos University's Director of Esports, Lydia Goh. Later, Goh and Markey were seen laughing intimately at Guildhouse, a 'Video Game Bar' where patrons can play computer games while enjoying beverages. We have reached out to Markey's agent, Andrea Morales, about the relationship but have not heard back with a response."

Besides Griffin and myself, the only other person who knows that the relationship is all a ruse is Landon. But only because I think he'd have some choice words with me if I decided to pursue it for real.

"I mean, I get it, but it doesn't mean I understand it," he says, while slurping on some pho. Griffin is in Canada for an away game, and Landon and I are eating lunch before we head to the grocery store to stock up on food for the week.

"I told you, it's because I wanted to bring more attention to the Esports League. Griffin even agreed to visit the university and talk about his love of gaming with the students. I need this so people can actually start respecting me in this job."

It took a lot of willpower to tell myself that this was *not* about trying to get Griffin to fall in love with me by fake dating him. No, this was strictly business. Besides, he already told me that he wouldn't want to date anyone because he doesn't subject whoever he's with to all the flashing photos, media attention, and incessant questions. So, it's better if I just live with the notion that we try to stay friends. Then once we each get what we want, we'll continue on with our lives as if we never accidentally met at that game.

"Yeah, but that feels like it benefits you more than it does him," Landon says. "He didn't ask for anything in return?"

"I mean, I told him that I would help him be less nervous about being in the public all the time. So, technically, he does get something out of it. I think he felt bad about hurting me, and we were in the right place at the right time at that game. He thought that he'd never meet me, so he let me down easy. But it's irrelevant now.".

"Yeah." Landon rolls his eyes as he reaches to take a bite of the spring roll. I love that we can find such good food in San Jose. We had to wait half an hour to even snag a seat, but with the rollercoaster of a week I've had, this is my happy place.

"He's lucky that I didn't break his nose."

I blink at him. "You would not have done that."

"No," he mutters as he looks down at his food, watching the eye-round steak slowly cook in the near-scalding hot broth. "First, I think I would have probably been arrested. Second, he's not worth the pain to my fist. Because while I think I'm strong, he's a lot stronger than I am, and any part of his body I hit would sprain my hand and do absolutely nothing to him."

I instantly picture Griffin's muscles, how they are still so defined, even with a hoodie on. The way he shoots the puck so efficiently around the ice. These angry feelings I have for him might be at the forefront of my mind, but in the back of my mind is the thought of him using those muscles to carry me, throw me on the bed, pin me down, and kiss me with those plump lips of his.

"He's not worth it," I tell Landon, "And now that we're 'together'," I say with air quotes, "You need to be nice to him. He's doing me a big favor, and I don't want anything about our fake relationship to be revealed. As far as you're aware, this is a very real thing, and I am very much in love with him."

Which is not necessarily true, but I can still be in *like* with his looks and body. Maybe we can see if, amidst the quid pro quo of it all, we might be able to have some *fun* along the way.

"Ugh, barf!" Landon says. "I feel like King Triton from The Little Mermaid when Ariel's like, 'But Daddy, I love him!' And I want to be like, 'I forbid you from seeing this man.'"

"What happened to me being an adult?" I countered.

"You can be an adult just…I have to keep this a secret until after April?! That's so long."

Landon starts whining like a baby, and I'm inclined to drown his wails in my soup. What's it to him anyway? He's not the one forced to spend all his spare time with Griffin to make this relationship seem convincing.

"Sorry, but we have to give enough time after the season so it doesn't look like it doesn't come off as a PR stunt. You seem so upset about this. You're not the one that has to fake date him."

His shoulders sag, and his face softens with a wince when he looks at mine, which apparently looks like I'm about to murder him.

"I'm sorry," he begins. "You know that I support you in whatever you do, even if I don't agree with it. I just…I still have to go along with it and I…was really rooting for you to date Mark, I mean, Dr. Brosamer. He seemed really into you."

If that's the case, then I wouldn't want to lead him on. I thought he was a nice person, and sure, he was interested in talking to me, but I didn't really feel any spark. I think we'd be better off as friends if he's okay with that. I haven't heard anything else from him since that night, anyway, even though we exchanged numbers at the game. He's probably not going to be super ecstatic to see me Monday, though. I set us up for success, only to tell him, "Sike! My online fling *did* end up working out, and we're dating now". Some things don't work out, while others work out in unexpected ways. Getting a fake hockey player boyfriend was definitely not something I put on my list of things I was manifesting this year.

On Monday, everything at work felt like it had changed.. I walked into the Student Life meeting that morning and everyone quickly looked up from their phones and blinked right at me, like I had made such a loud ruckus coming in that it had distracted everyone from their work.

I sit down at my seat around the conference table and Kristian looks at me, betrayal all over her face.

"Why didn't you tell me?"

"I'm sorry?"

"About your relationship?" she grits. "Come on, Lydia! I thought we were best friends!"

"I mean, I think we are..."

"But best friends tell each other everything, and you didn't tell me what could possibly be the most important thing to ever happen in your life."

I'm already dreading the direction this is going. I'm not worried about telling Kristian because I think that she'll get over the fact that I didn't tell her for obvious reasons, but my dating life is not that big of a deal. I guess I forgot who I'm dating.

Hopefully, the excuse of a celebrity romance gives me some slack. "I mean, given who it is, you have to kind of understand why I needed to keep it under wraps, right?"

She scoffs. "I guess so, but *holy shit* Lydia. Griffin Markey? How'd you bag that?"

I tell her the whole spiel I had rehearsed in my mind: we met while playing *Hero Seek*, but I don't tell her what really happened, that I tried to ask him out, and he turned me down somewhat gently, yet with no context at all. No, instead, I spin the narrative. We go on a date and I go to his game, and we're seen together later that night, confirming that we're in a relationship. Well, speculating, but that night, we post a selfie on our social media, and then everyone starts thinking that we're dating.

"Wow, of course you meet the love of your life on a video game. So what you're saying is, because I couldn't play with you that night, that I basically helped set you up."

"Basically." I'll agree with her if it'll make her feel better. Kristian is the Director of Fraternity Life, and her job can get pretty rough sometimes, especially over big party weekends like Halloween or game days. If this is what will put the pep in her step and avoid any bad blood between us, then awesome. "Thanks, Matchmaker."

"You're very welcome," she beams. "Although I'm glad it worked so well for you. If you can tell me the science of how to score a guy, I'd love that."

"Date didn't go so well?"

She shakes her head and tilts her head up, agonizing over the thought. "He just wanted to brag about work. And I don't blame him, he works for Google, but oh my god, I couldn't take it any longer. He wanted to talk so much about his job, but then I wanted to talk about my job, and he kept complaining that he didn't know how to relate. I was like, 'Really? You can't relate to frat members who are constantly getting in trouble for intoxication?' I found that surprising."

"Well, I'm sorry that your date didn't go well and that I didn't tell you about this earlier," I tell her. "It's all kind of a lot. I didn't think I'd ever seen my name so much online."

And some of them do not hold back.

"Yeah," Kristian winces. "People are crazy. I saw someone tag Griffin on a comment saying, 'Why would you want to date a nerd when you can have whoever you want?'"

I slump in my chair. I can keep telling myself all I want that this stuff doesn't affect me because these people are strangers and they don't know who Griffin is or who I am, but it does hurt a little bit. Is Griffin meant to be with someone who "looks good next to him on social media?" And what can I even do to make myself be someone like that?

"People are just jealous," I tell her.

"Yeah, and it's not a good look. But I know you," she smiles at me. "And you're better than these petty bitches."

Dr. Jones finally enters the conference room and starts our meeting. He goes into detail about everything going on in Student Life at the moment: the holiday bash that takes place right before finals, the calendar of cultural celebrations and heritage months, and how we're planning to celebrate each one. Kristian talks about the upcoming initiations for each of the Greek chapters and starting to plan spring recruitment, and when it comes to me, I forget what I'm doing. I want to talk about my personal life because that's been at the forefront of my mind, but we're at work now, and I have to start thinking about all the things that need to be done before the semester ends.

"Lydia," he calls. "Would you like to talk about what your department has been working on?"

"Um, yes. We have been planning our first tournament on LGU's campus in partnership with San Jose State. I have been talking with their esports club and booked the Grand Ballroom for our tournament. I am already in talks with vendors such as NVIDIA, Corsair, and some indie businesses. We'll be starting to market the event in January, and hopefully, we'll have a strong turnout both from schools as well as the community."

Dr. Jones blinks at me and he tilts his head at me like I'm missing something. My grandiose plan that I've been spending the last month on seems like it's missing something. Like it's not a great idea to have a tournament here to bring awareness to esports with all the schools in the Bay Area and local tech corporations.

"I think you're missing a key aspect of your work," he notes.

I look at him skeptically. "I'm sorry, what?"

"I saw that you've got a special someone in your life. When do we get to meet him?"

My mouth forms an "O," and I look around the room at the eyes blinking back at me. I didn't really have this laid out on my agenda of things to talk about because I literally just started "dating" a few days ago. I didn't think others were going to have opinions on what I was going to do about my relationship, but again, big hockey star.

"Um...I really haven't talked to him about visiting."

"What? Why?" Carley in Housing and Residential asks. She's not a particular favorite out of the people I work with. She isn't bad at her job, but she's not very fond of when Dr. Jones tells the group that there's a push for esports funding because we're new. But when she wants yet another new thing for the dormitory that was just built, then she throws a fit and wants to "see the numbers" that are supposed to be indicative of an ROI.

"Because," I stammer. "He's busy."

"Oh yeah, he just swept Vancouver this past weekend," Jay in Diversity and Inclusion says. "He's such a good player. You'll get me an autograph, right?"

"She should tell him to donate to esports," Carley adds. "That'd be a great help for the school."

"I'm not asking him to do anything," I snap, and suddenly everyone shuts their mouths, including petty-as-fuck Carley. "I'm sorry. I didn't mean to shout. I want to enjoy myself in this new relationship, and I won't ask him to do anything that he doesn't want to do. Besides being a hockey player, he is a person, too. We're, as you say, enjoying our honeymoon phase."

"Well, that's adorable, Lydia." Dr. Jones says. "We won't rush you, but of course any opportunity for us bask in Mr. Markey's greatness, we'd truly appreciate it."

"Of course," I nod. "I know that Griffin loves to meet his fans."

We go over more items on the meeting's agenda and finish up just before it's time for lunch. Dr. Jones dismisses everyone, but as I'm about to get up and leave, he calls out for me to stay behind for a moment.

"Can I talk to you for a moment, Miss Goh?"

Kristian stops, and I let her know to go to lunch without me, in case this conversation takes a bit of time. I'm hopeful that it doesn't, but I have to set aside time if Dr. Jones wants to talk to me, regardless of what it's about.

The room empties out, and Dr. Jones guides me to sit down next to him. The whirring of the air conditioning in the room surrounds us, and I feel uncomfortable that we're sitting so close, in two out of sixteen chairs, when there's no one else in here.

"What did you want to talk about, Dr. Jones?"

"Well, I wanted to talk to you personally without the rest of the team in the room. I wanted to ask if there's a way you can convince your boyfriend to...give some of his wealth to the esports program."

"Uh…" I thought we had already gone over this. It was easy to lash out when Carley said it, but I can't think that way when it comes to my own boss.

"We just started dating. I don't think it's appropriate to ask him for money so early into our relationship, if ever," I tell him.

He sighs and looks at me, guilt canvassing his face.

"Lydia," he begins. "I haven't announced this to anyone else but you yet, but considering it is your department, I should tell you first."

His solemn face starts to worry me, and I brace for the worst as he begins to suck in a breath and tell me the words I never want to hear.

"We're not doing as well with esports as everyone had hoped. President Nulty has decided that it's been a risk to take on esports with the spend just as high as certain sports, and we're not seeing reward. We need to raise at least a hundred thousand dollars if we want to offer scholarships to students next year, on top of retaining staff and purchasing equipment."

I gulp. Of course, this is news to me. I mean, I know there has been a struggle to try to raise enough funds to accommodate all of the dreams and equipment, but after this year, if we don't have enough money, then that's it? That's the end?

"So you're telling me if we can't get the money by what, the end of the school year, then…"

"Then there will no longer be an Esports Department at LGU."

And if there's no longer an Esports Department, then my job will be eliminated. My dream job. A job that I had spent so many hours brainstorming ways to make successful, gone. Just like that..

"Great," I croak.

"So, yes. It's great that you're now with Mr. Markey. If you're able to have him help out in this way, it would really help you and the department."

"S-sure. I...will try and ask him as soon as I can."

"That's great, Lydia," he smiles. "You would be a big help if you're able to raise these funds."

Yeah, and also try to keep my job. I know that I went into this fake dating arrangement thinking that it would benefit me, but I was thinking more so about the awareness of the club and the respect that I would gain if they saw him with me. Asking for money, hell, a hundred thousand dollars from him? That's a down payment on a house. That's a fancy sports car. That pays my student loans and probably part of my brother's. I can't do that. Which is why I'm going to be almost breaking my back trying to figure out how to fundraise it myself and seeing if he'll use his reach to help me.

Let's just hope I do it in time to help save myself.

9

Griffin

Griffin Markey: hey, u busy thursday night?

Lydia Goh: no, why?

Griffin Markey: games night is at my house - wanna come?

Lydia Goh: uhhhhh yeah sure. will i get to meet your friends?

Griffin Markey: yeah. Ross and Micah. they're cool. they know about us, btw. i felt like i spend too much time with them for them not to know the truth.

Lydia Goh: that's ok. it makes sense. I told my brother, because if i didn't then you might need a restraining order against him.

Griffin Markey: ha ha. yeah that's fine. i'll text you my address - be here around 7?

Lydia Goh: ok sounds good. do you need me to bring anything? food? drink? both?

Griffin Markey: yeah, feel free to bring something to eat and drink. we like doing it potluck style. i don't really cook, but i'll make like lasagna from TJ's or something.

Lydia Goh: haha, always count on Mr. Joe for having such good frozen foods.

I DO THE LAST bits of tidying up in my house, making sure that there is nothing out that would cause a stir. When the guys come over, I put less care into how my house looks because I frankly don't give a damn if they think the house is messy. I'm busy, and I don't have someone hired to help clean the house. But with Lydia coming over? Now, that's something that I have to worry about.

I don't know if she's a clean freak or if she has more clutter around her place, but I want to make a good first impression.

Because even if this whole thing is fake, I still want her to like me. While we're both in the mindset that dating may do more harm than good, I still think about her a more than I should. And opening up my home to her is going to take our friendship-slash-fake relationship to a new, vulnerable stage.

Ross and Micah arrive before Lydia because I told them to show up half an hour earlier to go over a game plan. And by game plan, I mean things they can't say while Lydia's here that will humiliate me because I know they're going to say some out-of-pocket shit.

"Knock knock," Ross and Micah walk in, carrying a tub of fried chicken and hard lemonade seltzers. This is going to be tough to burn off at practice tomorrow.

"Hey," I greet them. "Wow, this takes me back to college."

"Well, we didn't want to bring a veggie platter, so this was our other option."

I shrug. "It's good. I'm just thinking of the chicken sweats tomorrow. Oh, by the way, Lydia is coming over."

Micah's eyes widen at me. "What?"

"Wow, that's awesome!" Ross squeals. "We get to meet the woman that's replacing us in Griffin's heart!"

"She's not replacing anything," I counter. "She's a fake girlfriend, you guys know that. I'm just trying to help her get her esports league off the ground, and she's trying to help me with my aversion to the spotlight."

"Yeah, but we also know that you don't want it to be fake," Micah says. "Are you sure that she's not into you?"

"Yeah," I nod. "Because she told me."

"Just because she said it doesn't mean that it's true. She might not even really know her own feelings," Ross explains. "You need to try and prove to her that you can handle a little bit of attention and be seen out in public with her. She fell for you once, she can damn well easily do it again."

I roll my eyes and put the drinks in the fridge. "I'm not going to force her to fall in love with me. She's made up her mind; she wants to keep this strictly business, and that's fine. I think it's be better if we we're just friends anyway if it reaches that point."

"Boo," Ross says, giving me a thumbs down. "That's no fun. You should be able to be with whoever you want to and not have to feel guilty about it."

"Too late," I tell them. Even if, by some magical coincidence, I was able to convince Lydia to date me, there are so many unknowns in being roped into a relationship with a pro athlete. The biggest one is where I'll go. My contract isn't up for another two seasons, but then, I don't know if I will be in San Jose. I might be in Canada or back near home. While I would love to stay with a team and staff I've grown to consider family, I don't always get a say in the matter. New talent is always pooling in, and now I'm unfortunately, nearing the way out. And with that, means the possibility of moving. Lydia has made her home here. Her family's nearby, and all she knows is the South Bay. Plus, she has her dream job. I would feel guilty if I had to take her away from that. Or put her through long distance, which is always a toss-up in terms of how well it will go or how long it will last.

"It'll be no-strings-attached fun," I determine. I know that I might need something to curb my hormones if I'm constantly looking at Lydia. Maybe some light physical touch here and there to make things believable. "If I convince her to fool around a little, great, but nothing that we're tied to."

"Agreed," Micah says. "Women have a lot of baggage."

"Ugh, you guys are so pessimistic!" Ross is the hopeless romantic of our group, but he barely goes out on dates. I feel like he's been withholding some important intel from us on why he's both so in love with love, and doesn't want to do anything about it.

I hear a knock at the door and start to race toward it. "That's Lydia. Be on your best behaviors!"

"We can definitely try!" Ross shouts. I shake my head and suck in a breath. Showtime. I open the door and smile when I see Lydia holding an aluminum tin of something and a bottle of wine.

"Hi!" She holds up the items in her hands. "I made some noodles. And brought wine. I hope everyone likes wine."

"Thank you," I grab the bottle from her and beckon her inside. "Did you make these?"

"Yeah," she nods. "They're like vermicelli noodles, but seasoned with soy sauce and there are some some spare ribs in there too. I hope it tastes good."

"I'm sure it'll taste amazing," I tell her. It definitely smells divine. It's really thoughtful that she brought something, especially something homemade. All of us can barely cook or don't really have much time to. This is a nice change from the fast food or takeout we normally opt for.

I lead her into the kitchen and introduce her to the guys standing rather suspiciously with their hands folded on the kitchen island.

"Lydia, this is Ross and Micah. We've been teammates for the past ten years and, ironically, all like different types of games, so we play weekly with one another."

"Hi," she waves softly. "It's nice to meet you all."

"It's great to meet you," Ross says, sliding up next to her. "Griffin's told us so much about you."

Her face reddens. "He has?"

"Not anything bad," I blurt. I think. God, I'm so nervous about how these guys are going to humiliate the shit out of me in front of this woman. "Right, Ross?"

"Of course not!" He grins. "Actually, nothing but good things. Like how good you are at *Hero Seek*. If you want to play with a good player instead of Griffin here, who is average at best, hit me up!"

"Ross," I elbow him. "I'm sorry for him. You don't have to feel obligated to play with him."

She starts chuckling. "He's not that bad," she counters. "I'm just a lot better."

Micah and Ross make an "ooooooo" sound, and I start smiling with my head down. This woman's going to absolutely ruin me, more than she already has.

I reach into one of my cabinets and grab plates and utensils for everyone, along with wine glasses for myself and Lydia. Micah and Ross both express their distaste for wine, which I can see makes Lydia feel a little bad that she brought it, but I tell her to pour me a glass so I can enjoy it with her. Ross and Micah open the hard lemonades that are going to run them off the rails.

I decide for our board game night that we should play Monopoly, considering the last time we were meant to play, I talked everyone out of it because I wanted to go home and play with Lydia instead.

When I pull out my luxury edition wooden Monopoly board, Micah and Ross groan. It is a favorite of mine, so I had to adorn my game collection with one that really makes you feel luxurious while playing it.

"What, now you two don't want to play? You were giving me such a hard time for not wanting to play it last week!"

"Yeah, but that was last week!" Micah says. "I really don't know if I'm ready to lose some friendships tonight."

"You guys are being dramatic. Whatever happens, we'll still be friends."

"You're just saying that because we have a guest over." Ross leans over and whisper-talks to Lydia. "Watch out, Griff's a menace at Monopoly."

"Don't listen to them," I warn Lydia. "I'm *not* a menace when it comes to Monopoly," I repeat Ross's accusation.

"He just gets super competitive. Be prepared to make it a living hell to trade anything with this guy. He will barter to no end until he gets what he wants."

"Oh gosh," Lydia giggles. "It's too bad that I'm really hard to convince then."

Fuck. I feel my insides tingle, and I'm willing myself not to get flustered. This is going to be a really tough game, not because, yes, I am very competitive when it comes to Monopoly, but it's going to be really hard to resist Lydia's charms.

"I am willing to trade you my Park Place for your Marvin Gardens plus my railroad! Why won't you accept my trade?!" Lydia groans.

"Because a monopoly on the yellow puts you at a huge advantage!"

"And the blue doesn't?"

"The likelihood that someone will land on my spaces versus yours is so much less. And one railroad will get me barely anything!"

Lydia throws her hands up in frustration. "I can't believe you'd turn down the chance at a monopoly because you're thinking about probabilities."

"No, I'm thinking about how you've already taken control of a good chunk of the board, and I won't let you have any more of it!"

She rolls her eyes. "God, you really are a pain to play Monopoly with."

Micah and Ross snicker to themselves, and I genuinely feel a little bad that I've created a shouting match between me and Lydia. Maybe the guys were right, maybe I do get a little too competitive over a game that'll mean nothing once we're done playing.

The game finishes, and Lydia comes out victorious. After a lot of asking, nay begging, that she trade with me to make her monopoly, I finally relent, and one by one, the rest of us start going bankrupt. First, it was Micah and then Ross shortly thereafter, and then it was down to the two of us. After I gave Lydia a hard time earlier, she was not going to go easy on me. She had more properties than I did going into this final showdown, and when I ran the gauntlet of her properties, it was inevitable that I was going to land on the one space that she decided to build a whole-ass hotel on and declare myself bankrupt.

She squeals when I admit defeat and begins clapping to herself.

"Oh my god, that was such a long game, but we did it. We defeated the beast!"

Ross and Micah high-five her, and she finally turns to me and holds out her hand.

"Good game," she tells me. "You really put up a fight. But in the end, I just edged it out ever so slightly."

"Yes," I laugh. "Yes, you did. Good job."

Ross and Micah decide that they're going to call it a night and both start making their way out. As they shut the door, I go into the kitchen to see Lydia doing the dishes.

"Lydia, you don't have to do those. I'll take care of them later."

"No, it's okay," she tells me. "You were already nice enough to open up your house and invite me over. Plus, after that humiliating loss, I figured this would help ease a bit of the pain."

"Suuure," I nod. "Well, thank you. And thanks for bringing over the noodles. They were really tasty."

"You're welcome," she smiles at me. It's the first genuine smile since we played *Mario Kart* together at Guildhouse. Although, now that we're alone, I can see that she's not doing this to put on a show. She's interested in talking with me, and I'm savoring every last bit of her beaming face. "I like to cook, so when I'm given a reason to, it makes me happy to spread the love to others."

"I wish I could cook more, but I have such a busy schedule that I haven't taken the time to learn much."

She finishes up the dishes and reaches over for a rag to dry her hands. "Did you ever, like, make things with your parents? Or what is something that your parents made for dinner that just screams 'home cooking'?"

"My mom makes some really amazing tonkatsu. That, with some rice...nothing screams comfort to me more than that."

"That's awesome," she smiles. "You know, when Landon first found out about us, he was kind of bummed. Not just because of what you did to me, but because he looked up to you for being a Mixed-Asian American in the NHL. There's not many people of color in the NHL, and to have one be on a team that he's grown up watching over the years, it kind of stung a bit."

My heart drops. I know that this can only apply to one person because it just so happened to be Lydia's brother who invited her to the game where we met in the first place, but I don't want my decisions to be the reason that he stops seeing me as an inspiration. It always warms my heart to talk to certain fans, especially children, who tell me that it's cool to see someone that looks like them on the ice. I don't want a mistake I made to be the reason that I don't inspire someone, especially someone who shares a similar ethnicity to me, to chase after dreams that have a history of not welcoming them.

"Really?" I frown. "I'm sorry, I didn't mean to..."

"I told him that he shouldn't stop looking up to you for something that happened in your personal life. I don't really know hockey, but people have told me how good you are since the whole dating thing's come up."

"Do you want to come to a game?" I ask her. I get free tickets all the time, but I don't have friends who are non-hockey players. Plus, my parents never want to see me, so I would be happy to give it to a guest to use.

"Really? Are you sure?"

"Yeah," I nod. "I don't have anyone that I would give them to otherwise. Come to Saturday's game. And bring your brother. Tell him that I'm sorry for what I did and that despite my...decisions in regard to us, I don't want him to think that I won't be advocating for diversity in the NHL. As long as I'm a player, I will always speak up about my heritage."

"Good," she smiles. "You should. And thank you, I'd be happy to come to your game. I'll like...buy a jersey with your name on it and everything."

I feel my heart skip a beat for a moment. Imagining Lydia in a Stingrays jersey with my name on it. It makes me want to scoop her up, twirl her around, and proclaim to the world that she's mine.

"You don't have to," I say, trying to mask my delight.

"I know, but I think it'll be good! I mean, it makes for good content."

"You're right. Do it for the 'gram..."

"Exactly," she nods. She looks over at the time, and already it's nearing midnight.

"Shoot, I should probably go home. I have to work tomorrow, and it will take me time to get home and do my nightly routine."

"Yeah, same." I have to practice tomorrow and try not to keep thinking about Lydia in a jersey when I should be thinking about shooting pucks into goals. "I'll walk you to your car."

We head outside, where the slight Bay Area breeze sends a chill throughout the air. The leaves falling on the street remind me that my favorite season is approaching, even if that season lacks the snow I'm so used to back home.

"Thanks again for coming," I tell her. "Despite my tough loss, I had a really fun time."

"Thanks for having me. I had fun, too. And Ross and Micah were really nice. They're good friends. Makes me think not all athletes are super douche-heads."

"Only me, huh?"

She smiles and turns her gaze away. "Maybe. Just kidding. You're alright."

"Good night, Lydia, get home safe. Um, text me when you get home, alright? Just so I know you made it."

"Okay," she tells me. "I will. Good night, Griffin."

I watch as she gets into her car and drives away from my house. I sigh and watch my foggy breath in the cold air. I don't know how much longer I'm going to be able to fake this because every time Lydia does something that makes me smile, I fall deeper into the hole, and she's the only one who can pull me out.

10

Lydia

"I can't believe you wanted to come back here," Landon says. "You are entering into the inferno, and not because they're playing the Flames."

"Har har," I reply sarcastically. "He invited me to a game, and I wanted to go. Keep in mind that I could have picked anyone to go with me, and I chose you. A simple thank you would be nice."

I was pinching myself a little that I was back here for the second time in a month after never watching a live hockey game in my life. The first time, when I was devoid of any Stingrays gear, I stood out like a sore thumb because I wasn't much of a fan then. Now, I'm wearing a black and teal Stingrays jersey with Griffin's last name and number sewn onto the back. I wonder if I'll see the return of the over-hundred-dollar investment I made on a hockey jersey. The good thing is, I feel like I'm fitting in better with the crowd of fans who are also wearing jerseys or other Stingrays gear, Landon begrudgingly included.

He huffs. "Thank you. I'm genuinely curious where we're sitting."

"I am, too." We pick up our tickets at Will Call, and I have to run through the whole shebang of telling the ticket person who I am and show them my driver's license before they can give us the tickets.

We grab them, contained in an envelope with my name on it, then head up the concourse. I start to feel uncomfortable with all these fans' eyes turning to stare at us as we walk by.

"Um, Lydia," Landon whispers. "Why are people staring?"

"Because they recognize us...I think." I gulp. No one has their cameras open for photos yet, but two pairs of eyes become three, four, ten. No one is ballsy enough to walk up to us, but I know what's going through their minds.

They're probably thinking something along the lines of: "Oh my god, that's the woman that's dating Griffin Markey. How can she be his type? Well, it seems like he's into nerds, so that would make sense," because I'm definitely not on anyone's hot list.

"Just keep walking," Landon tells me, and he reaches to put his hand on my shoulder to guide me ahead of him. "Where are we sitting?"

I reach into the envelope and pull out two tickets that read "PL8, Row 1, Seat 1 and 2."

"Um, hey, Landon?" I ask. "Where's PL8?"

His eyes widen, and he rips the tickets from my hand. "Hold on, PL8?"

"Yeah, that's a weird name for a section, right?" I've been seeing section numbers that begin in ones and twos but nothing about a section that says PL.

"PL stands for Penthouse Lounge," Landon says. "It's like, overlooking the rink from the very top, and there's a dedicated bar and lounge, and it's super fancy. It's basically a suite!"

My jaw drops. We're sitting in a suite? That sounds so much nicer than sitting in the stands with everyone else.

"Wait, really? So how are we supposed to get there?"

We walk around and finally head up the stairs, where we find the entrance to the Penthouse Lounge. The attendant scans our tickets and leads us inside.

"Holy shit," I whisper. The lounge is beautiful. There's a full bar with no line like the ones on the concourse have, with a full spread of food under heat lamps. You can either sit and watch the game on the rink in these plush leather seats, or you can enjoy a drink or bite on a dining table, watching one of the lounge's many television screens. There are a few people in jerseys hanging by the bar, and they nod at us when we approach it. I order a margarita and Landon opts for a beer. We sit down in our seats, watching the players continue their warm-up.

"Okay," Landon sighs. "I hate to admit it, but this is really nice."

"You hate to admit it?" I raise my brow at him.

He groans, slumping into the chair. "Yes, I hate admitting it. I'm not supposed to like your boyfriend."

"He's really trying to be nice," I argue. "It's not about what he said to me during that *Hero Seek* game anymore. I'm over it, and you should be too."

I wasn't fully over it, not yet. But I thought about what would come of us dating. Would people look at me and think I wasn't what they were expecting to be dating a celebrity athlete like Griffin? Because I didn't wear luxurious clothes or jewelry or fit a mold, someone already predestined Griffin's partner to fit into?

I know that I asked to have attention on me, but I'm not going to change my looks to fit someone's perfect mold of what they're expecting from Griffin Markey's girlfriend.

The warm-ups end, and the lights start flashing in Stingrays colors. The crowd starts cheering when the announcer finishes introducing the opposing team and hypes everyone up ahead of the Stingrays announcement.

When Griffin's name is called, I jump out of my seat and start cheering. Landon side eyes me but it only fuels me to start cheering louder and wilder. Some people sitting with us turn to stare, but I don't give a damn on who can see. I only wish that Griffin could see me in the sea of thousands cheering for him. Just so he knows, I'm here to support him as a friend.

The game starts, and Griffin is truly on a roll. He's kept possession of the puck throughout the game, and he's attempted to score a bunch of times already. The goalie has saved all of his shots, but by the second period, he finally gets one in.

In the next play, Griffin steals the puck from an opposing player and tries to make a shot but is unsuccessful. As the goalie gathers himself to shoot the puck again, something dramatic happens. The opposing player that Griffin stole the puck from shoves him hard. Griffin gives him a shove back, and immediately things escalate. They're ripping at each other's jerseys, and the other player pushes him against the wall.

"Oh my god, what's happening?!" I gasp. "He's going to get hurt."

"Lids," Landon puts his hand on my wrist. "It's okay, he's going to be okay. They're just fighting. It's normal in hockey."

The referee breaks up their fight, and the other player gets put in what seems like a timeout box while Griffin's teammates check in on him. I sigh when I find out he's not hurt, but oh my god, that was such a scary feeling.

"Normal?" I shriek. "In what sport is fighting normal?"

He narrows his eyes at me like I'm the one who just said the absolute dumbest thing. "Lids, you're the Director of Esports gaming, which arguably is all about fighting."

"That's different. They're not really fighting each other. It's a simulation."

"Okay, fine," Landon rolls his eyes. "Well, have you ever watched football?"

I look at him straight-faced. Well, I suppose he got me with that one. "Okay...fair. But I wasn't expecting it to come so out of the blue like it did just now!"

"Well, yeah, I mean, valid. Hockey is a very contact-heavy sport. You're pushing people out of the way so you can clear a path for yourself to shoot, right?"

I nod. I guess it does make sense. But I can't help but feel terror over the idea of someone being on a mission to hurt Griffin. Even with his protective gear on, it must still bruise a little from being pushed against the wall and getting knocked into.

"Okay, I guess you're right. Sorry, I'm still learning the ropes with everything."

"Hey." Landon pats my arm. "You don't have to feel sorry. You're still trying to understand the game. Maybe I should have been giving you a run down. That's my fault too."

The buzzer sounds off, signaling the end of the period. The Stingrays are tied 1-1, and this is their last chance to make their goals before...what? Is there an overtime?

"What happens if the period ends and they tie? Do they go into overtime?"

"Yeah," Landon says. "They go into overtime. But it's different from other sports. If neither team scores in the time-frame of the first overtime period, then they can go into a shootout. And that will determine who wins."

"God, how stressful."

"If it gets to that point, yes. But the Stingrays have been holding their own. I think they can score one more goal and prevent the other team from scoring one themselves to win."

And by sheer luck, or because Landon is a genius, he's right. The Stingrays end up victorious when Micah shoots a goal with Griffin's assist.

"You know Micah?" Landon asks after I finish cheering for him by name while the other fans whoop and holler.

"Yeah, I went to Griffin's house for a games night. I met Ross and Micah and then ended up beating everyone at Monopoly."

Landon's eyes go wide. "Wow," he says. "I, uh, didn't know he invited you over to his place."

"Yeah, it was really lax. I mean, his friends were there, and we ate dinner and played games. I brought rice noodles and spare ribs. Everyone seemed to enjoy it. And his friends are really cool. They get together once a week to play a game, and because they have such different tastes, they take turns choosing. They also play trading card games, which is really cool. Griffin told me they're getting back into Magic and wanted to see if I'm interested in going to buy some packs with him."

I've always wanted to get into trading card games, so I was happy when he asked. I'm simply happy to play games with someone. Nothing to do with any desire to try to impress Griffin to get him to like me or anything. That games night taught me that I can enjoy playing games and keep my feelings strictly platonic. While it was hard when Griffin was standing over me in his kitchen, watching me wash his dishes, I kept thinking about how we have a good friendship, and it would be a mistake to mess that up more than anything.

"Wow, Lids. That's really cool. I'm...happy for you. He sounds like a chill guy to hang out with."

"Thanks," I grin. I'm happy for me too. I'm already starting to feel more confident in what I'm doing and who I'm talking with. Never mind that I have to still raise a lot more money or else I'm out of a job, but Griffin doesn't need to know that, even if my new relationship with him means that he's dripping with money to spend on me.

The game ends, and I've definitely had more than my typical amount of libations for the night. I start to waddle out of the lounge, waving at everyone I see and cheering, "Stingrays win!" so that everyone has it engrained in their minds.

"Okay, Lids," Landon grabs a hold of me. "God, when is the last time you've had this much to drink?"

I shrug. "Benji's wedding?" Benji, our cousin, got married six months ago in a lavish wedding at the Hayes Mansion. I definitely took full advantage of the open bar and somehow found myself tearing up the dance floor to everything from the Cupid Shuffle to trying to teach my Yin Yin how to dougie.

"Oh. Yeah, you were having fun at that wedding, if you know what I mean."

Our mom might have had to shush me one too many times at the dinner table, so yes, I am now realizing what he means, and I'm not the most fond of my behavior.

"Yeah, yeah, Mom wasn't very enthused with me, but to be fair, I was going through a lot! I had just interviewed for LGU and already freaking out about whether I got the job or not."

"And you did. Crushing it, if I might add. Speaking of your job, do you need help with the Homecoming showcase?"

I groan. "Fuck, I need to make a list of what I need to get ready for that event. How is it already next week? I feel like I don't have anything ready."

Homecoming is LGU's alumni weekend, where they plan a bunch of programming around all the fun-filled things LGU has going on to, once again, urge alumni to donate. This is the first year that esports will be showcased, and I have been, for lack of a better word, slacking big time on this. I just don't know what else I can plan. The computer room will be open for alumni to come in and ask about our esports teams, with opportunities to play some of the games as well, if they'd like. I don't know if that's going to make them want to donate, but dammit, I have to hope so.

Since there are going to be so many alumni on campus, that is truly my first and last ditch effort to make an impact. Because I'm not relying on Griffin to make a donation and don't want him to feel forced to either..

"Are you going to ask Griffin if he can come and make an appearance?" Landon asks.

"Pfft, no." I tell him.

"Why not? Isn't that the whole reason you two set this shit up in the first place?"

"Shut up!" I put a hand over his mouth. God, if someone hears what we're talking about right now, my whole cover will be blown. "Don't talk so loud."

"There are thousands of people around us," he gestures. He notices that I've turned cold, and a look of worry crosses over my face, so he taps me on the shoulder to calm me down. "Fine, fine. Sorry." He whispers in my ear, and with my heightened, nay drunken senses, it tingles my ears, and I begin to shiver. "Are you gonna ask him or no?"

"I don't know!" I admit. "I mean, I should ask him because you're right. That's the entire reason that I wanted him to agree to this in the first place. But I was saying that because I wanted to get Jared and the players to start respecting me. It's a whole other ballpark when you're talking about alumni and their deep pockets. I can't force Griffin into that warzone!"

"Why not?" Landon asks. "I'm sure he does a lot of schmoozing in his line of work. He can figure out how to talk to people, so they'll give you money."

"Still," I counter. "It's next week, and I don't want what it to take away from his schedule."

"Suit yourself," Landon shrugs. "I can't believe it sounds like I'm on Griffin's side. But I really think that it doesn't hurt to ask him. Seems like he'd say yes."

I slump my shoulders, feeling the cool air kiss my face as I wait for Griffin to come out of the arena to greet us and his fans. Feeling a little bit of the alcohol drain out of me, I sober up and start to feel sad that I'm the one that's afraid, and it's hurting me more than helping.

"You're right. I'll ask him right now to see what he says."

"Good," Landon says. "I'm just going to wait with you until I get to say thank you for the tickets, then I'm waiting for you in the car."

"Fair. I can't complain that you're staying to say thank you."

"Hey, I can be a gentleman sometimes."

I watch a hint of softness open up on Griffin's face as he runs through his routine of saying hi to each of his fans, taking a photograph, signing a puck or a jersey, and not looking so stiff as he was last time. He looks up, meets my eyes for a moment, and waves. I sheepishly wave back, and two girls, maybe around Landon's age, wearing Stingrays jerseys—ironically, the same ones as mine that boast Griffin's name and jersey number—turn their attention on me.

"Hi," One of them says to us. "Are you Lydia?"

Uh oh. I don't know if I fully prepared myself for what would happen with a fan encounter.

"Yes," I nod. "I am."

"Oh my god!" The start jumping up and down, and subsequently, people begin turning their heads, Griffin included.

"Yeah," I try to force a laugh. "It's really not a big deal, though."

"What do you mean?" The other one squeals. "It's so romantic! Does Griffin support you at your events, too?"

"I...I don't have anything really coming up..."

"That would be so cute!" God, when did their voices get so high-pitched?

"Is everything okay here?" Griffin asks.

They screech in unison, and I feel like my eardrums are about to burst. "Griffin! We were just telling Lydia how excited we are to see that she supports you at your games!"

"Yeah, you two are such couple goals!"

Griffin chuckles, and he gives me a look that makes me want to melt in place. His hair is slightly wet from the sweat in his helmet, but I like how it looks, knowing that it got like that from all the work he did on the ice.

"Thank you," he tells them. "Would you mind if I talked to Lydia in private?" He rests his hand on my shoulder, and my breathing picks up from how warm his hands feel.

"Of course, of course!" They tell us. Griffin nods at them in thanks, and he asks security to open the gate so Landon and I can be on the same side as him.

"Oh, go ahead," Landon says. "I just, uh, wanted to say thanks for the tickets, man. It's always been my dream to sit in the Penthouse Lounge, so...that was really nice. That's all. I'm going to wait in the car. No rush, Lids."

"Hey," Griffin starts. "Uh, if you want, I can take Lydia home."

"You sure?" Landon asks. He then looks straight at me. "Are you sure, Lids?"

I'm feeling the after-effects of tequila and wanting Griffin to wrap his big arms around my body.

"That's okay with me," I tell him. "I'll ride home with Griffin."

"Okay," Landon nods. "Text me when you get home, alright? And make sure she gets home safe?" He doesn't look menacing, just genuinely concerned.

"Yeah, of course," Griffin says. "Lydia will get home safe. That is a promise."

"Good," Landon nods. "I'll see you tomorrow, Lids. You two have a good night."

"Night," I wave goodbye.

Griffin looks down at me. "Thanks for coming tonight."

"You're welcome. Thanks for inviting us. I had a fun time, even though I barely know the rules."

"I'm glad." He smiles. "And hockey isn't too hard to pick up. Bottom line: shoot the puck into the goal, and the team with the most points wins. There's other things to be aware of as well..."

"Like fighting?" I butt in. "Yeah, learned about that too."

"I'm guessing you saw what happened?" he asks.

I nod. "Landon let me know very gently that fighting is a very big part of hockey...as it is with other sports like football, and...football, and..."

"Football?" He laughs, but my face turns grim as I remember him being pushed against the wall and thrown around by the other player. "Wait," he says, concerned. "Were you worried I was going to get hurt?"

I nod, trying not to let my inebriated state cause my eyes to water.

"Sorry," I sniffle and use my jersey to wipe off some tears streaking down my face. "I...get emotional sometimes. It's not a very pretty look, I know."

"Hey, it's okay." He wraps his arms around me, and I'm surprised at first, but once I feel his body pressed up against mine, I return my arms around him. It's nice. I like the protective layer he gives me. Even if he smells like sweat. "We wear a lot of protection to keep us safe. And I know that anything can happen, but I take extra caution when I'm on the ice so I don't worry anyone."

"Okay," I nod. I trust him. He's been doing this a long time, and even though anything can happen, he looks out for himself and I just have to let him do that.

"I hope the hug's okay," he says. "I'm very sweaty. But it seemed like you needed one."

"It was very needed, thank you."

"Hey, just want to be a good friend," he says.

Yeah. Friend. That's all we are and all we will remain. It's better that way.

"Are you doing anything this weekend?" he asks. "I figured we can get lunch. Get to know one another, as friends, of course."

"Oh, uh. I actually have to work. It's our Homecoming weekend and it's this big thing where a bunch of alumni come back to the school. I'm doing an open house in hopes that they'll donate to fund our program." Because this is my one shot.

"Nice. Did you...want me to come? I know we were talking about how part of this arrangement is me helping you with work stuff."

"Yeah," I reply. "For like, rude and stuck-up coaches who don't take me seriously. Not alumni with fat checks, that's too much ."

"No, it isn't Lydia," he shakes his head. "Tell me what time, and I'll be there."

"Okay." I croak. "Thank you. I can text you the details."

Who is this man I've been waiting all my life for? And why did it have to be someone who doesn't want to commit to anything more than a fake relationship with me?

11

Lydia

Pacing around the room is doing nothing to help calm me down from the ball of nerves I am feeling right now.

"Girl, you look hot as hell," Kristian says. "Stop worrying so much."

"I can't," I tell her, ready to pull my hair out, even though that will ruin the curls I spent all morning perfecting. I'm dressed in a blazer and a blouse that shows a hint of cleavage, and honestly, I haven't felt this sexy in a long time. I didn't dress this way to attract anyone, well, maybe except for Griffin, but if I was going to look like a bad bitch in a male-dominated industry, then by gosh, I'll wear a top that might be a little tight, so the girls can peek through.

"You're going to do great," Kristian tells me, gripping me by the shoulders. "You're going to get those donations secured, no problem."

"All one hundred thousand of it?" I whimper.

"Okay, probably not," she says. "But you have a bit of time to make that up! Think of this as a way for you to get ahead so that after the holidays, you can worry less about making up the rest. Plus, Griffin can totally act as arm candy around these stuffy donors."

"Yeah, crossing my fingers," I tell her. "You going to the happy hour tonight?"

"Hell yeah," she says. "The one weekend where LGU gives its staff and alumni free alcohol? Plus, I think the people at campus dining would definitely give us a double pour because we're staff."

"I would hope so. We're the ones stressing out, trying to impress everyone on behalf of the school."

The year after I graduated, I was so gung ho to go to a Homecoming. I felt that hot girl energy, thinking to myself, "I'm a big adult who has that big girl job, and I can participate in things like networking mixers with free alcohol and talking about the working world." Then I got older and still kept feeling that, but there became a point where things changed. I didn't really have any friends who were still in school, and people were less enthusiastic about going back every single year. Now, with my staff ID and university-branded business cards, I have to put my best smile forward again for LGU and everything that it offers. Go Condors?

The room is quiet for a moment as I wait for people to come and visit. I spent the majority of yesterday just standing by the printer waiting for these brochures I designed to print on fancy glossy paper. I guess it'd be okay if no one came. Then I won't need to shake myself out of a socially awkward funk.

Not long after, two couples come in and peer around the room.

"Hi!" I grin widely. I think my voice raises three octaves. "Welcome to LGU's Esports Computer Lab."

Each one of them are probably around my parents' age, maybe slightly older. They all have mostly grey hair, or…no hair. I forget that my parents are about to turn sixty. So I guess these guys can't be much older.

They peer around at the rows of computers, which all have a different game booted up for anyone to try. I walk up closer to give them a spiel about the setup if this whole "esports thing" is new to them.

"This is where members of our Esports Club and team can come to play various competitive multiplayer games with each other or other schools. Each desktop is equipped to run these games at blazing fast speeds, and we even have licensed gaming mice and keyboards that the pros use."

"So when did this…club become a thing?" One of the ladies asks.

"Oh! Well, this year, we started a pro team. Kind of like athletics? We're working to compete in tournaments with other schools and host one of our own."

"But playing video games isn't a sport."

I hold my tongue. It's okay, I rehearsed this. I have crafted the near perfect response to their skepticism.

"Actually, esports has recently been televised on networks like ESPN, and as it is two teams competing for entertainment, then it is, by definition, a sport."

"But they're not exercising," someone else mentions. "It doesn't require any physical energy."

"Actually, it has been proven that you do burn calories while playing a video game."

They stare at me like I'm spewing nonsense at them. *Do you want me to show you a chart or something? You can still be doing physical activity even if you're sitting in a chair!*

"There are some sports that use different parts of the body. Esports require you to be quick with your hands. If you are interested, I'd be happy to walk through a game with you."

They ponder the thought for a moment, but somehow, as a collective, they all agree that this is dumb, and they'd rather spend their time and their savings elsewhere.

"We are going to pass, actually," a lady says in a sweet, sarcastic tone. "But this was...interesting. Thank you for showing us around."

"Of course," I smile. "I will be here for the next two hours if you have any questions."

I slump in one of the gaming chairs. Two hours left? Of possibly the same routine of trying to tell people this is the shit and ending up deterring them away from it? Fuck this.

A bit of time goes by, and still some of the same type of people come in: old, presumably rich, decked out in LGU memorabilia and struggling to see why this should warrant their donation. And on top of that, I asked a few team members to come in and do a mock game for some of the attendees, but no one showed up. I know it's difficult to ask students to make plans on a Saturday, but shouldn't they be excited about this too?

As I'm about to sit down yet again, a family of four walks in, and I want to roll my eyes, certain that the same shit's going to happen again, but I need to keep a smile plastered on my face.

"Hi there," I beam. "Welcome to Los Gatos University's Department of Esports Gaming!"

A boy, probably around middle school age, nudges his mom's arm. "Mom, look, this is what I was talking about. I can play video games as a sport in college."

"Is that true?" She asks, staring at me. Am I supposed to feel intimidated by her stare at this seemingly innocent yet seemingly accusatory question?

"Yes." My nod turns into a near bow with how much force I'm exerting with it. "Yes, actually. We are fundraising money to give students the opportunity to receive scholarships to play competitive esports and have the opportunity to host and participate in tournaments with schools both in the Bay Area and around the country."

"And students would be able to...receive scholarships for their tuition by being recruited for a team? Like how Athletics works?"

"Exactly."

"Isn't that cool, Mom? If I keep playing League, I can become good enough to be on a college pro team!"

"Yeah, but what about basketball, Mason? You like basketball, and you're good at it!"

He throws his hands up. "But that's the thing, Mom. I'm not that good at basketball. I score points, but I'm not as good as Jace or Adam, and that's okay. But I can get a bunch of kills in League, and if I keep at it, I'll be a shoo-in for when I'm thinking about college, and I can play for LGU."

The mom looks at me as if I just brainwashed her child. But he's right. Everything takes practice, and with enough of it, we'll have a pool of players who are good enough to play esports at the collegiate level.

"Can I play a game here?" he asks, racing to the computer. "You can leave me here with..." He searches my face for a response respond.

"Lydia," I answer him.

"Lydia. If you need to go and do other things."

"Mason, I'm not leaving you here to...get you brainwashed by these computers." She glares at me, and I try to keep my face positive and professional, even though I'm terrified of her and the aura she's radiating right now.

"I can't believe they spend our donations on this. Do you see what you did? Now my son thinks that he can make it big by playing on the computer all the time. He's learning skills are going to go plunging down the drain!" Thank god her kid has earphones on right now.

"I..." Do I apologize? I want to because I want to be on everyone's good graces, but I'm sick of how many times I've heard that this department is brainwashing children or how it's not a sport. And I'm actually starting to get frustrated that Griffin promised me he'd be here, and he hasn't showed up while I've had to suffer with people who don't want to hear what I have to say.

"I can assure you that video games do not brainwash your child," a familiar voice appears at the door. She turns around and almost trips over herself at who enters the room.

"Oh my god," the younger kid standing next to her mom says. "It's Griffin Markey!"

"Griffin Markey," the dad stammers and stands straight up like he's a deer in headlights. "It's an honor to meet you. I didn't know you were involved with the school."

"Only recently. I thought I would come by to support my girlfriend while she's working."

"Girlfriend?" The mother squeaks. "This is who you're dating?"

"Yeah," he beams confidently. I blush a little. Even if it's a front, hearing it warms my insides.

"Awesome." The dad nods. "Yeah, I think I read somewhere that you were in a new relationship. How'd you two meet?"

"Online, actually," Griffin notes. "We were matched in a video game together and actually got really close. Turns out we both live in San Jose, and I've enjoyed the time we've spent together since we started dating." He looks down at me and grins, and I'm struggling to form any sort of response, so enamored by the way Griffin seems to say these things with such ease. And the way his eyes peer into mine. God, my heart is racing.

"Excuse me, Griffin?" The kid taps on Griffin's wrist. "Do you think that we can play a game together?"

Griffin's eyes widen a little. Guess he only thought he had to utter sweet nothings to these uptight alumni. "Hey, yeah, sure thing, buddy. Can I speak to Lydia first? And then I'll hop right in."

"Okay!" He skips back to his chair, and his parents sigh once they realize they definitely have no other choice but to sit and wait until Mason and Griffin are done with their game.

"Excuse us a moment," Griffin tells Mason's parents, pulling me aside to a corner of the room.

"Hey," I begin.

"I'm so sorry I'm late," he cuts in. "I had made a note to get here right at one o'clock, maybe a little earlier, so we could walk through a game plan, but the container that my leftovers were in exploded in the microwave, and my smoke detector went off. I don't have a fire extinguisher, so I made a note to order one, but long story short, I had to wait for the fire department to arrive, and it took longer than I thought to clean up, and I'm so sorry again, Lydia. I wanted to be here for you and for this, and I feel so bad that you had to do this by yourself for as long as you did."

"Griffin," I put my hand to his chest, then quickly retract it. I did not want to have it linger there for too long and grip those delicious pecs living under his button-down shirt. "It's okay. I'm not mad. Are you okay? You literally just had a fire in your house."

"I'm fine," he reassures me. "I'm microwave-less and don't trust containers that promise they're microwave safe anymore, but I'm fine. Nothing in the house burned down, thankfully. How's it been here? Besides that mom that thinks you've brainwashed her child."

"More or less the same shit," I sigh. "People come in, they look around, they think that what I have got going on is not really worth their time, and then they leave. I don't know what to tell them that will convince them that we're worth giving a chance."

"I'm sorry," he says. "But I'm here now. Put me to work!"

"Well, it seems like you've got a game queued up with a nice boy named Mason."

"Yeah, but I can easily tell him that I've got other responsibilities that my girlfriend has set up for me."

My heart flutters at the way the word *girlfriend* escapes his lips, and I lose my train of thought. "Um...I...can't think of anything right now. Go have fun. You're probably making this kid's year by playing video games with him."

"Okay." He nods and grips both sides of my arms before giving me a peck on the cheek. My face goes red, and he steps back.

"Um...I did that for show," he whispers. "You know, to look convincing."

"Y-yeah. Totally. Thanks. I'll let you know if anything comes up, okay?"

"Sounds good." He skips over to Mason, who is practically jumping out of his seat when the game boots up, and they're playing alongside each other.

"You know," Mason's mom slides up next to me, her face a little softer than when she accused me of essentially ruining her kid's life. "He hasn't been this excited about something in a long time."

"Oh yeah?" I ask innocently.

"Yeah. I mean, it's been tough. He's been having a rough time at school, and we found out he has ADHD, so we tried to figure out things that would be good for his focus. And we thought basketball would be it. He likes it, but he doesn't show nearly as much excitement for it as he does video games. And we didn't want him to spend so much time behind a screen because we thought it would do more harm than good. But he actually looks happy and invested in something."

Mason shouts, "Oh my god I can't believe I killed that guy!" and Griffin congratulates him with a high five.

"Good job, buddy," he says, and I grin. I shake my head out of its trance once I realize that I've started thinking about how good he is with kids.

"So, I'd like to apologize," the mom says. "I didn't mean to come off so harsh. This is really cool, what you have going on here. And if all works out, I think our son would love to be a part of this when he goes to college. We want him to go to

LGU, of course, but we'll support him with whatever decision he makes."

"Thank you." I nod at her. "And it's okay. It is a very new concept for a lot of people. That's my job, to educate people on our ever-evolving world, and this is just one part of it."

"Absolutely. You had some brochures out that mention something about donations?"

I sharply turn my head at her. "Yes?"

"I'd like to see if I can make a donation to the Esports Department."

"Oh! That's wonderful. Thank you so much. Here," I lead her to a table I've set up my laptop on. "Just put *esports* in the text box on where you'd like your donation to go."

"Excellent, thank you."

Griffin looks up at me from his computer and gives me a thumbs-up. I stick mine up at him, and he smiles, going back to his game with Mason.

Suddenly, my phone vibrates, and I look at who's calling me.

"Hey, Kris," I answer. "What's up?"

"Lydia. Be prepared. I am letting you know right now that the computer room is about to be flooded with people."

I gasp. "What do you mean?"

"Word got out that Griffin's there, and people want to see him. Someone must have said something about it, and everyone just got up and left from the fraternity open house. I'm just warning you, it is going to get very chaotic in there very quickly."

"Great," I respond. "Just...great."

"You got this, Lids," Kristian reassures me. "Just tell people they can't have a photo or autograph from Griffin unless they hear your speech about donations."

"You know, that's not a bad idea," I tell her. This shit shouldn't come for free.

"You got this. I'll see you after the open house."

"Alright, thanks, Kristian. Sorry I stole everyone from FSL."

"Eh, don't be sorry. These kids have to learn how to fundraise for their own chapters. Talk to you later."

And as soon as Kristian hangs up the phone, madness ensues. People rush into the room, and clearly, no one understands the meaning of personal space.

"Okay, hold on!" I chase after people who are coming in and trying to catch a glimpse of Griffin. They're sitting next to him and trying to interrupt the game Griffin and Mason are in the middle of.

It makes my blood boil because it's an absolutely horrible feeling to be suddenly bombarded by a swarm of people, and a fuse in me goes off, and my defensiveness go on full blast.

"Hey." I push someone encroaching in on Griffin's space. "I'm going to have to ask you to stop getting into Mr. Markey's space until he's ready to talk to you. If you don't comply, then I have no problem calling campus security to escort you out."

Griffin reaches over, grasps my hand on the table, and gives it a light squeeze.

"Uh, okay," the man, a younger alumni, says. He gets up and walks backward to create space around where Griffin is sitting, and I start leading them back to the table where the donor information is.

"While you're waiting to see Mr. Markey," I continue. "May I suggest reading about our fabulous Esports Program?" I hand out the flyers to each person standing in line. "And maybe consider a donation to keep the program going."

Once I am successfully able to maintain some line control, Mason and Griffin finish up their game, and Mason thanks me over and over again for the best thing that's ever happened to him. His parents appreciate it, too.

"Okay." Griffin comes up next to me. "How are we doing this?"

"How should we be doing this?" I ask him.

"Everyone can get a photo, but if you donate, you get an autograph?"

"I don't want to force people to donate..." I tell Griffin. "But I'm not going to force you to do anything you don't want to do."

"I'll do what I need to do. Don't worry about me."

Griffin stands next to the donor table, and I start ushering people in. Everyone's being respectful now. They calmly walk up to Griffin, ask for a photo, and a few ask him to sign a piece of their Homecoming badge. People are also using their spot in line to go up to the computers and donate. I walk out of the room to see how long the line is, and it spans all the way down the hall, the stairs, and out the door of the student union.

"Holy shit," I whisper. It looks like the entire campus might be standing in line for this.

"Hey," Landon walks up to me, standing outside of the student union. "This all for Griffin?"

"Uh-huh," I nod.

"Well then. I sure hope they donate for basically being at the right place at the right time."

"Me too," I tell him. I really did not think that there would be as big of a showing for Griffin, not like this, but it really shows how huge of a name he is and how, without him, I really would just be no one at all.

12

Griffin

MY CHEEKS HURT FROM all the smiling, but it warms my heart to see this room so full. Every seat is occupied with people who are playing various games on the computers. Some doing well, while others are dying left and right, but they don't seem to mind.

People who have come up to me and asked for a photo or autograph have been fairly respectful. They don't encroach on my space or spew inappropriate comments like "I want your babies," which somehow surprises me. It's been a lot of "You're a huge inspiration to me, Griffin" and "I'm really excited to see an Asian hockey player." Maybe Lydia was onto something. Was I too stubborn to see things through?

I lose track of how many people I've spoken to, but it's probably in the hundreds at this point. The open house is over, but people are still waiting in line to see me, and I don't want to disappoint anyone by ending the event, especially when there might be more opportunities for Lydia to receive more donations.

Sigh. Lydia. I peer over at her every once in a while at how beautiful she looks in that blazer and corset combo. She's dressed up more than her usual casual flair, complete with a sensational shade of dark pink lipstick that I want to kiss right off. She's calmed down since I first got here, and she's so entrenched in conversation that she doesn't even notice that I've been staring at her for the past few minutes. I really shouldn't have kissed her. It was on the cheek, but still. My lips tingled on her skin, and I've dug myself in so deep that every little move she makes fills me with a rush. I resist the urge to rub my hand over the hard-on forming in my pants.

Finally, after hours of smiles and standing, the line ends, and we're allowed to clean up and turn off the computers.

"Wow," Lydia says as she's scrolling through her laptop. "We raised ten thousand dollars today."

"Really? That's amazing!"

"Yeah," she whispers quietly. "Really is."

Her face looks sad, and I'm confused about why that is.

"Everything okay?" I ask her.

"Yeah," she murmurs. "Everything's fine."

"You don't seem fine," I tell her. "What happened?"

"Nothing!" Her voice raises, and it jolts me for a moment. It doesn't seem like nothing, and now I'm starting to get frustrated that she won't tell me what's going on.

"Your tone sounds otherwise," I retort back.

She rolls her eyes at me. "I can't even tell you what's wrong because you're not going to even think it's your fault, and I'm really trying not to blame you, but it's just...I can't do it."

"Blame me for what? What did I do?"

"You...exist, Griffin!"

I...exist? When did that become a problem for her?

"I'm sorry, I'm just...frustrated? I guess? I know I shouldn't be complaining. I'm happy you're here, and I'm really thankful you took time out of your busy life to meet all these people, but I'm just thinking that if you had left the room at any stage tonight, the swarm would have followed you. And it made me realize that...I put in all this hard work, but without you, it all would have gone to waste. I'm nobody when I'm in the same circle as you." Tears begin streaming down her face, and I instinctively rush to wrap my arms around her, even if there is no one around. It's what I'd do for any friend.

"Lydia," I say, rubbing her back to comfort her. "You are not nothing. You're the farthest thing from nothing." You're amazing and one of the hardest-working people I've met, and I'm really starting to feel a deep connection with you. That's what I want to tell her.

I rest my chin on top of her head. "I'm sorry. If my being here made you upset."

"No," she reassures me. "I don't want you to be sorry. And that's why I hate that I feel like this. It's just that I work hard to prove myself as a woman, and it makes me wonder whether anyone would give me the time of day if it was just me running this show."

"If they don't," I tell her, looking into her eyes. "Then they're making a mistake. Because you're one of the most hard-working people I know."

"Thank you." She rests her face on my chest, and I pull her in tighter to me. "You did an amazing job with all those people. I really appreciate it. How do you feel?"

"Surprisingly, it was pretty easy. People were very calm, which makes me realize...have I been freaking out for no reason?"

"I wouldn't say no reason," Lydia notes. "I think it just depends on the environment. We're at a school during the day versus after a hockey game, where people can be really riled up. I mean, aren't there fights that happen after the game between fans?"

"Yeah, fights happen." I don't see it, but hockey games are notorious for fights between fans. Maybe because they see the players fight, and so it makes them want to. Or a lot of drinking. That could very well be the reason too.

Lydia breaks away from our hug to do a once over of the room. After we've checked that every computer has been turned off and chairs have been tucked in, she puts her computer into her backpack and leads me to the door.

"Are you doing anything tonight?" she asks, pulling on the handle to make sure the door's locked.

"No," I shake my head. Maybe playing games alone, but I think about asking if she wants to play games with me. I'm not sure if that will bring up any sour memories, though. "Why?"

"Well, as a thank you for helping me out today, can I buy you dinner?"

"Ah." Our first time out together, just because. She has an eager grin on her face, and I don't want to turn down her offer. I mean, dinner with her sounds perfect, but typically, when I go out somewhere, I try to see if I can get a private area. I don't know where she's thinking of going to eat, but a little part of me dreads that it's somewhere busy because it feels like a lot of the popular restaurants in San Jose are packed to the brim at five o'clock on a Saturday.

"Okay, sure. Sounds great. Where are you thinking?"

"Well, I'm the one treating you, so wherever you want."

I'm trying to think of what I might be craving, but then I realize I crave a lot of the same things: ramen, dumplings, pizza. Oh, tacos. I run through my list of staples in San Jose, and I think that I'm overdue for a helping of dumplings, but I want to make sure that it'd be okay with Lydia.

"Do you like dumplings?"

She responds by laughing in my face, and I don't know if laughing back is an appropriate response, but I do.

"What's so funny?" I ask.

"You asked if I like dumplings, Griffin. Rule number one is yes. I like dumplings."

I relax my shoulders. Shit, I thought I had ruffled another feather, and I would be stuck trying to figure out how to apologize.

"But Landon and I had dumplings the other day. So it's not like I don't want it, but..."

"It hasn't been that long of a time to go without it," I reply.

"Yeah, I know what you mean. So let's do what you want. I trust your cravings."

"I feel like we share similar interests in food, which is most foods." she tells me. "There's a cute French spot not too far away in downtown Los Gatos. It's kind of small, I like it. Makes it feel intimate."

"French food?" Gonna be honest, that cuisine is not one I'd immediately think of when I told Lydia to suggest something. I know her favorite cuisine is Chinese food, and if she could eat one food for the rest of her life, it'd be wonton noodle soup. But if she has a good restaurant recommendation, I'll trust she knows where to go.

"Yeah." She tilts her head. "Is that okay?"

"Yeah," I nod over-enthusiastically. "It's totally fine. I didn't mean to sound so unsure. I just don't remember the last time I've had French food."

"You know, it's been a while for me too. But we'll go to this place sometimes for department holiday dinners. It's a nice treat."

"Okay." I open my hand out her for to lead the way. She suggests that we take one car to the restaurant, so we don't have to worry about parking.

We drive out of the hills where campus is and through some windy roads until we reach downtown. Like many downtown areas, it has one main street with a bunch of small shops and restaurants. There's a mix of small businesses and more well-known companies, and truthfully, you know when you're in a high-income town like Los Gatos when your options for furniture buying come in the form of a Restoration Hardware.

Lydia finds a place for us to park. We get out of her car, and are seated almost immediately in the restaurant. Lydia's right, it is a cute French bistro-style spot that doesn't have many chairs and tables, but each one is filled, and above each one are cute photos of France and different cookware hanging from the walls.

We are handed menus, and Lydia gives it a quick once over before closing the menu and placing it down.

"We should order a bottle of wine, right? It feels fitting for the occasion. But if you're not feeling wine, then we don't have to order it. I was just thinking because it fits the ambiance."

I chuckle. She is really cute when she rambles. "We can get a bottle of wine to share. I think you deserve it after the day you've had."

"Okay, sounds good."

The menu has a good variety of things for us to feast on. I know it might be the most basic thing I can get, but I could absolutely go for a steak Frites right now.

"How about escargot?" she asks.

I wince. Now this, I'm not completely sure about. In the grand scheme of things, escargot doesn't sound all that weird. Sure, it's snail. But people have the same visceral reaction to different sashimi. Especially uni. And I absolutely love uni.

"Never had it," I tell her.

"Would you like to try?"

I shrug. "Why not? Have you?"

"Oh yeah," she nods. "It's so good. When you're tasting it, you don't even realize that you're eating snail. They season it with a bunch of herbs and butter that make it as good as it is."

"Well then, let's try it out."

We tell the waiter our order, and promptly after he puts it in, a legit sommelier comes over for us to try the wine. Lydia motions for me to take the first sip of a bold Cabernet he's chosen for us because we've each opted for dark meat meals. I take a sip and instantly smile over the rich flavor.

"It's good," I tell him.

"Wonderful," he says, pouring a full glass for each of us.

The elegant atmosphere and service truly makes me feel like we're on a date. This is the kind of effort that should be put into trying to impress someone. If we chose a restaurant based on the fact that we're just friends, then I would have been okay with hot chicken sandwiches, even though those aren't very cheap anymore.

"This is nice," I tell Lydia. "I haven't had a chance to sit down and enjoy a nice meal in a while."

"Really? Do you not go out to restaurants super often?"

I shake my head. "I've always had fears that I'd be bombarded by fans during my meal, and I just resigned myself to only eating at home. I'd disguise myself in a hoodie and hat and then just sit at home and eat by myself."

"That...sounds so sad," she frowns. "I mean, I'm sorry if that sounds really judgmental. I don't know if I could do it. As much as I don't like talking to people, I like the times when I can go out, let loose, and enjoy a nicely cooked meal."

"Well, I think it's a little different for me because people can recognize me."

"Oh yeah," she whispers. "Sorry, again," she says, taking another sip of her wine. "I kind of forgot for a moment that you're famous. But maybe that's not such a bad thing...because you're just like anyone else for me. I don't see you as someone famous."

"It's okay," I reassure her. "I'm not mad at you. I get that it's hard to understand all the feelings associated with being a famous person. But you know something funny? I think that today was a step in the right direction for me—actually being tolerant of talking to people. I really enjoyed the kids and students coming up to me and mentioning how much they look up to me." It was a nice change from the DMs that tell me I'm a total babe or something along those lines.

I might always have fears of how people are going to react, but I have to remember that certain people do really look up to me and think I'm an inspiration, and I have to remember that their adoration for me really trumps any fear that I might have that someone will come up to me and take advantage of me for whatever reason."

"That's great," Lydia grins. "So you'd say that this was a success? The talking to people and getting out of your shell for my personal gain?"

"I think it benefitted both of us, for sure." I smile. I can tell that Lydia's warmed up since we've left campus. She's got a lightness to her, and as she continues to sip on her glass of wine, she's starting to feel more relaxed and letting loose a little bit, which makes me happy.

The waiter returns to our table and puts out a dish with small holes in it. I'm guessing this is the escargot. The obvious giveaway is that these individual bites are all encased in the snail shell still, but what intrigues me is that you can't see what the inside looks like. There's a lot of that pesto-looking sauce covering it.

"So, how do we eat it?" I ask Lydia once the waiter disappears.

"You grab the...tongs?" she says, picking up these small baby tongs with little saucers at the end of it. "And hold the shell with this, and with this," she holds up a small fork, "you grab the actual meat from the shell."

She slurps up the snail from its shell and starts chewing. "Oh yeah," she says, covering her mouth. "That is so good."

"Really?" I'm still feeling a little hesitant from looking at the literal snail shell that's in front of me.

"Just...you really can't taste the meat because the sauce is so good," she says. "Try it."

I follow the motions she made, grabbing the shell, twisting the meat inside like I would for an oyster, and slurping the snail up. The texture of it is rather slimy, but it's very easy to chew and swallow. Lydia's right. The sauce is what makes this good, and if you fixate on the buttery, pesto-like sauce, then it really doesn't feel like you're eating snail at all.

"What do you think?" she asks.

"I do really like the sauce. The snail itself, is fine. Actually, the texture doesn't really bother me all that much." Dare I say, I think I would get this again if I ever go to a French restaurant.

"Oh good," she beams. "I was a little afraid that I was pressuring you to try something that you might think is gross."

"Yeah, it's definitely not gross. I could slurp up this sauce all day, and I think I'll be just fine."

She giggles, and I smile back at her. Even if she doesn't think this is a date, this is definitely the most intimate we've been thus far, and I'm really enjoying it. I don't feel stressed, and I'm perfectly content being in Lydia's company. So content, in fact, that I want this night to last forever.

Our meals come out, and I'm enjoying every last nibble of my steak frites while Lydia's eating her scallops, which look just as appetizing.

"So," I ask. "I don't know if you ever told me how you got into esports."

"Have I not?" Her eyebrows perk up, and she bites her lip for a moment. "It's not actually that exciting of a story. Landon and I used to play video games all the time, and I wasn't good by any means, but I liked playing them. When I was a student at LGU, I was trying my best to get involved in everything I could because I wanted to get the full college experience. One day, I just showed up to Esports Club and asked to join."

"Oh yeah?" I nod. "How did that go?"

"It went as I expected. Sexist men who tried to convince me that I didn't really belong. But, I didn't back down and I ended up becoming the Vice President of Recruitment. Ironic, huh? That girl that everyone was so skeptical of when she first walked through the door ended up making such a huge impact. I got more people to join that weren't just men and actually left with a lot of friends. That guy that was so skeptical of me at first? I ended up hooking up with him not too long after that."

I almost choke on a fry with the thought of Lydia with another man. She's not...still hung up on him, right? This wasn't a story to tell me that she's actually using this fake relationship to get him back, right?

"Oh, you did?"

"Yeah, but that was like ten years ago. He's very much married with a child now. But it was fun in my wild college days. You had to have wild college days too? I would be so surprised if you didn't."

"Yeah, I'd be lying if I said they weren't wild." I don't know how I calmed down from the high of being a top hockey athlete and the partying that came with it to be recruited into the NHL. Lots of hungover mornings to only have history repeat itself.

"I'm lucky that I made it out with a spot in the NHL. There was a point where it felt like I was on thin ice, ironic as that sounds. I was throwing these huge ass parties, getting drunk every time, and paying absolutely no attention to my grades. I was so close to being on probation and losing my scholarship."

Lydia looks shocked. "Really?"

"Yeah." It was a bad part of my life that I wish I could redo. But you know what they say, everything happens for a reason, and it did serve as a good learning opportunity to absolutely never do that shit again. "I learned pretty quickly after that, with my spot on the team dangling over my head, to not make that same mistake again."

We finish up our meal, and I almost reach to pay for the check, but Lydia keeps her eyes on it and snatches it before I do.

"I told you that it was my treat!" she says, putting her credit card in the folio.

"I know, but I can still be nice and treat you for doing such a good job fundraising."

She blushes. "Well, maybe I'll let you get the next one. Maybe. I guarantee you in a week, I'm gonna want those dumplings."

"And I'd be happy to treat you to those."

She goes quiet for a moment after that, and I'm having trouble reading her expression. Does she not like my responses because they sound like they're laced with a bit of flirting?

We head back to campus without saying much on the journey back. She pulls back into the parking lot of campus, near the student union.

"Where'd you park?" she asks. "I can walk you back to your car. I realized I forgot something in the esports room, so I have to head back inside anyway."

"Oh, I didn't park too far away, just a few rows back. I...can walk with you to the student union if you'd like?"

"Um...yeah. Sure."

We walk up to the student union, my hand itching to find its way to her lower back. A man dressed in a suit and holding a glass of wine beams at us as we enter the building.

"Lydia!" He holds his arms out, and Lydia, puzzled at first, walks up and takes him in a side hug. "And you must be Griffin," he says to me. "I'm so excited to be meeting Lydia's rather famous boyfriend."

"Yes, nice to meet you as well...um...Mr..."

"Dr. Jones," he says, emphasizing the doctor part. He grabs a hold of my hand and shakes it with both of his, "Vice President of Student Life."

"Dr. Jones," I nod. Lydia's boss. I look over, and Lydia looks anxious to try and get out of this. I wonder if she has a poor opinion of her boss. Like if he's hard on her and makes her job even more stressful than it already is with everything else going on.

"We were just coming to grab something from the computer room," Lydia says. She grabs onto my hand and squeezes it like she's clinging on for life, then pulls me in the direction of the computer room

"Oh, well, do you have a moment, Lydia? Just for a quick chat since your boyfriend is with you."

"Um...of course, Dr. Jones. What's up?"

"Just wanted to talk to you about the open house today. Amazing to hear that Mr. Markey helped with showcasing the computer room. I heard that you made a bit of money in donations today."

"Yeah," she confirms. "We did."

"Good work. Although, I think it would have been easier to have your boyfriend assist with that fundraising."

What is he talking about?

"I...just figured I would have my computer out during the open house. You know, as protocol. To give people an option."

"I understand," Dr. Jones smiles. "Well, I'm sure lots of people really appreciated meeting Mr. Markey. I'll leave you to it then, enjoy your night. Good to meet you, Mr. Markey."

"You as well." I nod while being pulled by Lydia, who is speed walking through the hall to the room.

"Lydia, Lydia!" I try and meet her pace. She quickly unlocks the door and rushes to grab something from her office.

"Lydia," I barricade the door with my body so she isn't able to skirt by me to get out. "What did Dr. Jones mean by assisting with the fundraising?"

"I don't know!" She looks away from me and fumbles, trying to get her purse on her shoulder. "That was the first time I'd heard about that...weird fundraising thing..."

"Lydia, don't lie to me." I'm starting to get frustrated that she's not telling me the truth about what just happened. "I think we're past that point of you hiding things from me."

"And I think that there are things that I don't need to tell you. It's not like you mean something to me or anything," she retorts. She tries to use her petite body to get through a small opening between me and the door, and I grab a hold of her waist to stop her.

"You don't mean that," I grit out. "Tell me you don't mean that."

We're inches apart. So close that I'm almost kissing her forehead.

"No," she says, her eyes downturned.

"What is it that you can't tell me? I thought we were friends, Lydia."

"We are," she sniffs. "But there are things I'm allowed to keep to myself, and this is one of them. I'm not getting you involved with this, even if Dr. Jones wants you to be."

"Are you in trouble?" I hold my hands on her shoulders. "Please tell me if you need help."

She shakes her head. "I can't."

"I'm not letting you leave until you tell me. I don't care how long it takes. I will do this all night."

"Fine." She wipes her eyes. "But you have to promise me that you'll let me take care of it. I refuse to let you be responsible for something that concerns me and my job. I've reached a point where I care about you too much to let you get this involved with me."

She sets down her bag and takes a deep breath. "A few days ago, Dr. Jones told me that the president of the university told him that esports was 'too big of a gamble' to invest in. So unless I fundraise a hundred thousand dollars by the end of the year, the Esports Department is basically going to be defunct."

I start blinking rapidly when it dawns on me. "Wait, but then that means..."

"Yeah," she chokes out. "If the department shuts down, I'll lose my job."

"Let me help you." I rush out. "What, you need ninety thousand dollars? I can wire that amount as soon as I get home..."

"No!" she yells. "No! This is exactly what I didn't want to happen. I'm not taking the easy way out, and I'm not letting you spend this much money on me. I'm not worth it. I can't ask you to make such a big financial decision. I made ten thousand today, and what? There's like...six months left to go? I can do it. I'll raise the rest of the money. Don't worry."

"Lydia." I want her to know that she is worth it. She's worth so much more than the money that's in my bank account. I would drop anything to give her what she needs.

She slings her purse over her shoulder and wiggles her way past me now that I've let go of her. "I need to go. I'll talk to you later."

"Lydia," I grab her hand. "Please let me help."

"No, just...forget it, Griffin. I'm not letting you do this. Not for me."

She races off, and all I can do is watch her disappear from the windows of the room. What can I do to get her to change her mind about this?

13

Lydia

I SHOULD BE FEELING happy that I'm en route to a work trip where I'll be in the presence of other excited collegiate esports professionals, but I'm still fixating on what transpired last week and wondering if I acted the right way about everything that went down with Griffin. I thought I had a good enough reason to not tell him about the fundraising. I just wanted to feel like I was in control of something because it was my job to do so, but I paid the price.

Am I a coward for refusing to accept help from someone I know has enough money that it feels like he's not even making a dent?

No, but I am extremely humble. And it's what's torn our friendship apart.

I haven't spoken to Griffin since what happened. He's messaged me to ask if I'm okay and after a beat of no response, he just left our texts with, "When you're ready to talk, I'll be here."

I wish the ball wasn't in my court. He's been traveling for games, so his response time would be delayed anyway.

We're about to board the plane for Las Vegas, and I'm slightly stressing over the fact that I have to be a chaperone the entire weekend. We're going to a conference held at one of the newest hotels on the Strip: a cyberpunk-themed hotel called the Cyberscape. It's the first time I've attended anything conference-like for work. Back in my tech days, there would be big conferences dedicated to our job field, like RSA or Dreamforce, but those were held in San Francisco, so it wasn't very far of a trip to attend. Plus, while it is rather cool to see Moscone Center completely transformed to appease all of the techies that attend it, I didn't feel the love for cybersecurity or CRMs as I do for esports. When I was younger, I would fantasize about attending E3 one day, the conference where all the news about the hottest video games would debut to the world.

The students all seem to be excited that we get to travel for an esports conference. They might just be happy that they get to skip classes, but a few of them were giddy in their seat when they learned they might get to meet some of the biggest names in gaming when they play their exhibition matches at the Esports Arena at the Luxor Hotel. I'm more happy that I get to connect and network with fellow Directors of Esports. I'm also speaking on a panel about "Women in Gaming," which I hope means that there'll be several women there who share in my commiseration about trying to compete with the guys.

Once the airplane makes its way from the gate, I peek at my text messages before turning my phone to airplane mode. No text from Griffin, even if my stubborn ass is supposed to tell him when I'm ready to talk.

In about an hour and a half, we successfully land in Vegas, and I gather up the students so we can make our way to the shuttle stop, where a bus will take us from the airport to the Cyberscape.

"Lydia." Drew, one of the students, taps my arm. "Do we have a curfew?"

"Uh, no. Not really." They're college students, I think they're old enough to be making their own decisions. "My rule is that I'm going to be taking attendance at every morning of the conference, and if you're not there, then I will find you and you will suffer the consequences of missing whatever programming you had signed up for. But I'm not going to say you're not allowed to be out past a certain time. I will make a big note, though," and I say this, by pointing to everyone on the team. "If any of you participate in anything illegal and get caught, you are heading straight back to San Jose.

I also will caution that you are responsible for your own money, should you try your hand at gambling. It's not like a video game where you get unlimited tries. You pay for those tries and it is very easy to blow through your money if you're not careful."

They nod to acknowledge my warnings and soon, we're loading our bags and heading to the Cyberscape Hotel.

Off the bat, the hotel perfectly encompasses that Vegas grandeur. There are fancy shrubs that line the driveway up to the hotel and screens on the walls leading into the lobby. While some hotels have a specific kind of grandeur—the Bellagio with its Italian flair or the Blossom that has flowers dripping from the ceiling—the Cyberscape radiates technological advancement. While there are valet and bellmen who help us unload our luggage, there are also autonomous robots that are moving up and down, pulling guests' luggage on a wagon-like extension, small but mighty creatures that will soon make these bellmen obsolete.

We walk into the lobby, which looks like it's straight into the future. Behind the check-in desk are large monitors that display any and all information that you need to know. The weather, breaking news of the hour, and what the wait times are for each restaurant in the hotel. And a very nice welcome sign that lets everyone with the "National Association of Collegiate Esports Gaming" know that the hotel is so happy they are staying here.

I check in with a front desk agent, opting to not check-in with a robot even though they present the option to you, who gives me my keys for myself and the five rooms that are set aside for the students. I take note of who is sleeping in which room, sound off each room assignment, and hand them their room keys. Makes it easy when you have only boys.

The kids get dismissed and excitedly head up to their rooms to settle in. The conference doesn't begin until tomorrow, so tonight is a free night to settle in and enjoy being a tourist before a busy two days. They have to choose their own dinner options, but that's easy to find. The hotel itself has seven restaurants at different price points, plus we're close to a lot of other hotels on the Strip, so they are not short on options at all.

I make my way up to my own guest room, perched on the hotel's sixty-third floor. These hotels are truly on another level of grandeur. Imagining the thousands of people occupying these rooms right now is unfathomable.

I press the key fob to the door, and when it blinks green, I open it to a spacious king-sized room. There's a bed and a small armchair, but the amenities are high-tech. There are LEDs along the headboard that are flashing rainbows and a smart remote that controls everything from one tablet: the lights, the curtains, the AC.

I gasp when I see two joy cons resting on the TV stand.

"Oh my god, you can play games in your room?!" I squeal and hurriedly set my bags down to boot up the console. Maybe I should be an adult—unpack my things, and figure out what outfit I'm going to wear tomorrow, but I think I deserve time to unwind, play a cup, or a few. I wrangled up a bunch of kids and successfully got them to the airport. I deserve a break.

I start it up and smile when the familiar Mario voice announces what game I'm playing. I'm about to start a grand prix when my phone starts blowing up with text notifications.

LGU ESPORTS CREW

Drew: holy shit there's switches in our rooms!!

Noah: damn this place is high tech

Blake: come to mine and Dev's room for some versus action

Dev: yeah so i'll school your ass

Drew: Dev Lydia's in this chat rmbr

Dev: oh shit sorry. you can come if you want Lydia!!

I roll my eyes playfully. These kids. The coaches might give me grief because they've reached the threshold where they think they're high and mighty adults, but the kids aren't like that. They're no-nonsense and fun to be around. And they don't berate me for the decisions I make for the team. They're just happy to be here. While they'd probably play in good fun and low stakes, I'm not going to interfere with their time alone for the night. I want my time to play my games, too. Just me and the NPCs.

> Lydia: haha it's okay, y'all have fun. don't forget to eat.

> Noah: you got it, Lydia. speaking of which, I'm hungry guys. can we eat and then play switch?

> Dev: ...yeah that's probably a good idea.

The chat goes quiet, and I decide that I should find my own food to eat. The hotel has many different cuisine options, even one from an up-and-coming celebrity chef who serves elevated Mexican food, but I'm in the mood for something comforting. Something that hits close to home. And I know I'll find something that checks my boxes next door at the Blossom Hotel and Casino.

I walk down the expansive block of South Las Vegas Blvd. These hotels are like campuses, with how large they are and how much is going on at their fronts. Sure, everyone knows the Bellagio fountains, but even some of these entryways are just as grand.

I walk into the Blossom and smile at how elegant and Asian the interior looks. I have never been to China, but the intricate palace-themed architecture in the Blossom is stunning. It's surreal to think that my ancestors might have been people who worked on building these palaces or the ones the Blossom tried to replicate.

I walk up to the food court, which is all Asian-fast food. I'm unsure of where to start or how much food I'll actually be able to eat versus what I'm inhaling with my eyes.

My eyes catch on a food stand with the words "Happy Noodle" at the top. The menu is simple: there are only three options for noodle soup, and the first one, the Signature Beef Stew Noodle Soup, sounds delightful.

I place my order and sit down. My eyes fixate on a couple who are enjoying noodles and playing flirtatiously with one another. It makes me happy but also makes me want to gouge my eyes out.

This is unlike myself. I'm not the kind of person to get jealous over strangers engaging in PDA,

Maybe it's because I'm missing Griffin's small, friendly touches. The strictly platonic touches that somehow have me feeling very romantic things for him. I don't want him to hold anyone else the way he held me when I needed some comfort. And I'm trying to wrap my head around how he can so effortlessly do those things and only think of me as a friend when I'm over here losing my mind over him.

I feel my lip wobble, and tears start to splash into my soup. What is with me crying in the most inappropriate places?

"Um, excuse me?" A soft, high-pitched voice has me looking up. Oh, it's the lady sitting over there with her...boyfriend? I assume. Maybe they just met. What happens in Vegas, am I right?

"Hi," I sniff. "Um, can I help you?"

"Oh! I'm sorry," she says. "I just wanted to ask if you were okay. You were crying into your soup. You know the place is called Happy Noodle?" She points at the sign above the order window, of a drawn logo of a woman smiling and pointing to a steamy bowl of soup. "There shouldn't be any sadness while eating it."

"Yeah, I get it. The noodles taste amazing, by the way. I'm just...going through some shit, apparently." Shit being a jumble of emotions of being attracted to someone while also stressing out about a job that I'm passionate about.

She chuckles. "Yeah, I've been there. A bunch, to add. I know I might be a weirdo for coming up to talk to you, but I saw you were crying, so I thought I would ask if there's something I could do to help."

"Thank you." It unexpectedly really helps to know people can care. "I'm just going through...relationship stuff? Yeah, we'll say that."

"Ah, relationship stuff," she nods. "I know that feeling."

"Really? You and your...boyfriend, I assume, look like you're madly in love."

"Well, we are, but that wasn't how it always was. When we first started having feelings for one another, it felt like the universe didn't want us to be together. We were both working here, and the former manager wanted to kill us. I know it sounds wild, but when in Vegas, right? Anyway, we got through it because love survives all, but not with some hiccups along the way."

Wait, why does this all sound so familiar? I heard something about this on the news...wait.

"Hold on," I hold my hand out to stop her. "Are you Marissa Waters? Like famous poker player Marissa Waters?"

"Oh," she perks up and nods. "You know who I am?"

"Yeah!" I exclaim. "I love seeing you at the World Series tournaments. Any time I see a woman playing poker, actually. And you're doing so well this season. It's always awesome to see a fellow Mixed-Chinese do well at something they love."

"Oh!" She blushes. "Thank you. Do you play poker as well?"

"No. Not well, anyway. I'm more into esports and video games. But card games are cool, too!"

"Don't worry," she reassures me, "I definitely love a good video game every once in a while. Kellen plays them all the time. By chance, are you here for the Collegiate Esports Conference?"

"Yeah..." How did she know about that?

"Taylor, the General Manager of the hotel, is Kellen's best friend. He gives us the rundown on what's going on there. Apparently, this is a huge deal for collegiate esports. He's a video game nerd, too, so he's hoping everything will go well."

"Me too," I note. "For my own personal reasons. Networking and hoping that my students are going to be on their best behavior."

"Oooh, are you a coach?" Her face lights up at the thought.

"No," I correct her. "I'm a Director for Esports Gaming. So all of the business stuff related to esports. Fundraising, operations, marketing, all that jazz."

"That's really cool," she replies. "Are you enjoying it?"

"It has its ups and downs. But that's like with any job, right?" I don't think that I could want any other job; this is my dream job. But with many dreams, you have to work hard to chase them.

"Yep," Marissa nods. "I don't know if any job really comes easy. But as long as you're happy."

"I think I am. I know it may not seem like it." I make a motion around my face. "But I think things are looking up."

"Good. It was good to meet you..."

"Lydia," I tell her. "Thank you for coming to check on me. I feel a lot better now. The whole...relationship stuff hasn't magically fixed itself yet, but I think things can only go up."

"That's great! I hope things work out for you, Lydia. Have a good time in Vegas!"

She walks away and grabs her boyfriend's hand. I smile as they happily look into each other's eyes and share a kiss. I unlock my phone and type "San Jose Stingrays" in the search bar. Right now, the Stingrays are losing to Colorado, but only by one goal. I debate sending a text to Griffin to wish him good luck but ultimately decide not to, in case he loses and he doesn't want to hear from me to add salt to his wound. Instead, I finish my noodles and decide to gamble a few dollars before it's time to go to sleep and prepare for the first day of festivities.

14

Griffin

THAT WAS A BRUTAL loss.

My teammate's heads are all down, and the locker room is quiet as we all get lost in our own thoughts about how that could have ended up better than it did.

It wasn't a blowout by any means. We actually only lost by one goal, but I think that's why it stings more than if we had lost by five. Because it was in our grasp, and they just happened to score another goal with two minutes left in the period.

Mack is hurting that he missed that goal. I've reassured him that he shouldn't harp too much on it, but he does anyway. He knows that he's had a solid record, and this will definitely be something that the commentators talk about tomorrow. This loss doesn't define anything other than an additional number against us on our record. I'm still confident that we'll make the playoffs, which is when we're going to have to put our heads in the game to come out victorious.

Ross announces to the team that we're going to work to turn those frowns upside down and go out to a bar. I don't feel wholly enthused about going out because I fear that someone is going to recognize us, especially because we're going to be huddled in a group as a team.

"So what if someone recognizes us?" Ross says. "Besides, you had that whole signing with those students at Los Gatos University and didn't freak out."

"Yeah, because they weren't drunk or in enemy territory." Who knows how riled up the fans are going to be once we step foot in the bar and someone shouts that it's us? It'll be like West Side Story, except instead of dancing interludes, it's drunken fist fights.

"We'll be fine. We'll just go somewhere where there will be so many people that they won't recognize us."

I sigh and let Ross lead the way. Our hotel is close to a lot of bars, so it's an easy walk to a nearby spot that is already packed to the brim with hometown fans.

"I don't know if this is a good idea. It looks like they were done with the game and traveled over here. They're probably still riding the high of winning."

"Just keep your eyes on the prize," Ross advises. He keeps his gaze forward and enters the bar once we all show the guard our IDs. I join Ross at the bar, and he asks me what I want to drink.

"Just a beer," I tell him. "Um…whatever this West Coast IPA is."

"Shot?" Ross asks me.

"No shot!" I yell. I'm way past the point of shots. Tomorrow might be a travel day and we don't have to be ready for practice, but I would still like to be somewhat functioning.

"Party pooper." Ross sticks out his tongue at me, and I roll my eyes. The bartender gives me my beer, and Ross and the other guys find a booth where we all sit down.

We get ourselves acquainted, and as the loud music plays throughout the bar, I look up to already see some of the rookies talking to a group of women.

"God, these kids, am I right?" I nudge Ross.

"I'd recommend that you do the same thing, but I already know you have a certain name tattooed on your heart."

I look away. I might have Lydia's name engraved on my heart, in my body, everywhere in my mind, but I fucked things up with her. She hasn't even talked to me since Saturday, and I'm losing it. She's fully got me wrapped around her finger, even if she doesn't know it.

The only thing I've let her know since then is that she can take as long as she needs to think about things between us. I hate that I've put the ball in her court because it truly shows that she doesn't want anything to do with me and that I ruined a very good thing. I don't want her to lose her job. The circumstances are really not in her favor. She has to try and raise almost a hundred thousand dollars by the end of the school year or risk being defunct. Of course, I want to help. I have the money, which, hearing that, it does make me sound like a spoiled brat. But I worked hard to get where I am, and I want to help.

The idea comes to me as I'm sipping on my beer and watching a few players now on the dance floor, grinding with strangers. I don't need to write a check for the amount of money they need; I can do my own work to fundraise and be the spokesperson. It worked well to get people in the door during Homecoming, and it can work for this.

"Hey," I yell at Ross over the blaring music. "I need your help with something."

"What?" he yells back.

"I need your help to get the team to donate to Lydia's esports team."

"What?" He looks at me, confused. "I thought you wanted my help getting you drunk or something. What's this about Lydia's esports team?"

"She needs to raise money so that they can keep esports at her school, and she can keep her job. I tried to just cut a check for the rest of the money, but she got mad at me for 'wasting my money on something like this.' And then she stopped talking to me."

"Wait!" Ross scoots back in his chair. "Are you and Lydia fighting?"

"No!" I don't think we are? But I'm also not enjoying the position that we're in right now. "She's...kind of angry with me and hasn't responded to any of my texts. But I really care about her, and I want her to keep doing what she loves. So I'm going to fundraise the money as much as I can and contribute the rest. To show her that I did something to help out."

"Wow," Ross pretends to wipe a tear from his face. "You're really in love, aren't you?"

"What?! Love? No. Love's a strong word." I don't think I love Lydia. I'm enjoying the connection that I have with her. Even if the intent was to be fake at first, I'm done playing fake with Lydia. I want to see if there's a way to give us a real shot.

"I really like her," I tell Ross, smiling when I say "like her." I don't think I ever stopped from the day that we started playing games. Now that I've spent time with her, it has only reinforced the fact that she's just as amazing in real life as she was online.

"I'm just trying to do what I can to make it better. I know that it was originally all a ruse, but I think I'm ready for something real." I already passed the test of interacting with fans. I think I'm feeling a lot more confident in my ability to be approached and not get anxious about the outcome. It hasn't been long since Lydia and I met, but I feel like I've made really good progress.

"Okayyyy," Ross says. He doesn't look convinced. "You have to walk the walk if you're going to talk the talk."

"What do you mean?" I ask.

"Dude. I feel like you're being too casual about this because you had one good experience with a group of fans. What happens when you get stormed by the paparazzi, and you can't protect Lydia?"

I blink my eyes shut and turn away from him. I don't want to think about it. I'd like to think that I'll just deal with it when it happens, but maybe Ross is onto something. Maybe I'm underestimating how badly this could get out of hand. Regardless, in the moment, I'd protect Lydia at all costs. It doesn't matter how I feel as long as she's taken care of.

"I don't want to think about it," I tell him.

"Suit yourself," Ross shrugs, sipping on his colorful cocktail. "I'm critical because I care."

Then care less, I want to tell him. I'm starting to not like the feeling of people telling me they know what my best interests are, and not letting me figure it out for myself.

I scoot to the end of the booth and stand up to get another drink. Screw other people's contradictory best wishes. If I want something and think I have the willpower to get it, then I will.

I stand up at the bar next to a short, blonde-haired woman. I can only see her side profile, but that face looks strangely familiar.

"Hey," I nudge her. "Tori?"

She looks up at me and gasps, her pearly white teeth on display. "Oh my god, Griffin Markey?"

"Yeah," I grin. I reach down to give her a hug. "Funny meeting you here. You live in Denver?"

"I moved here last year for work. Before then, I was in Jersey, but I wanted to move West and experience a new city for a change."

"That's awesome." Tori Lambeau and I met in college. She would frequent our parties. As a cheerleader and Homecoming Queen, she was highly sought after. At the time, I was one of the people who chased after her. We spent a night together here and there, nothing official. She's great company, and I think a part of me will always think of her as a friend.

"Yeah," she says, paying for her drink. "I cheer for the Denver Broncos now, which is really fun. And I see you're still on the rink playing for San Jose."

"Yup. My tenth season. And I'll only stop if they force me to."

"That's super cool, Griffin. It's nice to see that you haven't changed a bit." She steps closer to me and caresses her hand over mine. I swallow, frozen in place. I did enjoy Tori's company when we were together, and it seems like she's used to being in the spotlight, with being on a football cheerleading team. Is this the kind of person that I'm meant to be with?

"Would you, by chance, be free tomorrow? Maybe drinks? Catch up?" She leans in closer to me, like she's wanting something more from me. And while the memories appear of us fooling around back then, I'm not feeling any attraction to her right now.

I breathe and retreat from her. "I'm sorry, Tori. I'm not really looking to date if that's what you're trying to imply."

"Oh!" She steps back. "No, no, I'm so sorry. I was reading this all wrong."

"It's okay. I...I think I have feelings for someone else too." My intoxication is starting to cause my brain to spill some feelings that I haven't yet admitted out loud.

"And are these feelings something she knows about?"

I shake my head. "She's...not like me. I mean, she's smart, fun to be around, beautiful, but she's not famous. And I'm afraid that if I thrust her into my very famous life, I'm not going to be able to protect her from a lifetime of people constantly watching her every move."

"Well, I think if you really care about her, then you'll figure it out. I mean, shit. Do you know how many people comment on my photos when I'm dancing and tell me I'm not pretty enough, or my body looks a certain way? It's every damn day that I get these jabs at how people think I need to be a perfect person if I'm going to be documenting my life online. And you know what I do? I keep on going. I'm not living my life to appease them. I'm living it to appease me. So do the thing that's going to make you happy. Who gives a shit what other people think? You shouldn't. You'd never feel like you're doing enough, then."

"Thanks, Tor." I wrap an arm around her and pull her in. "You're right. I'm going to do what I want because I deserve to be happy and find love."

"There you go. And hey, next time you're in Denver, I hope you'll bring your girlfriend with you."

"I hope so, too." I nod. "I'm gonna go give her a call right now."

I take my drink outside, where the cool air blows against my face, and the loud noise of people talking over one another is nowhere to be heard. I take a deep breath and press the phone button on Lydia's contact page.

It rings for a few seconds before I hear her pick up.

"Hello?"

"Hey," I croak. I forgot how much I love hearing her voice. "Um. I...wanted to check to see how you were doing."

"Oh. I'm doing well. Really well, actually. Today was the first day of this esports conference here in Vegas, and I was kind of bracing for something bad to happen. Like people would just make sexist comments like I've heard daily, but it's the complete opposite."

I start to grin. "Oh yeah? How so?"

"I had a panel today, um, about women in esports. And the panel was full of people who were excited to hear about the things women are doing in esports. I was on a stage with, like, Esports Community Managers, and professional women gamers...it was surreal. A student came up to me afterward and told me that I was an inspiration for her to go into the industry after she graduates. It's...I really wish that you could be here to see it."

"I wish I could be too." If there was a way that I could take a car right now to Vegas and surprise her, I would.

"Lydia..." I begin.

"I'm sorry, Griffin," she cuts in. "I shouldn't have gotten angry with you over the donation. It's this instinct in me to work hard for something I'm passionate about. I don't want everything to be just handed to me like it's on a silver platter. But this week, I came with the goal in mind I wanted to network and meet as many people as I could. And everyone I met shared their insights with me on how to make it in the industry. They advised me that I should take the help that I can because if one person believes in what I do, that's enough to keep going."

"It's okay," I reassure her. "You know I just want you to be happy and continue doing what you love."

"Yeah. I do."

A beat of silence passes before Lydia speaks up again.

"I miss you, Griffin."

It feels like my world stops at those four words. It's what I've wanted to hear for so long from her, reverberating through my ears. The four words that snap something in me to not sit here and let time pass by. The four magical words that tell me I need to tell Lydia how I really feel.

"I miss you too," I reply. "How long are you in Vegas for?"

"I leave Wednesday. So another day of some programming, a banquet to end the night, and we fly out the next morning back to San Jose."

I start looking up flights on my phone. I can take the first flight out of Denver and make it to Las Vegas in two hours. I don't have to be back in San Jose until Wednesday anyway, so what's wrong with making a slight detour?

"Okay." I act nonchalant while watching my phone tell me my flight to Vegas has been confirmed. "Well, I'll see you when you get back then?"

"Yes. I'll see you then. Dumplings included."

"Dumplings included. Later, Lydia."

"Bye, Griffin."

She hangs up the phone, and I quickly race back inside to tell Ross about my plan.

"Hey," he greets me. "Where have you been? I saw you talking to a woman at the bar... are you and Lydia..."

"We're good. That was someone I went to college with. But Lydia and I, I think we're going to be okay. I'm actually flying out tomorrow morning to surprise her at her conference in Vegas."

"What?!" Ross's jaw drops. "You're flying to Vegas? When?"

"Tomorrow morning. We don't have to be back home until Wednesday for practice, anyway."

"And Lydia has no idea you're doing this?"

I shake my head. I'm hoping that when she says she misses me, she truly means it. Otherwise, it'll be awkward that I just bought a plane ticket to Las Vegas without any other reason than to "get the girl." I guess I can enjoy a nice meal and play a couple card games to make it feel like it wasn't completely for just one person.

"Boy, you really are in love," Ross says. "Well, I'm eager to see how you'll pull this off. Mind if I tag along?"

"Um...I mean, I guess so. If this whole thing with Lydia goes well, then I'm probably leaving you in the dust."

"That's okay," he shrugs. "I'm gonna have my own fun in Vegas. You get your girl, dude."

"Alright then, looks like we're heading to Vegas tomorrow."

MATCH GAME

15

Lydia

IT'S A STRUGGLE TO wake up the next morning and get excited for another day of programming when Griffin is waiting for me at home.

The confessional came out of left field last night. I wasn't drunk, wasn't under the influence of anything else except a longing for wanting things to be back to the way they were, and boom. The words just slipped out. I confessed that I missed Griffin and almost reached a point where I told him that I was falling in love with him.

I should be happy that Griffin misses me back. That he wants me to be happy, so he tries to help me out just like any other friend would, except his is on a hundred-thousand-dollar scale. He's just saying all these things to be a good friend. That's all that we are. Friends.

I take a deep breath as I peer at my body dressed in the mirror mounted on the wall. I straighten out my blazer and ruffle some of the waves in my hair. Today, the only responsibility that I have is to show up. I should be talking to people and continuing my networking efforts, but I did my panel, I did the happy hour mixer, and I checked in on the students, who all seemed to be having a good time.

I head downstairs, say hello to a few other directors I've only met online through setting up tournaments with one another, and take a seat in a free row towards the back of the very large ballroom space that has to be filled with close to a thousand people.

As more people start taking their seats, I shoot a quick message to the students to get down here to fill up these chairs before the program begins.

> Lydia: Y'all better be at the opening keynote and not sleeping.

> Dev: We are!! We see you sitting near the front.

> Drew: But we'll confess, we may have stayed up a little too late playing at the arcade.

> Lydia: That's ok. I did too at the...adult equivalent of the arcade aka the casino.

The conference organizer walks up the stage and takes his place at the podium. He wishes everyone a good morning and begins by telling us he has a special announcement.

"Every year, we are in awe of those who have dedicated their lives to the improvement of esports in the community. This year, to recognize the directors who have gone above and beyond for their esports community, we will be awarding, for the first time, a Collegiate Esports Director of the Year. All Directors of Esports are eligible to win, and we will choose based on the answers that directors will be submitting, as well as testimonials from students and coaches.

But you all might be asking, what is the big deal about this award? Why would I submit myself for consideration? Well, that's where the exciting part comes in. The Director of the Year will be awarded the prize of a lifetime: brand new gaming equipment provided in sponsorship with Alienware, plus an all-expenses-paid trip for them and their teams to the League World Championships happening in South Korea."

Danny and I look at each other wide-eyed. Holy shit. This is the honor of a lifetime. If I can somehow sound convincing enough for this award, it could mean so many things. A state-of-the-art esports room and the chance to go to South Korea to see one of the biggest esports tournaments in the world.

But there's one big problem. While I can bullshit my way through a really convincing personal essay, I have absolutely no control over what the students or coaches are going to say. I'm afraid that I'm going to have to try and bribe them with booze or whatever college kids like to give me a glowing recommendation. I mean, I'd hope that they'd want to go to South Korea and have a new room just as much as me.

"Now, we know that anyone can write testimonials if they submit them online, so that's why, as part of the selection process, we will be spontaneously contacting students via phone to answer some questions about their respective directors."

Oh. So that's how they find that loophole.

"Applications are open now and will be due a month from today, in mid-December. Best of luck to all the directors who are considered for this opportunity."

They speak a little bit more about the different events happening today, but all I can think about is how I'm going to make a game plan to tackle this award. I want to win, and if I do, maybe that'll prove to the school that they don't have to worry as much about getting new equipment. I'm sure Jared's picky ass would be happy. But then I look at people like Danny, like other schools who seem to have their shit together, and I very much don't. So, as much as I want to chase the dream of being known to a community as Director of the Year, I definitely don't think I am deserving of such an honor when I look around the room and see much more established, much more knowledgeable people than me.

"Thank you all again for coming. We will see you at your respective panels, and there is no closing session after this, so please feel free to explore the area. Esports Arena at Luxor is offering drop-in times for the day for teams to tour and play. And from all of us here at the Collegiate Esports Association, we thank you for your participation, time, and dedication to furthering esports in the community."

Everyone gets up, and as I start to gather my bag, Danny makes a note about the award.

"Well, this is cool," he says. "I'm eager to see who gets chosen. It'd be cool to go somewhere like South Korea to watch the League World Championships. I went to the one in San Francisco the other year, and it was amazing how much that arena filled up with excited fans. I'm assuming you're going to apply, right?"

"Yeah," I nod. "But I don't think I'm going to get chosen."

"Why's that?"

I look down at the floor. "It just feels like I don't have anything really figured out. My higher-ups set outrageous expectations about how much return on investment we should be making, but they don't do the same thing for athletics. I can tell you that there are some sports at our school that are seeing more love than esports, and the school will pour money into them. Also, some of my coaches are super misogynistic. They don't respect me in my role. They don't believe that I can run a successful team. It's...hard to be a woman in esports."

"Yeah." Danny rubs my back and gives me a one-armed hug. "You're doing really well, though. The first year of running a team is super hard. I went through it, too, when we were first starting out. Trying to give people reasons to believe and all that. But you're doing a really good job, and from what you've told me, I can tell you're really dedicated to what you're doing. And that's what's worth it. If you can make your students see that, then that's all you need. We work in higher education. It's about the students, not the money."

"You're right," I laugh. I didn't take the job because the pay was nice. I took it because I wanted to make a difference to the students I was serving.

"Thank you," I tell Danny. Honestly, I have tried to introduce myself to several directors, but he is the only one that I've felt like I've been able to pour my life story out to. Everyone else has really made it feel like it's a competition to be the best director, bragging about how nice their equipment is or how many tournaments they've won. As a school that has neither of those things, Danny hasn't judged me for any of it. And he's got one of the most renowned esports programs in the country. "If I don't win the award, which I don't think I will, I hope you do."

"Thanks, Lydia. But I don't think I'm all that. It's funny. I think the students know how to do my job better than I can."

"Yeah, these are smart kids."

"Well, I'm gonna head to my panel. If I don't see you, have a safe trip back home, and good luck with the rest of the year. And with that special someone, too."

"Thank you." I give him a quick hug. "Safe travels to you and your team as well. And hopefully, we'll see each other at a tournament sometime."

"Do you have any you're registered for?"

"One." The only one I signed up for because I didn't know how equipped the students really are to participate in a tournament. But it's in April, so I'm hopeful that by then, they'll be raring to go. "It's the Valorant tournament in LA."

"Oh yeah? We're going to that one too. Looks like I'll see you in LA in April."

"See you then. May the best team win!"

Danny gives me another wave before making his way to a conference room, and I do the same to the "How to Market Your Team" panel, where I think what they're about to teach might be things I already know, but it was either this or "Understanding Your Esports Team's Financial Well Being." I don't know why Danny decided to attend that panel, but I also think his students really know how to market a team. Somehow, they are going viral on social media for just...showing off their game-playing skills.

After an entire panel dedicated to what the teacher dubbed "Gen Z Marketing," I head out to find the students. I don't have any other panels lined up for the day, but now I want to do everything right by the students so they look up to me enough to give me a glowing review when it comes time to select a Director of the Year.

"Hey, all." I walk up to them as they're talking to students from another school. "How was your panel?"

"It was fine," Dev says. "I feel like you'd like it but I would have just preferred to play in mock games with other schools."

"Yeah, that's how I've been feeling, too," Drew chimes in. "Like, these are all really cool and important things that we should be learning, but do they expect students to sit through all these things to learn something? We do that already for school; we want to be able to, I don't know…meet other players and play games!"

The rest of the team nods in unison, and I'm surprised. In a good way. I'm happy that they're expressing themselves on things that they feel strongly about. To me, that's a step in the right direction. At least they're not bullshitting anything for my benefit.

"Well, is there something that you all want to do that can actually be to your benefit? Like go to the arena and play?"

"Wait, can we?" Dev's face beams.

"Yeah, why not?" I shrug.

"Well, we didn't know if you wanted to go with us to these things. And maybe we haven't been super vocal about what we want either, so that's on us. But sorry to break it to you, Lydia, but panels and networking are boring. Is that what we have to do when we're in the working world? If so, I'm not ready to work."

"It's not always about panels and networking, but it is a part of the job. In all honesty, I don't love that part either, but they teach me a lot. Like how these social media platforms can garner a lot of attention from students as the marketing tool of choice."

"Ah," Brent nods. "Yeah. It's not hard, though. You just do some fun lighting effects and show us playing games, and you'll get noticed easily. It helps that we're good at what we do." He winks, and a laugh spills out from me.

"You guys are good at what you do. I don't get sentimental very often, but I really appreciate all of the work that you all have put in for this team. We're still very much in our growing stages, and some days may seem hard, but thank you all for being so kind to me. I want to make sure you all have a team to come back to next year."

"Thank you, Lydia," Drew says. "You're the one that does all the work, so we get to do what we love. We may not say it a lot because we've got a lot on our minds—school and playing and all that—but you've been a huge help in making all of our dreams come true. We're sorry if we don't speak up and defend you as much as we should. Jared and the other coaches say some mean things, and I should speak up against it because I definitely don't think you're bad at your job."

"Neither do I."

"None of us do."

"Really?" I raise my eyebrows. "Well, thanks guys. That really means a lot."

"When it comes time for those people to come and ask us what we think about you as a director, we're going to tell them that you're the best, most hard-working director there is. And we hope you win, not just because it means we'll get to go to South Korea or have a newly decked-out game room. But because you are the best director."

I try not to get emotional again, but I love these guys. This is the most they've spilled out to me since I became director. I want to envelop them all in a hug, but I save my feelings because I think they'll try to squirm out of it.

"Thanks, everyone. I really enjoy working for you all, and hopefully, one day, we'll bring home a tournament win and get our name on the map. And I hope all of you get to become pros one day, and I'll get to watch you in some world championships."

We begin to head to the lobby to catch a shuttle that will take us to the Luxor for a tour of the Esports Arena. I'm mildly excited about how grand this place might be. Maybe I'll try to get onto one of the games myself, just to say I've played in a venue that grand.

As we head out of the double doors, my eyes lock on someone very familiar wearing a blackout Stingrays hoodie and sweatpants. No. It can't be. I blink to see if I'm just hallucinating. But no, he's standing there, smiling at me as I gape at his presence.

"Griffin?"

16

Griffin

I DROP MY DUFFEL and softly wave to Lydia, whose mouth is agape, obviously shocked that I'm here in the flesh.

"Hey," I smile.

She thinks for a moment, then runs up to me and jumps up into my arms. I stumble back a little, but once I regain my footing, I wrap them around her waist and tug at her a little tighter. I bury my face in her neck and grin as her hair droops over my shoulder.

"Oh my god!" she exclaims. "You...you're here. In the flesh. In Vegas."

"I am." She's still holding on to me, and I don't let her go. I love the feeling of holding her, and even though people are probably looking at us, I don't care.

"Wait, why? I...your next game is back in San Jose."

"It is." I'm waiting for her to figure out that I'm here to see her, but her clueless face is really cute to watch. "Have you figured it out yet?"

"No! Wait." She smirks at me. "Did you come to visit me?"

"Bingo," I whisper, my face inches away from her.

She gasps, and I chuckle. "You said you missed me, right?"

"Y-yeah," she stammers.

"So I thought I'd fly to Vegas to surprise you."

She shakes her head. "You're...something else, Griffin Markey."

"By something else, I hope you mean the best fake boyfriend in the world."

Her face drops, and she moves her arms from around my neck, gripping my shoulders. "Yeah. You're the best fake boyfriend I've ever had." She squirms a little, and I let her down. Shit. Mission 'confess my feelings for Lydia with Vegas as a backdrop' is off to a stellar start.

"How long are you here for?" Lydia asks.

"Just until tomorrow morning." I look past her to see a crowd of students wearing LGU sweatshirts staring at us. Those are probably her students on the esports team.

"Um..." One of the kids speaks up. "Sorry to bother this love fest, but are we still going to go to the Esports Arena?"

"Yes!" Lydia blushes. "Sorry, everyone." She turns around and opens her hands to show me off. "This is Griffin. He, um, surprised me here on his way home from a game."

The kids walk up to us, their faces starstruck and eyes all fixed on me.

"Mr. Markey, I love watching you play."

"Thank you," I nod. "Have you guys been having a good time?"

"Yeah," another kid chimes in. "Although Lydia was just about to take us to the Esports Arena, and, um you're kind of stopping her from doing that."

"Oh." I frown. "I'm sorry. Here, you all can head on your way. I still need to check in. Um...Lydia, will there be a time that we can hang out?"

"I don't have anything to do after we head to the Esports Arena."

"Okay," I nod. "Great."

Ross wheels his suitcase over and lets out a groan. "God, you are such a little baby. I'll check in for you. Lydia," he says, turning to her. "Mind if Griffin tags along with your field trip to the arena?"

"Ross, that's okay. I don't want to interrupt anything that Lydia has planned with her students." And turn into a bumbling idiot in front of a bunch of college kids because I'm trying to formulate a grand plan to confess my feelings for Lydia, which seems like it's all gone to the wayside.

"You can come if you want," Lydia says. "We're going to take a tour and play a few games. The kids have been wanting to play because the networking stuff is boring them."

"Oh." At first, I shied away from wanting to tag along because it felt like maybe Lydia wanted to keep her distance from me, but I need to be honest with myself—I didn't come all this way to see Lydia one time, give her one hug, and then leave. I'm going to tell her that I'm falling in love with her and I'm going to plan the perfect time to do it.

"Okay, sure, I'll tag along."

"Mr. Markey, can you play a game of *Overwatch* with us?"

"Yes, Mr. Markey, pleeease?" Another student begs.

I'd much rather be talking to Lydia while these kids play on their own, but I suppose that if I need to win her over, then I'll have to get in her students' good graces.

"Sure," I chuckle. "But I'm not going to be very good," I warn them.

"That's alright, we can go a little easy on you," they giggle.

"You can come too, Mr. Nathan, if you want." another kid chimes in.

Ross's eyes look like they're sparkling under the bright LEDs in the Cyberscape. He's like a kid on Christmas. "Really?"

"Yeah, the more the merrier."

"Hell yes," Ross pumps his fist in the air. "Okay, I'm gonna check in. Give us like 5 minutes, and we'll be ready to head over."

"Sure thing," Lydia nods. I look back at her, mouth a "thank you" and rush over to the check-in desk. We grab our room keys and head inside the Cyberscape's futuristic-looking elevator.

"What happened, man?" Ross asks when the doors close, and we're alone in the elevator that will take us up forty floors to our rooms. "I was expecting the run-and-jump hug, but then Lydia just kind of shut off all of a sudden. What did you say to her?"

I slump my body against the wall and begin my slow descent down until I'm squatting on the floor. "I said that I was the best fake boyfriend in the world...which was true, but I guess it might have made her think that I just want this to be fake or she wants this to be fake...I don't know."

"Or maybe she also wants it to be real, but she had some existential crisis about the strength of this relationship."

"I guess." I bury my face between my legs. I don't know the right words to say or what I should avoid. Should I be forward with telling her how I feel, or do I feel it out and let her tell me what she feels when she's ready?

"Just...be a good friend to her. She has to have her work face on right now, and maybe she met someone who made her question if she's good at her job or not. These...work conferences might do that to you."

I wouldn't know. The only real conference that I went to was a concert competition where I met a bunch of musicians who were all vying for the top prize: an all-expenses-paid trip to New York City to play at Lincoln Center and tour Juilliard. I didn't win, but I lived so close to the school that I could have toured whenever I wanted.

"What do you think a professional athlete conference would look like?"

"Fitness challenges, hookups, drinking copious amounts of alcohol. The rookies during a club night, in a nutshell."

I stand back up. "Yeah, you're probably right."

We make it to Ross's floor, and he heads out to drop off his bags in the room. My room is just a few floors above his, so after I ride the elevator for a little longer, I get out and place my duffel on the bed in my room. I try not to get sucked into playing *Mario Kart* on the Switch console that comes standard with the room.

I head back down and see the crowd waiting by the lobby doors for me. I start walking towards them and plant myself next to Lydia.

"Sorry I'm late," I said. "I was really trying to resist not playing on that Switch."

"It is very tempting," Lydia nudges. "Although a *Mario Kart* race sounds like the perfect plan right now."

I raise my brows at her and make a note to myself to boot up the Switch later so we can play. Although if we're playing cross-legged on the bed, I'd be more tempted to tackle her and lay on top of her than play a little *Mario Kart*.

"Okay!" Lydia claps. "Let's get a move on then."

It's a bit of a trek to get to the Luxor from the Cyber-scape. Thankfully, we're able to take a monorail to the MGM

Grand and then cross the street to get to our destination, passing across our go-to place, the Aria, when we're in town for games. I wish I had more time to enjoy myself in Vegas; I always have fun exploring all that the city has to offer, including a not-as-well-known but very delicious spot at the Blossom Hotel called Happy Noodle that does a killer job at Beef Stew Noodle Soup.

We arrive at the arena, and I'm in awe of how large it is. It has multiple floors and a stage where players can compete in front of a crowd. It's a dream come true. For so long, I would play video games just for fun, not even thinking about how people could turn this into something profitable.

"Do you want to play a game?" I ask Lydia. "*Hero Seek*? For old times' sake?"

She blushes and slowly nods. I lead her to two computer stations sitting next to one another. We boot up the game, and I invite Lydia to join my party. She joins, and our characters come into full view for the first time in weeks.

"I missed this," Lydia said. "I didn't realize it's been so long since we've played."

"Yeah. Me too." We enter the map, and I go through the motions of scavenging for materials and slaying the minions that stand in our way. At some point, Lydia cries out.

"Griffin, I don't think that I can shake these guys all on my own."

"Okay, I'm coming, babe."

She sharply turns her neck to me. Her eyes are flickering from the screen to my face. "Did you just call me babe?" she asks.

"I..." It slips out. "I'm sorry. It was an accident, Lydia."

"It's fine," she says, turning back to the game. "I just have a lot of these guys on me."

I didn't mind the name once I realized I said it. I liked calling her babe, but she seems to kind of brush it off. God, I am messing it up big time here.

I move my character to help her and start shooting arrows at the enemy minions. God, these are loaded. I'm trying to rapidly shoot them off, but they react so quickly.

"God, dang it!" I start getting frustrated. "These guys are not dying."

Lydia is trying to spawn her own Support to ward off the minions—hers are super skilled, and they're dropping like flies.

"Griffin, I don't know if I can't shake them."

"No!" I yell at her. "We have to win. We're so close. I know I can beat these guys. Just...keep working at it."

"You don't have to yell at me!" She throws off her headset. "This is supposed to be fun, and you're being so serious."

She stops playing for a moment, and her character rapidly starts losing health. She gets up from her seat and huffs.

"What are you doing?!" I raise my voice. "You could have totally stuck it through and defeated those minions."

"What is wrong with you?" she yells. "You are getting worked up over a game. News flash, Griffin: people lose all the time. You don't have to be so upset about it."

I fall back into the chair. I just want to have a good time. And part of having a good time is winning. Lydia isn't trying hard enough because I know she has it in her to win, so I don't know why she isn't trying harder.

"I just want us to have a good time."

She groans. "You can still have a good time and not win. I know it's frustrating, but..." She holds the bridge of her nose. "You need to chill out. It's just a game, and honestly, right now, I'm not having fun playing with you acting like this. I'm going to go take a break and think you should do the same."

She storms off, and I hold a hand out to stop her, but I can't grab onto her in time. Is there even a point? I fucked up. And Lydia definitely wants nothing to do with me right now.

I get up and search around the room for where Lydia's gone. I can't find her anywhere. I catch one of the students who's part of Lydia's esports team and pull him aside.

"Hey, have you seen Lydia?"

"No," he shakes his head. "I haven't."

Shit. I start getting frazzled. My pace quickens, and I look in every nook and cranny of the arena to see if I can find her. I pull out my phone and call her, but her phone keeps ringing, and it eventually goes to voicemail.

"Hello, you've reached Lydia Goh. Please leave a message, and I will return your call as soon as I can."

"Lydia," I begin. "It's Griffin. I...I'm just making sure you're okay. I've looked everywhere for you around the arena, and I can't find you. Just...call or text me that you're okay."

After wandering around the arena, I've given up hope that I can find her somewhere here. The arena is big, but it's still constrained within four walls.

"Hey," I walk up to the students playing games on a row of computers. "I think Lydia might have left the arena, and she's pretty upset. I'm going to check in on her."

"Hey," one of the kids stands up. "You go after her Mr. Markey. And tell her how you feel. But if you break her heart, we will never forgive you. Lydia is the best director in the world and she deserves to be with someone who is going to treat her how she should be treated."

"Um," I swallow. "Yeah, noted. I'll be...good to her." That's the goal anyway. I've just been kind of fumbling with my words and actions to get there.

I speed walk through the hotel and crane my neck over at almost every slot machine, but no luck. I don't want to think that she's left completely, so I try to look through other parts of the hotel. The Luxor isn't the biggest hotel on the Strip, right? I mean, it's a goddamn pyramid.

After walking in circles, it seems, I finally spot Lydia sitting alone at a table, eating some sort of ice cream or frozen yogurt.

"Hey," I sit down across from her. "I've been looking for you."

"Sorry," she mumbles. "I just needed a pick-me-up."

"Lydia," I begin. "I am so sorry for how I acted. I was trying to relive the good ol' days, so to speak. When we'd get so excited over a win. I...might have gotten a little too carried away."

She raises her brows at me. "A little?"

"A little. I mean a lot."

"Griffin," she asks. "Why did you come to Vegas?"

I try moving my mouth. "To see you."

"But...but we're supposed to be friends. Friends don't just hop on a plane to fly and see their friends."

"Do they not?" I ask her. I take a deep breath. I think this is it.

She scoffs. "I don't know. This is like shit that you see in a romance movie."

"Is that bad?"

"It is...if you are just doing all of these things, but you don't actually like me," she tells me. "Griffin...I..."

I reach out to grab her wrist. If we're confessing feelings, then I want to be the one to do it first.

"I'm falling in love with you, Lydia."

Her mouth hangs open while I move my hand down to hold hers. Our fingers intertwine, and I start pouring out the rest of my feelings.

"I've tried to let go of the feelings I have for you, Lydia, but you continue to amaze me every day. I know that you might want this to be fake, and I've rejected you before, but it's only because I was scared. I'm still scared because I don't want the media to paint you in a bad light, but I…I think I want to try this out. If you want to. But I don't want to just be your friend."

I wait for her to react, and I almost think that I might have poured my damn heart out for nothing. But Lydia reacts by grabbing onto my hoodie and roping me in so that my lips touch hers. I close my eyes and push deeper into the kiss, and she moans. It's one of the best sounds I've heard in my life.

She pulls back, and I grin. "I hope that means you feel the same way I do."

She rolls her eyes. "It does. But…are you sure you want to be with me? Like, if we do this, then there are real feelings on the line. We can't use the excuse that it's fake, so we can move on anymore."

I didn't even think that when we were fake dating, that I could even stand the idea of it being fake. I just had to prove to myself that I'm capable of being in a real relationship, and at this point, I think I have. I know that the road ahead is going to be hard, with real emotions and real hearts on the line, but Lydia is the only person in the world that I want to be with, and I'm gonna fight damn hard to hold onto her.

"I do, Lydia." I grab onto her and pull her to stand up, facing me alongside the table. I hold both of her hands in mine. "I want nothing more than to be with you and to do whatever I can to make you happy. I want to keep falling in love with you because you make me happy."

She wraps her arms around me and gives me another kiss. I reach my arms around her waist and lift her towards me. "You make me happy too, Griffin Markey."

"So, what's next?" I ask.

"Are you hungry?" she asks. "I haven't eaten much today."

"I mean, of course. But I think I'm hungry for more than just food."

"Oh my god," she chuckles. Was it too soon for euphemisms? "Okay, well, let's get something to eat. And then you can get something to eat after," she winks.

And I think that makes for the best plan.

17

Lydia

GRIFFIN TAKES HOLD OF my hand and kisses my knuckles.

"Come on," he leads me away. "We should probably make sure that no one's worrying about us."

My face drops. "Have the kids been worrying?" I thought that I could leave for a bit and not have them notice. A typical game can last about an hour unless the team isn't able to hold their own.

"No," Griffin says. "Well, I might have been freaking out a little bit and constantly kept asking them where you were."

"Oh," I pout. My heart sinks a little, making Griffin worry. I was just frustrated that he was taking the game so seriously. Turns out he was just nervous and grappling with his feelings for me. Turns out we were both victims of feeling things for one another but thinking the other person didn't feel the same way.

I needed to kiss him. How else could I respond when he tells me that he's falling in love with me? It's everything that I wanted to hear from his lips. I had an inkling when I saw him in the lobby that he was here with some ulterior motive, like to ask me out, but I got scared. I didn't know if it was for show because he still reminded me that he was my fake boyfriend, but now that I'm holding onto him, I've never been more excited to take a risk for love.

"Sorry I worried you. I needed to clear my head," I grip his hand tighter. "But you found me!"

"I did," he grins at me. "And I'm so glad."

He leans down and gives me another peck. I can't stop grinning. When we were publicizing our fake relationship, we didn't really talk about PDA. We shied away from it because I knew that I was going to start feeling things if I tasted him. And when I planted my lips on his, those thoughts were confirmed. I already felt the electric tingles shiver down my body when he reeled me in and held me in his arms with his broad shoulders and big muscles. Now I'm just eager to take off his clothes and explore every crevice of the body hiding underneath his clothes.

"Griffin," I ask. "When did you know? That you were feeling something more than just friendship for me?"

"I think it was a slow development," he tells me. "Obviously, when I didn't even know what your name was or what you looked like, I was having feelings for the girl that I loved playing *Hero Seek* with. But back then, I didn't know if you'd be the girl to change my outlook on dating. I didn't know if you could be, which is why I didn't agree to go on that date the first time. But then, I watched you in your element, talking to people about esports and the way you'd smile when you'd brag about your students. By the way, before I came to look for you, they told me that if I broke your heart, then they were going to make sure that I paid for it."

I rest my cheek against his arm. These kids. This past weekend, I developed a new kind of bond with these college students that I've been trying to connect with since the school year started. Bonding with college students is difficult; it's like trying to bond with a teenager whose only goal in life is to be noticed by the cool kids. And someone old comes along, and it's like their cool meter drops dramatically. I know video games, but I definitely don't think I'll ever have any accomplishments that will rival what they get on a regular day.

But they opened themselves up to me this weekend, and the moments we've had, talking about the desire to win an esports tournament and how much good work I've apparently done for this team, warms my heart. We're going to go back to Los Gatos and will be closer than ever before, which is great because I know that these kids have my back when the coaches might question my decisions.

"We've really gotten to know one another this past weekend. They told me how they should have made more of an effort to stand up for me against the coaches when they made sexist remarks, which meant a lot."

"Good," Griffin smiles. "They should be sticking up for you because you're good at your job."

"Thanks, Griffin. Have I told you lately how much I appreciate you?"

"You have, but I'm never tired of hearing it." He turns to me and leans down, kissing me again. At this rate, we're never going to get to our next destination.

His mouth opens up, and he holds me up a little so he's cradling me by my ass. He flicks his tongue against mine, and I groan. God, his lips are so full and taste so good. I tug a little on his bottom lip, and he chuckles.

"God, Lydia. Are you sure we can't ignore our responsibilities, go back to our room, and just...relax?"

I giggle. "Come on, Griffin. When we get back to the room, we are *not* going to be just relaxing."

His eyes turn dark, and he looks at me seductively, like I'm a snack he can't wait to devour.

"Well, now that you mention it," he murmurs in my ear, "you're absolutely right. I'm ready to throw you on the bed and let you experience me inside of you."

My face turns red, and I let out a little gasp. "Well, I guess we should get going then."

We meet the students and Ross back at the entrance of the arena, and everyone looks back at us with their arms crossed and smirks all over their faces.

"Took you two long enough," Ross grins. "Did you get lost?"

"No," I stammer. "We were only chatting, and we got a little carried away." Because we were kissing after practically every sentence. They're lucky that we're even here after the moment of seduction we just had, that I'm still wet down there from.

"Alright. Well, I'm starving, and so are the students. Can we go get something to eat?"

"Yes, of course." I'd make the decision to treat the team to a dinner in Vegas to say thank you for their participation throughout the weekend, as well as their hard work over the school year. I had a bit of money budgeted for food expenses on this trip so we can all enjoy a nice Vegas meal. Unfortunately, I don't have enough money to treat everyone to a beef Wellington at Hell's Kitchen, but there are plenty of other celebrity chefs that have more budget-friendly options and good dishes as well.

"Where did you all want to go?" I ask the students.

"Weeeelll," Dev begins. "I know you said you were going to treat us to something this weekend, but we wanted to see if we could go somewhere more expensive. Of course, we'd pay for ourselves."

"Oh." My brows raise. I do want to treat the students because we were all at the conference together, but it sounds like they have an idea of what they want, which might be more than my measly budget will allow. "Are you sure, guys? What were you all thinking?"

"We want to go to a buffet."

I sigh. Of course. What Vegas trip isn't complete without a trip to the buffet? And these kids are definitely not done growing. I know they inhale food like a vacuum cleaner, wiping out all of my promotional snacks during club meetings that are supposed to be for people interested in the club. Vegas buffets don't come cheap; I think we'll be spending upwards of seventy dollars per person.

"Ah, a buffet. Well, guys, I really wanted to treat you to a good meal here in Vegas and not have you worry about spending your own money. You're sure you still want to eat at a buffet?"

"We're sure. We talked about it as a group, and all of us were okay with dropping the money for a buffet dinner. You don't have to worry about covering for any of us. We can even pay for your meal, too!"

"That's very nice of you all, but I don't want you spending your own money on me." I guess I can just pay for it all myself. It'll be expensive, but I want these students to be treated to something special, and I guess that's going to be in the form of a buffet meal.

"I'll take care of it," I tell them. "Don't worry about me. I don't want you all to be paying for your own meals."

"Okay!" The students exclaim. "Thank you, Lydia. That's super nice of you."

"Don't mention it," I tell them. I need to rework my budget after this, but it's going to a good cause. I want to be in these students' good graces, and I know that money can't buy you love, but maybe it can get you a support system.

We walk to Caesar's Palace for their iconic Bacchanal Buffet, and after waiting in line to accommodate our large party, we finally head up to the machine to pay. I start going through the motions of selecting everything.

Eight adult buffet dinners.

Eighty dollars a person.

No one gets any drinks on top of that. That they can pay for.

After tax, it's looking like almost a thousand dollars for one meal. It's fine. I can definitely pay for this and not worry about paying for rent and my car this month.

As I'm about to put my credit card to read, a hand comes from behind me and grabs my wrist. With his other hand, Griffin reaches over and puts his credit card on the reader, and the machine notifies us that the transaction has been approved.

"Hey." I turn around. "You didn't need to do that."

"I wanted to." He looks at me with those devastating eyes. "Don't worry about it."

I already know that trying to argue with Griffin is pointless, so I don't fight him. Instead, I wrap my arms around his waist and rest my head on his chest.

"Thank you," I tell him. "That's very generous of you. When did these buffets get so expensive?"

He chuckles and kisses the top of my head. "Probably when food got more expensive. Luckily, it seems like you're at a table with seven guys who will eat up the entire buffet spread."

"I just like the crab legs. That's where the money is."

He grins at me. "You are the perfect woman for me."

I blush, and I'm counting down the minutes until we can get back to the hotel and spend the rest of the night in bed, exploring every nook and cranny of each other's bodies. My stomach grumbles, so I decide that I should probably eat something so we can continue what we started, but in bed and with a satisfied stomach.

We get seated, and the students immediately leave the table to fill up their plates with food. I eye the seafood area, fill up my plate with crab legs, and begin diving in. No one has come back to sit down yet. It's a buffet, so you can get as many plates as you want. Is there really that many options that beat seafood? I guess so. Seafood is a rather acquired taste.

Griffin returns with a heaping of meat and seafood and takes a seat next to me.

"Enjoying yourself?" He winks.

I nod, accidentally splashing a bit of seawater from cracking the leg in two.

"Oops," I turn to him. "Did I get you?"

"A little," he whispers in my ear. "But I don't mind getting wet." He shoots me a wink.

I choke on the crab, and start coughing.

"You okay, Lydia?" Ross asks as he's taking a seat.

"Yup," I mutter. "Just went down the wrong pipe."

Griffin chuckles, and I kick my leg to the side to hit his. This is going to be the longest dinner of my life. And it's not because it's all you can eat over the span of two hours.

Everyone finishes up, and we walk, nay, waddle out of the buffet. It's good that we're going to be able to walk it off with how far the hotel is from here.

We start making our trek down the Strip, and the street is illuminated by the lights from the hotel billboards.

"Oh, look!" Drew points. "The Bellagio fountain show is about to begin!"

The students try to squeeze through other tourists to get a glimpse of the famed water show. Frank Sinatra's "Fly Me to the Moon" starts playing, and I smile up at Griffin and thread my fingers with his as Frank sings about doing the same thing.

"This song describes how I feel about you," Griffin tells me.

The song finishes up with the chorus repeating itself again, and I hold on to Griffin's hands when they snake over my shoulders and rest on my chest. As the song recites its last "I love you," the water retreats back into the pool, and the lights come back on, signaling its end.

Griffin grabs onto my hand, and we walk across the street back to the Cyberscape, where I wave goodnight to the kids and tell them not to stay up too late because we have an early flight tomorrow.

Ross joins them, but not before turning around to face us and drawing a little heart around our heads with his fingers.

"Enjoy your night, love birds," he tells us before asking if the kids can hold the elevator open for him.

"So," Griffin pulls me in. "My room or yours?"

"I don't mind either way. I was surprised to see that my room had a balcony. But I am also fully okay with going to your room if they gave you a suite upgrade for obvious reasons."

"Not this time. I booked so late that I was lucky enough to get a room. My balcony doesn't even face the fountains."

"Well, looks like I have that leg up on you then." I wink.

"Lead the way then, Liddy."

I blush. He called me by my *Hero Seek* username. Barely anyone knows about it, but to hear it come from his lips sends my heartbeat skyrocketing.

"I like that. The way you call me Liddy. My parents haven't used that nickname since I was in elementary school."

"Really?" His eyebrows raise. "Why did they stop?"

"I asked them to when I got to be a teenager. Were you ever in that phase where nicknames screamed childish? That's what happened to me. So, they went back to calling me Lydia."

"Well, I enjoyed saying it when we were playing *Hero Seek,* and I enjoy saying it now." We walk into the elevator, and when the doors close, Griffin wastes no time. He gently slams me against the wall and starts to plant kisses from my lips down to my collarbone.

I giggle at how his lips tickle my skin. "Griffin, stop that tickles!"

"Good." His whispers sound more like growls. "I love seeing that beautiful smile of yours."

The elevator ascends, but it feels like it's not going up fast enough. Curse our rooms for being over fifty floors off the ground. While I can appreciate a nice view, the journey feels arduous.

Finally, the elevator stops, and as the doors open up, Griffin effortlessly lifts me by my ass cheeks, and I grip onto him with my legs. "You on tight?" He asks.

"Mhhhm," I say, clinging to him like a monkey climbing a tree. I bury my head in his neck as he traverses down the hallway.

"Shit, I forgot we're going to your room. What's your room number?"

"Oh. 61225." He has to turn around, but soon enough, we stop in front of my door and he puts me down so I can grab my room key from my backpack. I tap the key onto the door lock, and when the light flashes green, we step inside the guest room that is supposed to mirror a dream stream room with changing rainbow strip lights and 16-bit art renditions hanging from the walls.

Griffin stops in front of me and grabs a hold of my shirt to yank it clean off my body. I'm wearing nothing but my bra underneath, and he licks his lips while keeping his eyes fixed on my breasts.

"May I?" he asks while rubbing his hand over my padded push-up bra. "This is in the way of what I want."

"Yes," I breathe. "Absolutely, yes."

He bends down and kisses me again as reaches around with his hands and unclasps my bra. His tongue brushes against mine. His lips are so smooth, and when my bra drops to the floor, he immediately pinches my nipple between his thumb and pointer finger, and I moan into his mouth.

"Feel good?" he murmurs.

"Amazing." I haven't been touched like this by anyone other than myself for a long time, and Griffin handles my body with such care and gentleness.

"This is just the start, Lydia." He gets down on his knees, and while his hand pushes up on my breast, his lips begin to suck on my nipple. I groan louder than I thought was possible, and my knees involuntarily buckle at how damn amazing it feels when he licks and bites at just the tip.

He retreats from my breast for a moment and starts to undo my pants, hoisting down my underwear to reveal my pussy.

"Fuck, Lydia. You're a goddess. I've spent so long dreaming of this."

"Then worship me like the goddess I am, Griffin. Give me the pleasure that I deserve."

"Abso-fucking-lutely," he growls. He thrusts one of his fingers into me and starts swirling around my clit. I purse my lips and close my eyes at how nice his fingers feel inside me.

"Fuck, Lydia, you're so wet."

It doesn't take much. Just one look at Griffin and down there turns into a puddle. With the work he's done on my body, I feel ready to burst.

"Are you surprised?" I pant.

"Not in the slightest," he laughs. He pushes me onto the bed, and I splay out for him on the covers. He stands at the foot of the bed and begins taking off his clothes. I know that I was expecting him to be muscled and well-toned, but my imagination did not prepare me for the reality of how great he looks with no clothes on. He has a perfectly sculpted stomach and a thin layer of hair on his chest. His bicep is beautifully inked with Japanese characters cascading over a Manhattan skyline.

"What does your tattoo translate to?" I ask.

"It's an old Japanese saying that goes something along the lines of 'You stumble seven times but get back up eight.' Just something to remind me that I'm going to fall a lot, whether it's losing a game or, who knows, suffer an injury, but I'll always get back up. Everyone counts on me, and I don't want to let them down. I got it after I graduated college because my mom is against tattoos. For valid reasons, of course. I have to keep it covered when I go to Japan because they're banned in most public places. "

I feel tears prickle in my eyes, and I definitely didn't expect to feel this kind of emotion just as I'm about to orgasm. Well, from something other than sex, anyway.

"Hey," he leans over my body and cups my cheek. "What's wrong?"

"I'm okay," I reassure him. "You're amazing, you know that?"

"Well, I do have people tell me that after a game, so it is something I've been told."

"Okay, but besides the hockey skills, you're determined, and you're not selfish. You have other's intentions in mind, and you're looking out for them more than yourself. That's what makes you amazing."

"Well, I'm only really amazing if I can love you how you deserve to be loved and treat you how you deserve to be treated."

He gives me another kiss down to my breasts, and I tug a little bit of his hair.

"Lydia," his forehead touches mine. "I want to feel how I fit inside of you."

"Yes, please," I breathe. "Do you have a condom?"

"Yeah," he laughs and pulls one out of his wallet. "I had to make a pit stop at the convenience store to buy some because I didn't bring any with me, but I was hoping that I was going to get to this point tonight."

A part of me wished for that, too, and I'm happy that despite the hiccups, we're ending the night like this.

Griffin unzips his pants and pulls down his briefs. When I get a glimpse of his hard dick, my heart rate speeds up, and my mouth begins to salivate from how majestic it looks. He removes the condom from its wrapping and starts sliding it down.

"I'm done taking things slow," he says into my shoulder. He slides a finger inside me. I let out a short gasp, and he chuckles to himself as he slides another finger in and swirls around inside.

"Mmm, Lydia. You're so wet," he breathes against my neck, and the hot air makes me shudder.

"It's...been...a while."

"And now I'm about to make love to you every chance I get. Every night that we sleep at home, I want you in my bed."

He takes his fingers out and reaches to grab my nipple, pinching it slightly. While he's kissing me and our tongues flick against each other, he pushes his dick into me and exhales into my mouth. He starts a steady rhythm, slow at first and then picking up speed. He fills me up so perfectly. I know I'm not going to last much longer.

"Oh, Lydia." His eyes close. "God, you feel fucking perfect. I don't know how much longer I can last."

We find out that it doesn't take much longer. A couple more pumps, and Griffin lets out a sharp exhale, catching his breath as he puts some more of his weight on me. He gives me a quick peck and smiles. "That was amazing. You're amazing, you know that?"

I chuckle. "Well, I do now because my boyfriend's just told me."

"Boyfriend," he beams. "I do love the sound of that."

We clean up and return to my bed, where we fall asleep to gameplay footage of last year's League World Championships. And it's the best way I've ever gone to bed.

18
Griffin

YOU CAN ONLY STAY so high for so long, because eventually you have to come down. And when I do, I crash.

We return home from Vegas to a tough shootout loss against Boston. It especially stings when it's on our home rink because the fans filled the stands, thinking we could best a long standing good team, but success evades us. I don't love how many goals I missed this game. I lost control of the puck and our team had too many penalties that caused the other team to score one too many times for it to even go into overtime.

To make myself better from a loss that is just a blip on our record, I log onto my computer and look up cities for a weekend getaway. I know that I literally just came back from Vegas, but I want nothing more than to spend alone time with Lydia. I'm ready to be away from San Jose for a little bit. I love the city, and there's definitely a lot of good places to eat and drink within its city limits, but I haven't explored California nearly as much as I should have.

There are a lot of cities on my wishlist: Carmel, Napa, Santa Cruz. I'm surprised I have yet to take a trip to any of these places. I've done San Francisco and we go to LA for games. We've even done a Disney trip post-game in Anaheim. But these tourist spots that show up on lists of "Top Places to Visit in California" have evaded me.

I find a nice modern resort in Napa that I think will be perfect for us. It's a small, yet sprawling property with suites as the standard room type. Everyone who knows Napa, knows wine country. And there is plenty to eat on top of it. I think Lydia will really like it. She doesn't know that I've decided to plan this trip. I haven't really told her about the reasoning either. Since we've come back from Las Vegas, I can't help but smile that things are looking up for Lydia. She's returned to LGU with beaming confidence and a "not taking shit from no one" attitude. Her students have their first tournament next week, and Lydia's been beaming when she talks about their practice games and how the esports world is not ready for Los Gatos University's teams.

I book the hotel and attempt to pull some strings to get a dinner reservation at a top restaurant. The French Laundry would get me huge brownie points with Lydia. Hell, we're talking Boyfriend of the Year award. People make last minute cancellations for that place, right?

I don't have anywhere else to be for the day until Lydia gets off work, so I press refresh on the reservation site constantly, hoping something pops up. I keep my eyes peeled for anything this upcoming weekend and only to get up from my computer to use the bathroom.

Even when Ross gives me a call, I debate whether to pick it up. Well, I guess I can talk and keep my eye on the computer at the same time.

"What's up?" I answer.

"Hello to you too. Doing anything right now? I'm craving pho."

I realize that I haven't eaten since our morning practice. What an opportune time for my stomach to start growling as a means to tell me I should probably put something in there.

"Pho sounds so good. But...I shouldn't. I'm kind of working on something right now."

"What can you possibly be working on that's more important than eating pho?" Ross asks impatiently. He's definitely not going to like the response I give as a valid enough reason to bail on him.

"I'll have you know, I'm working on something very important. It's for Lydia."

"Oooooh. Okay, lover boy. Don't tell me you're already going engagement ring shopping?"

I wish he could see me rolling my eyes at my computer. It is way too early to be thinking about engagement rings and all the things that lead beyond that. Even though I've confessed my love to her, and I think that we're in love with each other enough to make big commitments like move in together, get married, and everything that might follow after that. But we just started officially dating. I want to be able to enjoy every minute of just being in love with Lydia. And showing that love in every way that I can.

"No. I'm planning a weekend getaway."

"Wait, really?" Ross sounds surprised. "That...sounds nice. What are you thinking?"

"I'm trying to plan a trip to Napa." And Ross is distracting me from my mission to constantly hit the refresh button to ensure I swoop an open reservation for this weekend. "Ugh, does anyone cancel their reservation at French Laundry?"

"Hold up. Are you trying to get a reservation for French Laundry? For this weekend? Good luck with that. You know people book like, three months in advance for that restaurant."

"Yes, I'm fully aware." Maybe I should have tried making this happen earlier. But three months ago I only knew Lydia as a character in a video game. I would've needed to be completely smitten with her to have booked a reservation for a three-star Michelin restaurant with what knowledge, or lack thereof, I had of Lydia back then. "I'm just hoping that someone cancels like...with two days notice. Like if someone is too sick to go or they broke up and can't go anymore." Man, I must be really fucked up to be wishing demise onto someone for my own personal gain.

"Well, I'm rooting for you, pal. You still want to go get pho?"

My stomach grumbles, so I think I need to give up trying for a moment and put some food in my stomach.

Ross offers to pick me up and drive to our go-to spot in Vietnam Town so I can keep my eyes glued to my phone and the restaurant's reservation platform. But after refreshing the page a total of five times as we approached the restaurant, I decided it wasn't worth the effort and instead, opted to book a table at the hotel's restaurant on-site. Apparently, they have one Michelin star, which is still an amazing feat.

"You are really dropping the dough for one weekend. A stay at a resort that costs over a thousand per night? And then a three-course dinner that'll rack up another, what, five hundred for you two? And don't even get me started on how many wineries you're planning on hitting up."

"So?" I shrug. I love Lydia, and I think that she deserves a weekend away. Money isn't an issue for me, and Ross knows that. I don't know what prompts him to start asking questions about my intentions with the money I earn.

"It just seems unlike you. That's all. You're one of the most frugal people I know, so sorry if I'm feeling a little surprised at this recent change in behavior."

"Sure," I mutter into my soup spoon. "Look, I know that I've spent much of my life being very minimal on spending. But...this time is different. I'm in love." It tickles my tongue, that L-word. They tell you love makes you do some outrageous things, and this might just be me seeing that. No person has ever made me derail my travel plans, spend an exorbitant amount on a getaway, and overall, just make me feel...unlike myself. I'm happier. I feel like I can go out more and not care who has their eyes on me. Maybe Lydia was right from the get-go, it just took someone to believe in me to make me do something that scares me.

"Lovesick," Ross counters with a wink. "Hey man, I'm happy for you. It's one of the best feelings in the world, being in love. Or so I remember. The last time I felt anywhere near to being in love with someone was the summer before I went to college."

"Really?" I slurp a heaping of noodles into my mouth. Ross and his love life are a tight-lipped subject. He's not the one to come home each night with a different woman. I guess maybe because there's someone still occupying his thoughts. "Someone from back home?"

"Yeah," he looks out the window of the restaurant. "She's...still living at home, I think. Her dad owns a pinball museum. They're like, super dedicated to the community. She's one of those people who will probably never leave the home she grew up in."

"Got it." I thought I could be the same, once upon a time. I had my eyes set on a New Jersey or New York team just because I wanted my parents to have the same level of support they'd given to my brothers and their endeavors. Because now I'm thousands of miles away and too "out of the way" to be supported at games. "Well, maybe your paths will cross again someday."

"Maybe." Ross has turned all melancholic now as he stares at the green onion and broth remnants in front of him. "This is why I don't think about these kinds of things. I get all sad about the one who got away and shit. Promise me whatever happens, it doesn't make you lose sight of the game. Because these women leave marks in your head that last forever."

I nod. It's easy for me to say, "Of course, I'm going to stay focused," but it's still early. We're in the classic "honeymoon stage," where it feels like nothing can shake up the love that we have for one another. That throughout the hardships, we'll survive. I guess this weekend will be the first chance I'll have to test those waters because now there's something worth fighting for. Something that I'm actually holding onto for as long as I'm living.

I try to keep our destination a secret from Lydia, as we drive two hours north from San Jose to Napa. I turn my head for a moment and watch her look out the window as we pass Emeryville and the IKEA alongside the freeway.

"Are you sure you don't want to tell me where we're going? Otherwise, I'm just going to keep asking until we get there."

"I'm sure," I reassure her. I extend my arm out to put my hand on her thigh, which is bouncing up and down in soft, fast movements. "You'll like it, don't worry."

"I'm not worried. That much. I just...I don't know. Surprises make me anxious, even if they're good ones. I like being in control and scheduling everything on my own. When things are out of my control, my mind fills with thoughts of what-ifs and what could it be."

"Well, let's do something that can take your mind off of things." I rub her thigh, and the bouncing subsides. "We should be there in about an hour anyway. We're approaching, what, Berkeley? Where the school is? Did you ever want to go there?"

"Eh, yeah. I feel like it was engrained by my college counselor, though. Berkeley was so many of my classmates' dream school. Valid, as it's one of the best schools in the country. I applied, but I didn't get accepted. I think I would've liked it though. There are a lot of opportunities—they have one of the best business programs and lots of chances to work with companies in and around the area with it being so close to SF. In the end, LGU felt like it was the best place for me to go. Sure, it was close to home, and I know people want to escape the home they grew up in, but a part of me thought that I needed to stay here to fulfill my life's purpose. Which I guess I learned later on in life would be to head up LGU's first pro esports team. Funny how everything falls into place when you least expect it."

"Yeah," I smile. "Funny, I was kind of thinking about that the other day. Ross and I were talking about things we left behind in our hometowns, and for a lot of my life, I wanted to remain close to my family. I went to college in New York, I kept my eyes on any New York or New Jersey team in hopes they'd draft me, and then I was drafted first round by San Jose. I was nervous to move to a team that was on the opposite coast from where I grew up, but it allowed me to explore a new place. And, whatever happens after my contract is up, wherever I go, I'll always think of San Jose as my home. Plus, being here led me to you."

"It did." She grips my hand resting on her thigh and interlaces her fingers with mine. "When's your contract up?"

"I'm an unrestricted free agent, so I technically don't have a timeframe on when my contract is up like baseball or basketball. I've been playing for the NHL for long enough that I have this thing called a 'Non-Movement Clause,' so it just means I can't be traded without approval."

"Would there be a scenario where you might consider moving?"

"If I get traded with a good salary, then I may." I know teams have their eye on me. It's just a matter of one of them spending what I think my worth is and extending a contract my way.

The car goes quiet, save for the sound of the radio playing the alternative indie music I queued up for the drive. This conversation curbed Lydia's anxiety for a little bit, but I might have just brought it back with talks of moving and the looming possibility of long distance.

"Everything okay?" I ask.

"Yeah," she sighs. She takes in a deep breath and exhales onto the passenger side window while we cross the bridge to Vallejo.

"It doesn't sound like you're okay," I counter.

"I...I'll be fine. I just...didn't realize that there's a very real possibility that you could be traded and move and be far away from me and...I never thought about long distance."

My heart sinks, and I frown, quickly glancing at my phone to ensure I don't miss the exit coming up in a few short miles. I don't want this weekend to be filled with negative thoughts, and I'm starting to feel anxious that I might've ruined this weekend, when we haven't even arrived at our destination yet.

"Hey," I squeeze her hand a little tighter. "We're not going to think about that now. I did not just drop an undisclosed amount of money on a weekend getaway for us to mope about the future. No matter what happens with me, where I might go if I decide to move on from here, I'm not going to just drop everything and give up on us because it might be hard. I'm never going to give up on us."

"I won't either," she reassures me, tilting her lips up into a small smile. As I stroke her knuckle with my thumb, I make a mental promise to myself that even if things get hard, I won't stop loving her. I won't stop working on ensuring I'm the best version of myself because Lydia deserves it. She deserves everything.

19

Lydia

It's only when we get off the freeway and venture in and out of roads, with signs indicating where these roads lead, that I realize where we're going.

It has been years since I've made the trip to California's iconic wine country. I went during college with a few friends for our own weekend getaway before graduating. It was so much fun. At least, from what I can remember. My mind went slightly fuzzy after winery number four. I think we went to a bar as well, but I was so far gone by that point that I don't think I needed to drink anymore. And that's the weekend where I learned what a wine headache was.

This trip is already different on so many levels. First, it's a romantic getaway. Griffin has kept me completely in the dark about our plans for this weekend, and all I know about is that we'll probably be going to a few wineries. Everything else is a mystery. I'm excited about the wine tasting, but how many wineries is Griffin going to take me to? And at what point am I going to drink too many glasses of wine that drunk Lydia is going to interact with Griffin for the first time and possibly leave him to be my caretaker for the weekend if I take a tumble off the deep end?

I close my eyes and rest my head against the window of the car. I'm going to try to clear my head for the weekend, so I'm not thinking about the conversation we had earlier about the future and how uncertain it is. Griffin might be going to a different team sooner than I want him to, and then we'll have to have some difficult conversations about us, our life, and its future. He was already feeling bad for bringing it up, so I shove those thoughts out of my head and hype myself up for what's about to happen. We're going somewhere that's supposed to be relaxing. And have like, our first date out as a couple. That feels so surreal to me. We've known each other for months at this point, but this is the first time we'll be in a public place as a couple. There might be press that will find us, and I'll just need to accept that this kind of publicity is going to be a part of my life if I want to be with Griffin.

"Tired?" he asks. "We're almost there."

"I'm fine, just trying to get all the bad thoughts out of my head in preparation for when we get there."

Griffin chuckles to himself. "Okay, babe."

"You like calling me that, don't you?" I grin at him. It's a classic nickname to call your significant other, but Griffin called me "babe" when we were in Vegas, playing *Hero Seek* at the

Esports Arena, and we weren't anything official yet. It was one of the first inclinations I had that his feelings weren't quite platonic anymore.

"Yeah," he blushes. "I kind of do. It's cliché, but it's a word that rolls right off the tongue. I smile every time I say it."

"I do, too." I'm blushing, and the sensation is making this already warm car even hotter. It feels like a sauna in here when outside, it's crisp and cool in the thick of the winter.

We veer off the road that we've been traveling on for a while to one surrounded by greenery and a few gated homes on either side of the road. After a few turns, we pull into a parking lot with a simple sign along a concrete wall that reads, "Auberge du Soleil."

I gasp loudly. "Griffin..."

"We're here." He turns to me after pulling up to the hotel. A valet promptly takes his car.

Auberge is certifiably the most luxurious resort in Napa Valley. Napa has a handful of five-star resorts. Resorts that cost more per night than my monthly car payment. I've never stayed here because I cannot afford to drop a thousand dollars, plus taxes and resort fees, and have spent my life never dreaming of it because it was out of reach.

"You got us reservations...here?" I ask, still awestruck, and we've barely even seen the hotel.

"Yes, I did."

"Why?" I can't help but question. Not because I don't appreciate the gesture, but because I can't help but list all the things I could buy instead with the amount Griffin probably spent.

"Because I love you," he responds with no hesitation. "And you deserve to have a getaway. I have generally been budget-conscious when it comes to spending. Aka, I don't. I've kept the same furniture since I moved to San Jose. I own two cars, which sometimes feels excessive, but I've wanted a sports car my whole life, and sometimes that's not a feasible car to drive around. So I bought a bigger one. My teammates constantly make fun of me for how frugal I am, but I've just never found pleasure in material things. If I am going to spend a lot of money on something, it's going to be on experiences. I try to go to Japan every other year and visit New Jersey to see my family. I'm going to drop a lot of money to explore the world. And now I'm happy that I get to visit somewhere new with someone special."

My heart is beating so fast it wants to leap out of my chest, and my hands feel clammy as they're shaking from the rush of emotions I'm feeling from Griffin's affectionate words. I feel like I don't deserve his kindness. I think about how everything fell right into place from the moment we were paired together in one of the biggest co-op games to exist.

"I'm excited about that, too. I hope that one day I'll get to go to Japan with you. I've never been before."

"It's beautiful," he grins. "There are so many amazing places to explore, and the best places are the ones that veer off the typical tourist cities. And the food is delicious. I already love Japanese food, but there's something that just tastes so fresh when you eat tuna that was actually fished near the city. I'd love it if I could take you. I can only go after the season ends. Maybe we can plan to go when the school year's up? Although I'll warn you, it gets very humid in the summer, and while I love everything about Japan, the weather at that time is nearly unbearable."

"I'm sure I'll still love it, humidity and all."

Griffin grabs my bags and checks into our room. The front desk attendant confirms with him that he has indeed booked a Deluxe Private Garden Suite for two nights. He goes through the motions of authorizing his card, answering the kind attendant's questions about what's brought us to Napa, with Griffin telling her that it's his first time but letting me answer that I'd been here before. Not the resort, just a few wineries that everyone makes a point to visit, like the one that looks like a castle. I don't know what Griffin's agenda is for visiting wineries while we're here, but I make a note to research wineries to bring up to him over the complimentary breakfast we receive with his suite reservation.

She gives Griffin the keycards to the room and a map of where it is, along with all the amenities available at our fingertips. Spa, pool, and the 24-hour fitness center that I'm sure Griffin's going to use as the sun rises. I'm going to spend my time laying out on a pool chair and reading a book, a wine bottle included.

Griffin thanks her, and she makes it a point to tell us if we need anything during our stay here do not hesitate to ask. She then hands us each a glass of wine.

"Please enjoy this complimentary glass of wine for you to enjoy on your walk to your room," she says with a polite smile

I carefully take the wine glass by the stem, take a sip of the crisp, slightly sweet wine, and let out a satisfied hum at how tasty it is.

"How is it?" she asks.

"Delicious," I say. I can't help the grin plastered across my face. I have to remind myself that I need to maintain a certain level of sophistication, which means I cannot just take this wine and down it like it's water in a place where I feel like my presence doesn't belong.

"Good," she nods. "I hope you have a wonderful stay."

"Thank you," Griffin replies, taking my hand and leading me out to walk down the path to our accommodation.

"What are your thoughts so far?" Griffin asks me as we begin the walk to where our suite is.

"I..." I'm speechless. So much of this resort has blown me away. The service, the design. I mean, this walk amongst the trees and the view of the mountainside is straight out of a postcard. I wouldn't be surprised if they sell art pieces of this very view and people swoop it up for thousands of dollars. "I love it."

I also love how being away from home is making me feel. Whenever I'm on campus, or even when I'm home after work, I tend to feel anxious. Nothing major has to be going on, but I automatically think about whether there was something I could have done differently that day or what the outcome of the future might be. Here, amidst the trees and vines, I feel peaceful. I don't have that tendency to check my phone and the emails that flood my inbox.

Griffin touches the keycard to our room, and when he opens the wooden door, my eyes widen. This suite is stunning. A full living room, complete with rustic, earth-toned furniture that is styled way better than my beat-up loveseat that has had lots of asses imprint themselves in it, a full-size bathroom with a freestanding tub and walk-in shower, but the piéce de résistance is that there's not just the tub in the bathroom. No, there is an outdoor tub with shrubs lined behind it.

"There's a tub in the yard!" I squeal, running to open the French-style doors to get a better view. "I never thought I could want something more than I want a yard with a tub in it."

"It's pretty nice, huh?" Griffin chuckles.

I turn around sharply to face him. "Pretty nice? Griffin, this is more than just pretty nice. This is...fuck."

"Woah!" he exclaims. "That good?"

I give him a light shove. "Shut up. This place makes me speechless, okay? I'm in awe. This is nicer than my apartment."

"I'll make a note to look into adding a tub to the backyard," Griffin smirks. "So it'll be up to your standards."

"Oh." I blink back at him. "You don't have to. I'm not going to be over that much."

That's a lie. I'm going to spend almost every moment that I'm not at work at Griffin's house. I love my apartment, but it's small. There's one bedroom, barely any closet space left for my unsuppressed shopping addiction, and a narrow kitchen. It works fine for one person, but it is also a reminder that I would rather be with Griffin than be alone. And having two people there makes the place feel very cramped. Griffin has a hillside mansion with five bedrooms, even though he's the only one that lives there. I always fantasize about playing hide and seek in his house, maybe rewarding him with something special if he can successfully find me amongst the many nooks and crannies.

"You don't want to think about moving in together?"

"I..." Do? I think? I would be ecstatic if Griffin and I woke up next to each other every day or most days since he's on the road a good amount during the season. But we've only been dating—officially dating—for the past two weeks, and moving in would be the next milestone in our relationship. I trace my fingers along the rim of the outdoor tub. I love Griffin, but was it too soon to take such a big step?

"I haven't given it much thought, I guess." I lean back so my hands can grip the tub behind me. "I'd love to wake up next to you and make meals with you and build a home together. But that is a big step and a big conversation. We need to give it some time before we talk about it." I didn't want the whirlwind of being in love to deter me from the very real commitment moving in was going to be, and I needed to be honest with myself for a moment. Because once my clothes are hanging from that closet, I'll be more than just "Griffin Markey's girlfriend." I'll be "the woman Griffin Markey's sharing his life with, under one roof and all."

"Don't get me wrong," I continue. "I'm gonna love getting to that point where we'll be waking up next to one another, but I want to make sure both of us are ready to take that next step."

"I get it," he reassures me, reaching to wrap his hands around my waist. "One day at a time. And I'm ready to absolutely ravish you during this one."

He bends down to plant his lips on mine and, in a swift motion, starts to turn the faucet on so water can begin filling the tub.

"What are you doing?" I ask, but it doesn't all sound like words because my lips are still firmly pressed to Griffin's.

"You're fangirling over this tub so much, so why not just use it? I am paying for it after all."

I titled my head. "You're right about that."

He burrows his face in my neck, splashing little kisses along its side. "Plus, I think I've earned seeing your naked body after that long drive."

I roll my eyes. "It wasn't even that long."

"Anything over five minutes might as well feel like an eternity," he grumbles. "If you won't take them off, I'd be happy to rip them off myself." He takes the bottom of my grey pullover crewneck and pulls it over my head. He then goes to show off a skill that he's somehow perfected by taking off my bra while keeping his arms around me and kissing me deeper, causing me to lean back into him. When my bra falls onto the floor, he lets out a deep moan as he cups my breast and pushes it up so my nipple is in prime sucking territory.

After a small pinch, he sucks at my breast, and I let out a loud groan.

"Yeah, babe? You like it when I take you in like that?" He looks down at my breasts again. "God, your body is a damn wonderland."

The water's filled most of the tub at this point, so Griffin turns the faucet off, and I wiggle out of my leggings and toss them aside. Griffin licks his lips at me, and my stomach begins to churn. The way he looks at me, ravenous for my body, makes me feel like I'm wanted. That I'm finally seen in someone's eyes with a desire to be chased after. It ignites something in me. I almost jump in his arms to kiss him, taking a fist full of the back of his hair and curling my legs around his thighs.

"God, Lydia. I want you so bad."

"You have me. All of me."

He carries me from the bottom of my ass and sets me gently into the warm water. Not long after my body submerses itself, Griffin hastily takes off his clothes and steps into the tub after me.

He breathes out, content when he feels the warmth against his body, and I glide towards him once he presses himself up against the tub.

"This settles it," he says, "When I'm getting home, I'm going to look into having a tub installed in the backyard."

"Really? It's nice, right?" It doesn't even have all the bells and whistles, like spa jets and color-changing LEDs. It's just a large soaking tub that has room for two people to snuggle up with one another, naked bodies pressed together, even if Griffin is almost six feet tall.

"I'll have to make sure that no one can peek in, but I think with enough shrubs and trees planted, I'll be able to make it work. Maybe I'll add in a pond as well, so we can hear the running water in our background to make it feel even more relaxing."

"That sounds amazing," I note. The idea of us living together sounded even more enticing now.

Griffin pulls me into him so that my submerged body touches his. I wrap my legs on either side of him and feel his hard dick up against my pussy. It's such a tease, and we'd never talked about having sex in places outside of a bed. I rub against him, and he lets out a sharp breath.

"Stop teasing me, babe," he grits. "I can't take any more of it."

He submerges his hand into the water and pushes one finger in and another once he stretches me a little more. He rubs a finger against my clit, and I shudder.

"My little Liddy," he says, an evil grin on his face. "I can feel how wet you are beyond being in this tub."

"It...feels...good...okay?" I breathe. His thick fingers fill me up, and when he rubs my clit, it sends sensations up my body, causing everything to feel ticklish.

"Here," he pants. "I'm gonna try something. You know how to float on your back in the water?"

"Uh, yeah." I nod.

"Okay. Tilt back." I do what he says, and lean back so I'm looking up at the sky and my back floats up to the surface. The tub is a little bit longer than my height. As I keep my body afloat, Griffin comes up next to my waist and splays his hand across my lower back."

"I'm going to have you spread your legs for me, babe, okay?"

"Yes," I blink back up at his head, shining through the sunlight. I start to spread my legs a little bit, so my feet almost touch the edges of the tub.

"Good girl," he whispers. He lifts one of my legs, startling me a bit so that I almost lose my balance.

Griffin tightens the hold on my back. "I got you. Always." He moves in between my legs and hoists one of them over his shoulder.

"What-what are you doing?" I ask, losing my breath.

"I'm tasting you," he responds bluntly.

"You...what? Are you sure?"

"Of course I am. Why are you asking?"

"Because..." I look away from him for a moment. "What if I don't taste good?"

"No such thing," he tells me. "Let me pleasure you, babe."

"Okay," I whisper. I grip onto the edges of the tub as he hoists my legs to wrap around his neck. Then, Griffin bends down and starts to suck and lick at my clit.

"Oh my god." I close my head and tilt my neck up, letting my hair sink deeper into the water. I let out a moan when he presses his tongue further into me.

"You taste amazing," he tells me, letting my legs fall back. He steps closer so our bodies press up against one another, and he goes back to working his fingers inside me. "You're out of this world. I feel like the luckiest man in the world right now, being able to make you come like this."

"I love you," I pant. "So much."

He brushes his lips against mine. "I love you, too. Now, what other parts of you can I explore while I got you all wet?"

20

Griffin

IF IT WASN'T FOR Lydia's excitement over the phrase "Complimentary Breakfast," I'd much rather be in the tub again than eating. Or eating something other than this egg benedict, if you catch my drift.

But Lydia argued that we can't pass up food that's included in our stay, especially when other guests who aren't receiving this complimentary are shelling out money to eat fancy breakfast food. What she wants, she gets.

The weekend has already been off to a great start, even if we haven't traversed much off the resort map. We haven't left our room much. We had a nice dinner reservation last night here at the hotel restaurant because I was unsuccessful in getting a reservation at French Laundry, no surprises there. Lydia didn't seem to mind. The hotel's four-course dinner menu was still delicious, and the view from our table overlooked the valley, which glowed orange from the beautiful setting sun. As I watched

Lydia glow from the radiance of the sun, it made my heart leap. I didn't want to spend any time away from her. But when we get home, I need to pack to go on a two-week trip filled with multiple away games in Canada. Maybe a weekend getaway where we're not interrupted by the hustle and bustle of our real life was more detrimental because it served as a reminder that my lack of presence during the season will only make Lydia feel more alone when she might need me most.

"What's our plan for today?" she asks me, after taking a large bite of her chilaquiles.

I had arranged for a private car service to take us to different wineries. I think there were five wineries that they put on our itinerary for tastings. I'd requested that as they were crafting this tour, they choose wineries that have private tasting areas or won't see much foot traffic. I don't want onlookers to take photos of us that will end up on the internet. While I feel like I've been better about handling the media thanks to Lydia, now it's about protecting her instead of garnering exposure for each of our gains.

"I asked a wine tour service to plan out our day for us. They said they have five wineries that might be perfect for our needs." I know that there will be people choosing to go there of their own accord anyway, but I didn't buy out the winery for us to have exclusive access. But maybe that would have been worth it so I could smother Lydia in my affection with only the person pouring our wine as a possible witness. Do wineries do room service but for wine tasting? I jot a note in my head to inquire about it when I plan our next trip to wine country. Hopefully, by then, I'll be successful in getting a reservation for French Laundry.

"That sounds awesome. I'm so glad that I can drink as much wine as I want without worry. Wine makes me do some wild things."

I raise a brow at her. Drunk Lydia is someone I've never experienced, and I'm not certain what I should be looking out for, but it might be that I'll have to drag her along the floor of the winery while she giddily laughs to herself.

"What kind of wild things?" I chuckle.

"Oh, just things like talking non-stop about *Hero Seek* lore and characters that I think are totally shippable. Romance novels that live rent-free in my head. On my birthday last year, I went on a rant about gamer girl bathtub streams. Who knows what unhinged topic I'll go off the rails with this time."

"Just be careful when you're talking to me about romance novel sex scenes," I warn her.

"Oh, yeah." She nods. "I don't think the people working at the winery want to hear that. Or maybe they do. What if there's a secret book club of people who read romance and drink wine? That's the kind of club I want to be a part of."

"No, silly," I wrap my leg around her ankle and make a swift motion to pull her chair closer to the table. "Because I'm going to want to recreate anything you talk about reading in your romance novel. I'll have to do it on the counter, or else I might explode."

Her cheeks heat, and I smirk, raising a brow at her. She gulps the remainder of her drink and clears her throat.

"Um, are you done?" she croaks. "We should probably go back to get ready. I don't know...how long it might take us. If you know what I mean."

Oh, this feisty little one. My feisty little one. I know exactly what she means, and the next thing I know, we're bolting.

The first winery that we go to is up the road from Auberge, so we walk up to meet our tour guide.

"Oh my god!" Lydia pulls my hand towards the sign of the winery. It shocks me how strong her pull is as I almost stumble over the flat concrete.

"What is it?" I ask. At first glance, I can't see anything that juts out at me. It's just a wooden sign with the name of the winery and its hours.

"There are CAVES!" she squeals. "Are we going to get to walk through the cave?"

"Erm, yes? We can," I answer. I let the professionals do the planning, which means I don't know what the full agenda is. I didn't even know that they had wine caves here until Lydia exclaims like Buddy the Elf when Mall Santa visits. "I'm sure it's not too complicated to ask. We'll get a tour if they haven't set up one for us already."

We check in with our guide, a cheerful man named Terrence (don't call him Terry because his dad claimed that nickname already) who has so much energy and excitement, it's like he drank a bottle of breakfast rosé. Lydia is all for it, though, matching Terrence's energy as she tells him about the resort, the delicious food, and how it's been years since she's visited Napa, and her goal today is to, gently putting it, get fucked up.

"Okay, but is it possible to get a cave tour?" Lydia asks. "I have no idea what is on our agenda this morning but if touring a cave is on that list of possibilities, I want in."

Terrence laughs and shakes his head. "Um, of course, we're getting a tour of the caves. How can you not go to a winery with a cave and not explore it?"

"That's what I was saying!" Lydia exclaimed. "Y'all know what the people want. I should have never doubted that."

I swallow a lump in my throat. I don't know what to expect from these caves Lydia can't seem to keep quiet about. Are these caves...spacious? Are they long? Is there a way to see the end of the cave? Is there any light to make me feel like I'm not going to be trapped under rubble if something catastrophic were to happen? I think I might be slightly nervous about the hypothetical entrapment. Am I claustrophobic?

"Have you been through this cave?" I ask meekly.

"Yeah," Terrence nods. "A bunch of times. Why?"

"Would you say the cave is...spacious?"

Lydia slowly turns her head towards me and raises an eyebrow skeptically. "Wait, are you afraid of going inside the cave?"

"No," I counter. Although, I don't know what the point of acting like I'm so strong is. I don't need to kid myself. I think I am scared of tight spaces. Or the feeling of being constrained. When I'm slammed up against the glass wall for just a moment, I brace myself and try to shove my opponent out of the way, or else I'll start panicking that I'm unable to move, to escape. The way that I want to breathe in and feel the air moving around me is a desire I never thought I'd want so badly until I started thinking about the possibility of being trapped in this cave.

"I might be a little afraid of going in the cave," I confess. "I've never thought of myself as being afraid of enclosed spaces before, but the more I'm thinking about it, the more I'm slightly freaking out at the possibility of getting trapped and feeling like there's no way out. Like, give me the gentle breeze, and I'll feel a little more secure."

"The cave has pretty tall ceilings," Terrence reassures me. "But if you walk through at first and feel uneasy about continuing on, then we can skip the cave. It is a nice day to have a tasting outdoor. The wind might be a little crisp, though. Hope that's okay."

"We're equipped for the weather." Lydia pulls at her sweater. "I want to make sure we all have a good time." She inches her hand towards mine, which is lodged in my pocket, and when I feel her fingers touching the back of my hand, I take it out and interlace my fingers with hers.

"We should go through the cave," I say while keeping my eyes glued on Lydia. "I'll be okay."

"Are you sure?" she asks. "I don't want you to feel panicked."

I smirk down at her, my body already feeling more secure with her being next to me rather than if I were to go at this alone. She unknowingly creates this barrier that acts like a shield from my own thoughts of dread and despair.

"I'll be okay. I already feel a little better knowing I don't have to go about this alone."

We walk through the cave, and I'm not going to lie, it is a marvel. And more spacious than I had originally feared. Maybe because caves that I've seen in movies and other sites discussing how they're wonders of the world have those dagger-like rock forms hanging down from them. I forget if those are stalagmites or stalactites. Either way, I feel like I can breathe better in this cave and not be worried about the possible bats that may be lurking in the ceiling like some caves in the movies.

The winery leads us to a room with barrels on the walls and a table laden with wine glasses. They ready a variety of wines for us to taste. I am more of a red wine person, but there's something good about each one of the wines we try. I know they give you that bucket to empty out your glass in case you don't want to waste your tastebuds on a wine that isn't to your liking.

I nudge Lydia as she's beginning to sip on her first glass of red. "How is it?"

"Really good," she grins, going to take another sip of the wine. "I don't really treat myself to a nice glass of wine as much as I should."

"Why? Is wine not your go-to drink?"

"I guess not," she shrugs. "I mean, I have a few bottles of wine at home. But I think they're all the ones I bought because of a five-cent wine sale. I don't spend my money on nice wine, but the more that I sip on this wine, the more I want days where I come home from work and unwind by pouring myself a glass of something like this."

I turn to jot down the wine that she recently tried so we can get a bottle of it to take with us. Wait, do they sell it by the case? That'll make it easier, so I don't need to make multiple trips for refills. But I wouldn't be opposed to joining a wine club as an excuse to make the drive up here more often. The sprawling greenery and chateau-inspired wineries are a nice change from the office buildings and suburban homes that surround me every single day.

"I wouldn't mind making this a semi-frequent trip," I smile at Lydia. "Or I can talk to my publicist about starting my own wine brand. It's very popular for celebrities to have alcohol brands. I mean, look at E-40. He has a champagne that tastes like cotton candy."

She giggles. "What would you call your wine brand?"

"I'm thinking 'Narwhal Wines.' I mean, gotta keep it in the aquatic family, right?"

Lydia rolls her eyes at me with her lips glued to the rim. "You're silly."

I am. But I feel accomplished when I can make Lydia laugh. Her smile warms every part of my body and makes me forget that we're underground with no windows that look out to the world above us.

We finish our sips, and as I'm about to hand over my order slip to get a bottle of that wine that Lydia liked so much and a case to ship home to my house, a lady wearing an olive green pants suit struts in on her high heels.

"I'm sorry to interrupt," she says. "But we have a problem."

"What's going on?" Terrence stands up.

"There is a swarm of cars with cameras outside, telling us that they were tipped off that Griffin Markey is here, and they are not going to budge until they get some footage of what they came here for."

"Wait." I stand up. "How do they know I'm here? I instructed Terrence to register for all our tastings under him."

Her hands go up in surrender. "I wish I could tell you. We've already asked all our staff if they've said anything, and of course, they're denying spilling the beans. It couldn't have been from another visitor because the next tasting isn't until eleven. I haven't had the time to interrogate all of our staff members, but I am deeply sorry that this has happened. We have other celebrities that have visited us, and we take all matters of confidentiality very seriously."

I sigh. I want to be frustrated, and I am, because I put in these measures to ensure that this didn't happen, but I have to remember who I am. I'm one of the biggest hockey players on this continent and if someone sees me walking somewhere, especially somewhere that can be classified as romantic, there will be curiosity. No one has really seen Lydia and me out in public together since we became official, except when we were in Vegas and shared that kiss. I don't publicly share snippets of my life on social media because of the people who will comment shit about Lydia and how ugly she looks or how we don't look good together. I know the whole reason we started dating, albeit fake, is because Lydia wanted to prove she had thick skin to overcome the haters. If something was said when we were fake dating, sure, I'd be upset because no one should speak about a woman that way, but now, the stakes are different. Any bad comment about Lydia ignites something inside of me. Something that people don't want to see when it'll inevitably explode.

I hold my head in my hands and rest my elbows on the table. Lydia reaches over to gently put her hand on my shoulder.

"Hey, we'll be okay," she reassures me. "We'll just walk out and not make eye contact. Sounds easy, right?"

"Yeah," I grit. But I'm bracing myself for disaster. Cameras getting in our faces, and people hurling questions all at the same time. Everyone demanding to know about me and my life and doing whatever they can to make it happen. Force included.

"Did you still want to plan to do the rest of the tour?" Terrence asks.

I pout. It'd be in our best interest not to, even though it's not the option that I want to move forward with. We've only reached one winery, and I had an entire day planned to travel around Napa. But I can't help playing worst-case scenarios in my head. They *will* follow us. They *will* take more photos. They *will* ask us more questions. The peaceful paradise I dreamed up in Napa has become a nightmare in a snap, all because of who I am and the way people put me up on a pedestal. It's moments like these when I wish I was a nobody. That I didn't go through with a career in the NHL. I would be your average Griffin, but still having fate map its course to Lydia.

"I think it's best if we don't leave a trail," I frown. "I know that cuts our plans early, but I fear that they'll follow us and get photos of us against my consent." I turn to Lydia. "I'm sorry, babe."

She blinks back at me, her expression unreadable, and I try to be patient before she lets me know what she's thinking.

"It's alright," she shrugs.

I quickly grab a hold of her hand that's in a fist on the table. Her nonchalant response worries me. "Are you sure?"

"Yes," she says with a little light in her voice. "I don't want you to feel like you have a target on your back for the rest of the day. We can spend the rest of the afternoon at the pool, share a bottle of wine, and relax. That sounds like a wonderful way to spend an afternoon to me."

I shoot her a soft smile and give that fist on the table a squeeze. We nod in agreement, and both get up to face the music. Before we walk out of the cave to sneakily hurry away without answering any questions, the winery profusely apologizes and promises to us that we can come back any time that we want, be lifelong wine club members, and every other concession besides wine ownership. Although, they tell me it's not completely out of the picture. Sans the snitch, I did really like their winery. I was slightly anxious that the cave might make me feel a sense of dread, but to my surprise, I was more wowed than worried. I would love to collaborate on a wine label, but all that's occupying my mind right now is how my day was thwarted by people who want to invade my personal space and my own mind not being strong enough to cancel out the noise and just go on with my day as planned.

We head out of the cave, and Terrence decides that he'll be our "knight in shining armor" and lead the way to, hopefully, shield us from any cameras. He was completely understanding about the situation and even gave us his personal cell for a raincheck tour. He jokingly added if there's an opportunity for tickets, he'll make the drive, and I told him I'd be happy to get some for him. It's the least I can do since he's no longer able to excitedly talk about all things wine and Napa Valley, something he reiterated is the best part of his job and brings him the most joy.

The moment we step outside, it's a frenzy. No one has any regard for personal space, and as much as Terrence tries to cover and lead us through the crowd, people and their cameras butt into any nook and cranny to catch a photo of me and Lydia. Their voices shout over one another, bombarding us with invasive questions that I'm refusing to answer.

"Griffin, do you and Lydia have plans to move in with one another?"

"Griffin, have you heard the backlash about how your girl-friend does not want to be in the public eye?"

But one question whisks me away to another planet. A hellscape that ignites something so catastrophic in me that I react in a way I didn't think possible because I've never done anything like it before in my life.

A bearded man comes up to us, right beside Lydia, almost to the point where their arms are touching. He stuffs his camera inches away from Lydia's face and asks her, in an aggressive tone:

"Lydia, what is your response to Griffin's fans who are saying you don't belong in the esports industry?"

Before Lydia's able to utter any form of response, I shove the guy and his camera away.

"What the hell, man?"

"Do not ever talk to her like that, do you hear me? You and your scumbag press can take your cameras and shove them up your fucking asshole. And if I see any photos of us circulating online, I will find you and destroy you with my own bare hands."

What happens after is a blur. It's like I blinked, and we were sitting in Terrence's car, heading not even a mile back to our resort. But we diverge from the hotel's typical point of entry and, instead, are escorted by the hotel's staff to enter via the valet parking entrance. Lydia's remained silent since my outburst. It's worrying me because I know that I reacted out of line. I can justify my actions all I want, but it was still highly unprofessional, and as much as I threatened to destroy that man, he has a right to his revenge after I more than likely sprained his nose, if not broke it.

Terrence puts his car in park and the resort staff are standing with their hands folded in front of them, ready to walk me and Lydia back to our room.

"Okay, here we are," Terrence says, his voice decibels lower than when we first met him.

"Thanks again Terrence," I say, trying to keep a positive demeanor. "Let me know when you're thinking of coming to San Jose for a game, and I'll set you up with tickets, alright?"

"Y-yeah," he responds weakly. "Okay."

Shit. I'm starting to get nervous that I may have scared him off. So much for having an "in" if we're making a trip back out here. I wouldn't be surprised if the winery ghosts me, too, even if I went back to say this is their fault in the first place. As we walk back to our room, I keep my hand on the small of Lydia's back, not pressing her to say anything. She doesn't, and it's messing with my brain. I need to let her have her space to recoup her feelings about this, but I'm afraid this might be the start of the worst descent we could possibly embark on.

21

Lydia

SINCE THE INCIDENT AT the winery, things haven't been the same between Griffin and me.

I wanted to be there for Griffin, and a part of me felt the remorse crawl into my bones that I wasn't as present in our relationship at a time when it was at its most vulnerable.

It has been four days since our escapade to Napa Valley. What began as a beautiful getaway soon turned south. It's not Griffin's fault, in my opinion. I would've acted out, too, but Griffin got to him first. And now, he's paying for it.

As expected, the guy that had his nose sprained a la "literal camera to the face" by Griffin posted the photo online from his camera's point of view, showing Griffin's hand outstretched before it slammed in his face. And then the other photographers took photos and videos of Griffin lashing out and posted that. The response from the public hasn't been stellar. It's been a shock to a lot of fans' systems, according to what I've read. I wish I hadn't read the comments because they enraged me.

"Do not mess with Markey. He'll break your nose and then some."

"I've lost a lot of respect for Griffin Markey. I know paparazzi can be invasive, but that doesn't mean you have to hurt them."

"What's dating done to you, Griffin? You're no longer a class act."

They weren't there. They didn't know what happened. They only see what happened through the lens of someone else, someone who's just hoping to make a quick buck by photographing a major hockey star. Griffin now comes across as someone who has an anger problem, and it's surprising to people because Griffin has spent most of his professional hockey career being the guy with the heart of gold and the NHL's sweetheart.

Griffin's been on the road again and three hours ahead in New York, so we haven't been talking as much as we would if we shared a time zone. He's also been in his head a lot about what happened and told me from the day he left for New York that he'll be busy. He apologized for when he'll be slow to respond to my texts because he's also going to New Jersey to visit his family. Is it bad that I've been too busy to care as much as I should? Over at LGU, the team has been practicing every day for a big tournament that's coming up soon. If we win this tournament, we'll have an automatic invitation to compete in the state finals in Las Vegas and potentially be in contention for

Worlds, taking place in Seoul. The victory is so close I can taste it, but there is a lot that we need to work on before even thinking about tasting victory. The kids keep manifesting, and this whole week, they've been staying in the esports room as late as ten pm, playing online to get practice matches in. I decided to stay late with them, catering different foods every night. For me, it's been fun to see them get so into something and be really good at it. The swiftness of their mice skating across the mouse pad, the clicks of the keyboard being tapped with such fervor. I almost feel like I have to force my mouth shut after it goes numb from being open for so long in awe.

As I'm wrapping up some marketing plans for potential fundraiser campaigns we'll need to do if we want to successfully make it to Vegas and not cause our pockets to bleed in the process, I hear my phone buzz and look to see that Landon's texted me.

Landon: Lunch plans? I wanna talk to you about something.

Lydia: No plans. What do you want to talk to me about?

Landon: I'll tell you during lunch. Meet you @ 1?

Lydia: Sure thing.

Landon's texts are so cryptic that I puzzle over why he's being so secretive. I hope it's exciting news. Maybe he received a job offer. But he would come across as more elated in his text if it was good news, which begs the question: what kind of bad news is he going to bear? Have he and his girlfriend hit a rough patch?

I jog down the stairs to the first floor, where all the food outlets are, and press my back against a wall to wait for Landon. I survey each of the different stations. My favorite one is the build-your-own pasta, where they sauté all the toppings and sauce right in front of you, but that one always has the longest line, and the current line of students is already almost to the door.

"Hey," Landon walks up to me and knocks me out of my thoughts about what to eat.

"Oh, hi! Sorry, just figuring out what to eat."

"You mean figuring out if you want to wait in line for the pasta, which happens every week." Landon starts chuckling. "Do you not like the Asian stir-fry station?"

"It's alright," I shrug. Should I like it more because we're Asian? I have to give it to the school and whoever's in charge of food outlets here. The beef and broccoli hits the spot occasionally. But whenever I settle for Asian food, I remember that my family can cook it better and wish they made food out of our school's cafeteria.

"Yin Yin makes it better."

Landon rolls his eyes. "Well, of course. It's college food. It's not supposed to be revolutionary."

"True. I should just be happy I don't have to pay for it, thanks to your meal plan."

We order our lunch. I ultimately decide to settle for the Asian stir-fry, and we find a table near the back corner of the dining area.

"Okay," I look Landon straight in the eyes before even taking a bite. Cryptic texts do not go well with my anxiety, and I need to know what he has to say before I can do anything else. "What is this *something* you needed to tell me over lunch? And why did you make it sound so vague?"

Landon sighs and puts the spoon down. Ha, he thought he could get a bite in before I interrogate him.

"I know you're my big sister, and you're an adult and fully capable of making your own decisions..."

I don't like where this is going.

"But," I interject.

"I'm worried about you, Lids."

I scrunch my nose in disgust. What on earth should Landon be worried about? My safety? I can assure him I'm safe. Griffin may have exhibited a violent side over one outburst, but this isn't an indication that my life was in danger, and how dare Landon assume that it was.

"Well, stop," I tell him straight. "Like you said, I'm an adult capable of making my own decisions. And I know what this is about. You weren't there, you don't know what happened."

He pinches the bridge of his nose. "Yes, I know. But he still reacted out of line."

"Yeah, because that guy got in our space."

"I know. And the paparazzi are completely out of line by asking those questions. But violence is never the answer."

"Don't you think I know that?!" I yell, loud enough for those sitting at the surrounding tables to turn around and eye us. God, I've never wanted to shrink back into nothingness as often as I wanted to in the past week. I'm starting to feel the embarrassment creep into every one of my veins, and now the walls I've tried so hard to keep together are starting to break apart, bit by bit.

"I'm sorry." I feel a droplet on my cheek. "This week hasn't been easy. And Griffin hasn't been talking to me much. He's been in New York for games and is making a trip out to see his family and...I want to be there for him because I know he's going through a lot, but he won't answer any of my texts."

"It's not your fault," Landon says, reaching to rub my forearm resting on the table. "Look, I'm sorry if I came off as condescending. It's just...people are talking, Lydia. They're spreading rumors that Griffin is violent and abusive beyond what they saw happen to that guy. You'd tell me if that was the case, right?"

"Y-yeah," I answer. It lacked confidence, but it should have been full of it. I just didn't want to believe that Griffin would ever do something like that. He wouldn't to me. But I wasn't confident enough to say he wouldn't to other people. "Of course."

"Okay, good. Just...stay off social media for a little bit," Landon warned. "It's a bloodbath out there. People are painting

Griffin in a bad light. He lashes out one time and everyone's focusing on the bad more than the good. People are putting Griffin's jersey up for sale on resell sites. It's bad."

I've suddenly lost my appetite for the sad-looking rice bowl that's losing steam in front of me. Griffin probably already knows about everything that's happened. Is a text reassuring him I've got his back going to even do anything for the heartbreak he must feel right now?

I pull out my phone and send him a text anyway. He'll either leave me on read, or he'll respond. I'd prefer the latter, but at least if it says he read it, then I can rest easy knowing that he's thinking of me like I'm thinking about him. I'm planning on spending tonight away from the university, for the first time this week, to watch the Stingrays take on the Islanders on TV. Griffin's parents and brothers are making the trip from New Jersey to watch him. I wonder what thoughts are racing through their minds about this. Are they disappointed in Griffin after the incident? I know that he's not the favorite child because he willingly left home, and they don't make an effort to fly to California to visit him because it's "too far." This probably just reinforces that Griffin is making poor decisions that they don't agree with.

> Lydia: Hey, I know you're busy with practices and spending time with your family, but I wanted to let you know I love you, and I'm here when you need me. x

I quietly walk back up to the food outlets and request a to-go box for the food I barely ate. Maybe I'll eat it later, but I feel a burst of nausea coming on, and I wish I could be at home now with my heating pad. I return to the table and tell Landon I have to get back to my desk. He simply nods and doesn't pry for me to spill my feelings and potentially showcase my ugly cries to an audience of judgy college students.

I plop down at my desk, not even moving to turn on the lights and rest my head in my arms crossed on the desk. It reminds me of when I'd get in trouble in elementary school and got "benched" for recess. I shut my eyes, and the drowsiness quickly sinks in. I'm awoken by knocking on the doorframe.

"Lydia?" A deep voice calls. I jolt up and gasp when I realize that I fell asleep. I peer over to the clock on my desk. I must've been asleep for at least half an hour! When I look up to the doorframe, and Dr. Jones is eyeing me coolly with his arms crossed over his chest, I want to gasp again.

"Dr. Jones!" My tone rises an octave. "We didn't have a meeting today, right?" I'm still red that Dr. Jones discovered me almost on the brink of REM. It's unlike me to fall asleep during work. I guess I was just so exhausted after lunch that I accidentally fell asleep. That was a mistake, because ,of course, I got caught in the act. Like my job is such a snooze fest when in actuality, I have a lot of work to do, and I just wasted time by napping. Maybe I'll put the game on my second screen while getting the rest of the things on my to-do list done today. Plus whatever Dr. Jones might have in store for me.

"No, Lydia. We didn't have a meeting. Is everything okay? Did you have trouble sleeping last night?"

"No, of course not! I just...wanted to take a little break since I knew I was going to stay late tonight. Gotta finish the fundraiser plan for the League Championships!"

"Lydia," he takes a seat across from me on my desk. "I wanted to check in on you because I know...things might be hard for you right now."

I bite my cheek. News has been spreading like a cold. And now, I have my boss asking questions about my overall well-being, over something that's not impeding my work performance. At least, not that I'm aware of.

"Um, everything's fine," I say with an ounce of confidence. "Why do you ask?"

He sighs and shoots me a look as if he's been through a hurricane. Scratching the side of his face, he purses his lips before extending them into a straight line.

"The Department of Student Life has been receiving some...comments on our social media posts about you and your relationship with Griffin Markey."

"What?" The color drains from my face, and my heart feels like it's on the cusp of shattering. The scrutiny against Griffin has spread too far. Beyond his social media and that of the Stingrays, now it's affecting me and my place of work, which is supposed to be using its social media channels to promote itself as a prized learning institution. "What kind of comments?"

He pulls out his phone and swipes up to unlock it. "Let's see…" His eyes flicker back and forth to read whatever is on the screen.

"How can you promote someone on your social media that assaults innocent people?"

"Save your employees from Griffin Markey, especially his girlfriend, Lydia Goh. I'm fearful that she'll be next."

I reel back in my chair. Why did it feel like everything expounded tenfold in a matter of minutes? I know I haven't been checking socials often for my own mental health, but this seems excessive for one incident with an invasive paparazzi that I could argue deserved what he got. Now people are saying to protect the school? Just because what? There was one post made about him dropping into our esports room and donating money to help the program. And because he's with me? Did I miss something? A catastrophic event that has led to Griffin being on the trending list for all the wrong reasons?

"Griffin is not hurting me," I begin. If I wanted to clear the air on anything, that was going to be the first. "I know he hurt someone, but it wasn't like it was unprovoked. They found us at the winery and…"

"There's been a recent development," Dr. Jones tells me. "Have you not seen the news?"

"No, I…" Fell asleep after lunch. And apparently, during that time, a lot has happened. "Took that nap, remember?"

"Oh yeah. I'll pretend that I didn't walk into you doing that. Not that you aren't allowed to...just...work productivity and all that."

I nod. I feel ashamed about it, too, I want to add. But I'm too anxious about what conundrum Griffin might have gotten himself into now.

"What's been on the news?"

Dr. Jones silently responds by typing something on his phone again and turns it around to show me. His eyes don't meet mine, instead, they look down at my desk, full of dilapidated papers strewn about. I didn't have time to organize them into folders, but I believe in the method to my madness. There was too much in my brain right now to take the time to organize my thoughts. I grab the phone, and my eyes widen when I see, in big bold letters, a headline reading:

"Griffin Markey Caught in Fight with Rival Davey Nettles at Puck Drop During San Jose vs NY Islanders Game

San Jose Stingrays player Griffin Markey was caught in a brawl immediately after the puck dropped with New York Islanders player Davey Nettles. It was not clear how the fight was provoked, but Markey made the first hit against Nettles. The two played hockey together at Cornell University, but it seems they may not have had a budding friendship. It was later decided that Markey would be suspended for the remainder of the game for violent misconduct. San Jose Stingrays coach, Brett Salter, has yet to comment on Markey's fight, but with the first period ending and the score 4 to 1 New York, we have a feeling he won't have many positive remarks regarding Markey's outburst."

My eyes start to well up, and I use my sleeve to wipe them before I full-on bawl in front of Dr. Jones. "I...I don't know why he did that."

"I know," Dr. Jones has a look of pity on his face. At least he agrees it's not my fault. "I just...just watch out for yourself, Lydia. And let me know immediately if anyone asks for your comment on anything. We want to protect ourselves."

"Yes," I quiver. "I will."

He gets up and exits my office, which only then is when I let the dam break and the tears shed. *Griffin,* I want to cry out. *What is going on?*

22

Griffin

THE VISITING TEAM LOCKER room whirrs from the faint air filling inside, with the sound of a commentator rattling off the play-by-play of what's happening on the ice.

This guy passing it to another guy, who's somehow able to maneuver against the normally strong Stingrays defense and SCORE!

The Islanders take yet another goal.

It's even more of a sting because we're not on our home turf, so Islander fans are just basking in this rare victory, as they have one of the worst records in the NHL. And then the icing on the cake is that my parents and brothers are here. Way to make your family proud, Markey. They drive the hour and a half to go to this game, only for you to be kicked out within the first two minutes.

I mean, hopefully, the fight was interesting.

Fucking Nettles. We may both have attended Cornell at the same time, and at one point, I was proud to call him a teammate, but he showed me his true colors tonight.

"Your reign's coming to a fucking end, Markey. You were never good at managing your emotions. Your girlfriend better run while she can."

Why does everyone think that because I hurt someone, it means I'm going to hurt my girlfriend? That my anger management, or lack thereof, will transfer to beating my girlfriend if we ever find ourselves in an argument? I want to scream to the world how wrong they are, but people are just so focused on the bad things I've done in the past week that it feels like a marathon to try and get them on my good side again.

I can argue all I want with Coach, and with the refs, and promise that I won't hit anyone again, or do something that will get me kicked out of the arena, that I just want to cheer on my teammates. But no. One outburst, one moment where I lost control, and a full-on line brawl led me to a game suspension.

The final buzzer blares over the TV mounted in the corner of the locker room, and I look at the final score. Stingrays, 1. Islanders, 6.

Everyone sulks into the locker room once we're off the ice but I don't meet anyone's stare.

"This is all your fault!" Lindley points at me. "We lost to the Islanders because of your little spat. We're fighting a wild card spot. We need every win we can get!"

I scoff. Rookies are always so melodramatic. Worst case we're dropping from first to second. Vancouver just so happens to be on a winning streak.

"We're doing just fine," I grit. "Know your place before you talk back to your captain like that."

Another player in my peripheral tsks. "Oh yeah. Great how our captain just happens to be in the headlines of every major news outlet as an abuser. You're some role model." He rolls his eyes and others are whispering in agreement around him.

"Enough!" Ross chimes in, and the room goes silent. "Before you go on bitching about who you're forced to listen to, maybe you should know that this fight wasn't unprovoked. Nettles made a comment that was uncalled for, and Griffin retaliated. Do not lie to me and tell me that you wouldn't have acted the same way."

Lindley hangs his head low and shuts his eyes. "Okay, I probably would've. I'm sorry for my comment, Markey. I believe you if it was warranted."

"Don't." I shake my head. While I wish I could be appreciative of Ross defending me, I am not going to deny that I fucked up. "Look, I'm not condoning my behavior. I could have left it at one shove, but I didn't. I don't think I'm setting a good example right now for anyone, and I'm already planning to take preventative steps to ensure that this doesn't happen again. I apologize for letting you all down. You deserved a win tonight and a captain to show up and help bring you there, but that wasn't me. I wasn't the bigger man, and I let my emotions ruin a game that we could have won easily. That's all I have to say about this, and I'd prefer it if no one asks for any follow-up tonight."

I gather my things, ignoring the outside noise, and brace myself to tell Coach I'm heading out of here before our post-game huddle. I wasn't in the game anyway, so if Coach and I could just sidebar on what we need to talk about so I can go be alone, that'd be fantastic.

Coach storms in. One look at him, and you can see the invisible fumes coming out from his ears.

"Markey," he barks and narrows his eyes at me. "You're requested in the press room."

Fuck. I thought that I only needed to make one vulnerable speech today. Who the hell knows the kind of vitriol that'll get spewed at me from the press? All they want to see is trouble, and I can't wait to have my words somehow twisted so I look like an even worse human.

"Alright," I get up and meet him at the entryway. He doesn't speak a word to anyone else before we head down the hallway to the press room.

Before I step inside to face the wrath, he holds out his hand to grab the door handle to stop me.

"Look, Markey. Just...don't divulge too much if you don't want to. We'll handle any damage control ahead of the next game. Don't get yourself into deeper water than you're already in."

"Yes, Coach," I reply. He's already had to sugarcoat shit to make me look better and try to comb up reasons for why we lost or why I had my outburst in the first place. He probably made up some shit about how we're working on my anger management and reassured everyone it won't happen again.

"Did you, um, did they already ask you about the brawl?"

"Yes," he nods. "They did."

"Can I...know what you said?"

He doesn't meet my gaze. With his eyes fixed on the floor, he just lets out a long sigh.

"I tried to make you sound as innocent as possible, Markey. That you're going through some things. But at some point, I can't justify your actions when you chose to make your private life public."

I want to scream, "It's not fair!" Like a kid who didn't get what he wanted from the store. But it's my fault. I chose to go outside of my comfort zone after playing it safe. I could have asked for security, but I didn't think I'd need it. I thought I would be strong enough to face my fears, that the power of love could counteract any fear that I had of strangers intruding into my personal life.

"Yeah, I know," I whisper. "Well, thanks for giving some kind of sugarcoated response. We'll see how it'll go over with me."

He squeezes my shoulder. I've been a Stingray for so long, and this might be the first time that I've had an actual intimate moment with Coach about something other than hockey. This moment makes me feel a bond with Coach, stronger than any bond that I've felt with my family in a long time. Hell, I don't even know if they're waiting around to talk to me or if they feel embarrassed to be related to me after the kerfuffle.

"Whatever happens doesn't take away from how good you are as a hockey player. And it never will. You've accomplished a lot, Griffin. This isn't your legacy. Your performance on the ice will be, even if this one mistake may carry more impact."

I try not to let my tears spill. "Thanks," I nod. With that Creed-esque speech, I feel like I've got enough in me to tackle anything these reporters hurl towards me.

Or so I thought.

When I walk into the press room, camera flashes blind my vision. I can barely see my way up to the stage area, where there's a table and microphone. After me will be members of the Islanders, probably gloating about how well they performed tonight, and Nettles will say something about how he just said those things to rile me up for the game, but he didn't think that I would react the way that I did. That I'm the one who is going to need help. And he'll get off clean like he has all his life.

I take a seat, and everyone's shouting my name, trying to wiggle their way in to ask me a question. I don't know how else to kick this off other than to point at one of the reporters sitting in the front row. A woman wearing a blazer and a frilly red silk blouse.

"Mr. Markey, what can you tell us about the fight at puck drop between you and Mr. Nettles?"

I sigh. "What I can tell you is that Mr. Nettles made some inappropriate comments about me and my personal life that struck a chord. As other news outlets have publicized, it has been a difficult week for me, and I can truthfully say that I overreacted. But this fight wasn't unprovoked. I want that to be on the record or whatever journalists say."

I point to another person, raising their hand and holding their recording device towards me. "Mr. Markey, due to your recent behavior, Stingrays fans, as well as hockey fans in general, are saying that you have an anger issue. Would you agree?"

I sigh. "Yeah. I will admit that I have an anger issue."

"And what are you doing to combat that anger issue?"

I blink back at him. Jeez, do you think that I have a plan yet for what I'm doing about this? I mean, sure, I've contemplated therapy. But I haven't made the appointment yet.

"I don't know," I shrug. "Maybe therapy? I...everything just happened. I haven't really had the chance to call to make an appointment."

I gesture to another person. "Have you spoken to your girlfriend, Lydia Goh, since the incident?"

Huh, that question kind of came out of left field. I saw that Lydia had left me a text not long ago, just a kind message, something along the lines of wanting to be there for me, but I had to warm up before I could respond. She's probably at work now, and I don't even want to imagine what kind of scrutiny she's been dealing with if news has already traveled to her. Shit, now I'm wishing that I was closer to her to play damage control if she's trying to fend for herself.

"No," I shake my head. "I haven't. Why do you ask?"

"Because she just shared to her Instagram story a post from Los Gatos University about you."

"What?" My jaw drops. "What kind of post?"

"I would check your phone," is all the reporter tells me, and I quickly end the press conference to race back to the locker room and grab a hold of my phone. Skipping through the hundreds of missed calls and text messages from my family, I open Instagram. Lydia's profile photo is the first one next to mine, signaling that she posted a new story, just as the reporter said.

All the post has is a Los Gatos University Department of Student Life letterhead and one sentence below it.

"We have deleted the photos of San Jose Stingrays player Griffin Markey from our page. We do not condone violence amongst our students and faculty and do not agree with the actions Mr. Markey has committed in the past week. We apologize for previously promoting Mr. Markey as a patron to the LGU community."

"What the fuck," I whisper. Who posted this? And was Lydia forced to repost this or did she decide to of her own free will? Is she in trouble? Like her job was hanging by a thread, so that's why she had to share this?

My head is spinning with anxiety, and I need to know if what Lydia did was her own choice and if she's doing it as some sort of retaliation towards me. When you think that being in love with someone means that you're going to be there for them through thick and thin, something like this makes you question it. But it's also making me realize that I did fuck up, and maybe

Lydia needs to be with someone who doesn't have so much baggage weighing them down right now.

Before I race to pull her contact card, my phone screen pops up with an incoming call from "Gordon Markey."

God dammit. I've avoided my family all night and their frequent calling and texting showed me that maybe they might care about me, so I should reciprocate whatever feelings they might have.

"Hello?"

"Hey, Griff."

Gordo's greeting lacks any sort of enthusiasm to be talking to me for the first time in almost a year, so now I'm not so sure what he might want.

"Um, hi. What's up?" I return similar levels of weariness.

"Um, are you still at the arena by chance? We wanted to know if we could see you."

"Oh," I sit up straighter on the bench. "Yeah. I'm still here. Let me pack up my things. Who's all here?"

"All of us. Me, Graham, Mom and Dad. We couldn't leave your game without taking the chance to see you in person."

I scoff. "Even if I barely played in it?"

"Well, yeah. Shit happens, Griff. I'm not going to press more about it."

"Okay." I can be appreciative of that. "Thanks. I just need to gather my things and I'll meet you...near where the visiting team enters? You know what, I'm going to let my coach know and we'll see if you can come in here."

"Sure thing. We'll see if we can find our way to the player entrance. We just say we're here to see you?"

"Yeah, I'll tell a guard you're my family and stand with him. See you in like...five minutes."

"Sure thing," Gordo's tone lightens a bit, like he might be excited to see me. Gordon's always been the favorite of the three Markey boys and embraces it by touting his successes any chance he gets. That also includes the occasional snarkiness around me, emanating some sort of jealousy every time I'd talk about my success. But I'm eager to see if that's been turned around.

I walk to the player entrance, and next to the guard, there's a group of four people huddled together, dressed in warm clothing appropriate for the crisp New York winter that I don't miss much.

"Hey guys," I sheepishly wave.

My mom moves forward first, a petite Japanese woman with a full head of grey hair now. She used to color it when we were younger, but now looks like she's embraced her inevitable aging.

She envelops me in a bear hug.

I wobble backward a little bit; Momma Markey is a force and probably where much of my strength comes from.

"Hi, Mom." I wrap my arms around her, giving her a light squeeze. "Dad, Gordo, Graham. Um, thank you all for coming. I'm sorry that I didn't get to play as much as you were expecting. Or really, at all." I allow my vulnerability to absorb into my bones. "I feel like I've disappointed you all. I'm so sorry."

"Oh, Griffin." My mom starts rubbing circles on my back. "It's okay," she tells me. "We're not disappointed."

"You should be." I shuffle between each word, fully accepting that I'm a snotty mess in my mother's arms again. I feel like I'm a child again, crying after I'd lose a game or miss a goal, and my mom would be there in a snap to comfort me. It's actually kind of nice, feeling like I'm loved again.

"I didn't want to fight him," I confess. That sounds pretty dumb for a hockey player. Hockey fights are an essential part of the game, and I'll partake in a fight if it's the most strategic move to make. But never to the point where I'd get ejected from the game. "To that level, anyway. But he said something that involved Lydia...and I just snapped."

"Lydia's your girlfriend, right?" Graham asks. "She seems very sweet. You two look really cute together."

"Yeah, you think so?" My face drops when I remember the post she reshared, basically alluding that she wants nothing to do with me so she can protect her job. I don't blame her; she's worked so hard to get to a point where she's respected by her peers. It still hurts, though, the realization that if I want what's best for her, I'm going to have to set her free. "I don't think that she's very happy right now. After everything that happened."

"Have you talked to her?" My dad asks. "If she really loves you, she'll stick with you no matter what."

"It's not that I don't think she loves me," I counter. "It's that...I think she deserves better than me."

"Wait," Gordon holds up his hand to stop me. "You're not thinking of breaking up with her, are you? Just because of one fight?"

"It's more than a fight, though! I thought that I could take on a relationship in the public eye, and I've failed. Twice. I need to take a step back and work on myself before I'm worthy of being with anyone. Especially Lydia."

"Well, if you want to take some time off...I know you really can't because of the season, but we'd love it if you'd come home. Or hey, maybe Dad and I will stay with you in San Jose? Help out where we can?"

My eyes widen. "You'd...you'd come and visit? But I'm so far away."

"We haven't made as much of an effort as we should've to be there for you, Griffin," my mom continues. "But we want to. We want you to get better. And if that means coming to San Jose and helping around the house a little, we'll do it."

"Yeah." My dad places a hand on my shoulder. "We'll be there for you."

I wipe any remnants of tears on my face. "Thank you, guys." I might be feeling a lot of emotions right now, but what's taking over is the feeling of compassion my parents are giving to me when I'm feeling my lowest.

I know that I'll need it when I make the worst and hardest decision of my life, even though I know it's the right thing to do. Because I need to work on myself, before I can be the man Lydia needs.

23

Lydia

Why did I even do this?

Oh yeah, because if I didn't, then I was going to kiss my job goodbye.

I was forced against my better judgment to repost on the LGU Esports Department's Instagram a simple text on a blue background condemning Griffin's behavior at the Stingrays's most recent game in New York. An incident that I only found out about because my own fucking boss was sent a video of the incident by an alumni who donates a large sum of money to the school, specifically to the Esports Department, because they have a "deep connection to video gaming." Then where have you been this past year, you dunce? I haven't seen a single dime trickle in from this person, which is something I fact-checked after looking at our donor history. He told Dr. Jones that he and a network of other affluent alumni are not going to support the Department of Student Life if they promote athletes who are "threats to society." And the only pro athlete on the department's Instagram page is Griffin.

"I'm really sorry, Lydia," Cat, the department's social media manager, apologizes after a department-wide meeting about maintaining our "esteemed brand identity" and for the mistakes we've made and how we're going to amend them. The safest way to do that is to publicly say sorry and announce that we're not going to be professionally involved with Griffin anymore. Note how we didn't say personally because, well, last I checked, I'm still dating him.

We haven't really talked much, though. He still hasn't responded to my text. And I know he's en route to San Jose today. Do I call him when he touches down to meet him at his house after work? Is it completely bonkers to just drive to his house and say I have a right, as his girlfriend, to see him? I try to tell myself that he needs space, but when I'm going through something hard, like right now, I want to be in Griffin's company. I want to tell him that I don't know if I made the right decision, choosing my job over him. That I had to take a stance that I didn't agree with because money was hanging over my head.

"It is what it is," I tell Cat. She's a new grad who started as an intern when she was enrolled as a student. Someone eager to spend another chunk of their life roaming the same halls and being around ambitious students, and then later, suffer from the inevitable burnout that college brings.

I took this job because I always felt like I had a connection to Los Gatos University, and I wanted to be like those alumni who give a good sum of money and the school recognizes them in a good light. But at the end of the day, a school is a business, and they need to make decisions that bring money, even if it hurts others as a result.

"Have you been receiving anything on any of your personal accounts?" She asks.

"My Instagram account is private." So I can't receive unsolicited direct messages. My email has received a few requests for interviews from journalists, but I just drag them to the trash. If I say something that comes from my heart, it'll be skewed against Griffin. Plus, the whole "representing the school" thing and trying to look out for my students before myself.

"Okay, good. You'd let me know if you receive something that can be considered harmful, right? We can help."

I flash her the smallest smile, the most I've given in the past twenty-four hours. A closed-lipped, tight one that takes a lot of effort to make it seem like I'm okay. That I'm happy that it feels like someone has my back.

"Thanks. I'll let you know."

Cat leaves the room, and I walk away from my computer because the only thing that I want to do right now is doom scroll, even though it's the last thing I should do.

Instead, I walk over to one of the gaming stations, sit down, and click open up a game that's not my usual go-to. *Hero Seek* was the game I used to escape to, but now it just feels strange. I can't boot it up without thinking about Griffin, what he might be thinking about right now, and how he hasn't made an effort to talk to me. Even a thumbs up to acknowledge my text would be better than the crickets he's been giving me.

I need to play something to release some of the anger bubbling up inside me, ready to boil over. I pull up a first-person shooter. These games aren't typically on my playlist, because the stakes are too high, and the people get too toxic in the chat. If I spoke and people recognized my feminine voice, they'd go ballistic. But right now, little can make me sadder than how I already feel. I'm like a glass pane, and the toxic words people will probably be spewing at me are like little balls that bounce off me, unable to make a dent in me.

I'm paired amongst other players in the lobby and we ready up. I put on the headphones just to take cues from my teammates in case I need to retreat or meet someone at a point. The object of the game is to get the most kills, and when the clock counts down, I strategize my way to get those kills. I don't think I'm good enough to blitz in front and make myself an easy target. My reflex time isn't fast enough to react when it comes to who's gonna shoot who first. I've equipped myself with a gun that works best if you're up close, so I look over at the corner map and find a way to sneak into the opposing team's base and get someone from behind.

I get a kill and almost get another one, but when someone shoots me from behind, I scowl.

"Fuck!" I whisper.

"Hey P-Diddy, stop lolling around and start playing."

"My name is not P-Diddy," I grumble. The nickname irks me a bit, and I start to feel a headache start to form at my temples from the stress of toxic players when this is supposed to be a stress reliever.

I ignore my teammates' suggestions for what to do next because I know that I've set myself in a direction to be good enough to go solo and try and rack up kills for my team.

But when I'm stuck in a shootout, and I get myself killed again, I rip off my headset and yell a loud "FUCK!" at the computer.

"Hey, Lids, is, uh, everything okay?"

I look up at who's walked into the room, and my mouth drops when I see Griffin approaching my chair, dressed in a Stingrays hoodie and sweatpants. He's so casual but it's the best look on him. His hair is unkept, and he has bags under his eyes but he's still the most beautiful sight. It reminds me of us behind the scenes. What I'd never allow the media to see as long as we're together.

"Griffin?" I whisper. I don't care what is going on with the game now. I'm away from my keyboard, standing at my post while teammates are racing to finish out this game. I can hear their muffled calls through my headset, yelling at me why I'm AFK, and I ignore it. In fact, I quickly exit the game and whisper a silent apology, even though I don't give a shit if I just cost them a victory.

I stand up and throw my arms around him, my hands making a fist as I tug onto him as tight as I possibly can.

"What...why are you here?"

"I wanted to talk to you as soon as I got to San Jose," he says. He's exhausted, I can tell, because he doesn't sound as enthusiastic as I hoped he would be.

"Oh. Yes, of course. What's up?" I'm trying to stay positive but faltering as he doesn't seem to lift his voice. Not even slightly excited to be seeing me after days apart.

"I, uh. I saw the story reposted...on the Esports Department account."

Shit. Well, I figured he must've. Hopefully, I can convince him that it wasn't something I wanted to do.

"Oh. You did? Look, babe, I didn't want to..."

"I don't know if we should keep doing this."

My heart stops beating, and I try and spin the narrative for my, our, own good.

"Keep doing what? Like...you want me to leave my job?"

"No, Lids," he shakes his head. "I...I'm sorry."

He's sorry? For what? No. No, no, no, no, no.

"What are you trying to say, Griffin?" My lips start trembling.

"I don't want you to leave your job. I don't...I fucked up Lydia. I'm a fucked up person, and I don't think that you deserve to be with someone that everyone sees as their biggest enemy right now."

"But…it's okay, you're fucked up." I try to say whatever I can to save this situation, but it doesn't come out right when I hear myself say it. "I know why you're acting like this. And I think we just need to take a beat, and maybe we'll put out a statement that we're working on it. We can get through this…"

"NO!" he shouts, and I take a step back out of his arms and almost trip over one of the chairs. "I…I'm sorry. See this, this mess. You don't deserve to be with someone who's like this."

"But," I start sobbing. "I love you. Shouldn't love be enough to conquer whatever…obstacles we're put through?"

"Not…not when I need to work on these things alone. So I can fix myself. Until then…I…need some time. I'm sorry."

I couldn't have predicted something like this happening. This can't be it for us. I wanted Griffin to come home so we could talk through whatever monsters were in his head and conjure up a game plan so we could take care of the haters together. Instead, we're breaking up, and nothing I can say or do will change Griffin's mind because he's going through a lot in his head right now that he needs to fix. Without me.

"I…There's nothing I can say that's going to make you change your mind?" I whisper.

He shakes his head. "No, Lydia. I'm sorry. So so sorry."

"Are you?" I blink away the tears. It feels like this is the lazy way out of what I was prepared to work so hard for. "If you loved me, you'd fight to keep me."

"No." His voice sounds strained. "You don't understand. I love you so much that I need you to be with someone who doesn't carry all these burdens. I...I need you to be with someone normal."

"I don't want normal!" I scream. "I want you. Please don't let me go, Griffin."

"I'm sorry." Again with that phrase that means bullshit to me right now.

"Yeah," I turn my head to look away from his gaze. "I guess I am too."

He turns around and walks out of the room, and when he leaves, my legs go limp, and I drop to the floor. I start crying so heavily that I forget how to breathe. I just got dumped, and there is nothing I can do about it. There is no battle I can fight and come out victorious. Love's a game, they say, but how am I supposed to feel like it is when I can't win?

"Lydia," Kristian calls for me as she's entering my office. "Lydia, I think you should take the rest of the day off. Shit, take a week off."

I can't, I want to scream. My legs feel so heavy that they can't move, and my face is stuck to the desk calendar on my desk, which is sopping wet now from the tears. I have tried so hard to get up and look at my computer, and answer an email or a few, but when I will my head to tilt up and stare at my computer, I am reminded of how my job constantly exposes me to video games.

The kids just wrapped up a tournament.

There's a tournament we're hosting next week.

Red Bull wants to finally sponsor us.

And worst of all, Griffin is still the face of *Hero Seek*. It's an even bigger deal now because the Stingrays are poised to claim the division and receive a bye in the first round of playoffs. Even though it's only been a week since our breakup, that was enough time for people to forgive him for his behavior and worship him again. I think the video that he made of him in his living room, wearing a black shirt and hair unkept, basically being vulnerable and apologizing about what happened, how he reacted, and why he did it, helped. (Yes, he did say it was because he was in love, and no, I did not continue the video after that.) The comments were generally positive, and that's how I found out that Griffin started going to therapy.

Am I completely over this breakup and Griffin? No. It hurts that I've been left in a position where I feel helpless, that my existence is putting more harm on the person I love than good. But he told me he needed to do this to work on himself. So I can only hope that means we'll find our way back to each other again.

"There's so much to do," I groan. "We have the tournament next weekend, and I need to make sure everything's ready for it."

Kristian takes a seat across from me and gently pats my head like I'm a puppy. I lean into her pats. Any touch is welcome after lamenting the past week about how alone it feels to sleep in your bed when you've grown accustomed to waking up in another person's arms.

"You can coordinate everything from home. You can set up your laptop in bed, and no one will know."

"I know." I finally get enough courage to hoist myself up and sit upright in my chair. My spine still wobbles a bit, and I don't sit straight along the back, but at least I can give my desk calendar a much-needed break from being smooshed. "I just can't leave the kids, you know? I'm trying so hard to not rain down on their parade. They deserve to have someone be there to hype them up."

She grabs a hold of my arm and gives it a quick squeeze. "I get it. Just...take care of yourself too, okay? I hate seeing you like this."

"I'll try. Thanks, Kris."

"Anytime. Love you, Lids!"

"Love you, too," I whisper.

As much as it pains me to be detached from my students and campus, I decide Kristian's right. Being here only serves as a reminder that I need to flee from the negative thoughts invading my mind. I draft a long email to Dr. Jones, telling him that despite university policy stating guidelines against working from home full time, I think that it is in my best interest to do so in my quest to "heal" as best as I can. That my productivity is better suited off-campus, for once.

I hit the send button, and as I'm packing up my things, my phone pings back with a text.

Dr. Jones: Hi Lydia, I just finished reading your email and wanted to let you know it is okay to take the day and work from home. If you'd like to take the rest of the week and work from home, that is okay too. I just want you to know I'm here if you need any help navigating through this difficult time. Dr. J

Lydia: Thanks, Dr. Jones. I'll try to use this time to recoup as best as I can so I can be ready for the tournament next week.

I get into my car, and as I leave LGU and the students milling about, I wonder to myself if there will ever be a point where I feel like I can be the best director for the team. And if I can't, then how will I tell them it's time for me to embark on a new path?

24

Griffin

♥ 🎮 ⬤

A MONTH AFTER THE breakup

I should be happy that I'm not the NHL's public enemy number one, but I'm still hurting. I miss Lydia. While my therapist, Cindy, has told me I have made great strides in our sessions the past few weeks, I feel an emptiness in my body that can only be filled by the presence of Lydia. The touch of Lydia. The love from Lydia.

"Why did you decide to break up with Lydia?" Cindy asks me after a few sessions. I finally opened up about a lot of buried feelings about my career. I know a big part of why I decided to go to therapy was to talk to someone about what's been bottled up inside me for my entire professional career, but the vulnerability is something that I could never have prepared myself for.

I slump in the loveseat and tilt my neck up to the tiled ceiling. Cindy keeps her office very welcoming. She has some weird obsession with ficuses, and I have to try to swerve my head around the leaves so I don't knock into them with the force of my body, and they bend or break.

"I needed to work on myself before I could be a good boyfriend. When the incident happened, it pulled me down to a new low I didn't think existed. I hated myself. I...I wanted to hurt myself over how I reacted. I might be a hockey player, but that fight was an unacceptable reaction. It was embarrassing, it was harmful, it was...it wasn't what I wanted to be. I mean, it's great now that people have seemed to forgive me. They praise me for doing something about it. But I still don't feel like I'm what that Lydia deserves."

"And what does she deserve?"

I don't know why the question stumps me, makes me think a little more. Shouldn't I know all that Lydia deserves because it's everything I'm not? That's what I told her when I decided we should break up. "Um...well. Someone who doesn't have a lot of baggage. And before you ask to elaborate, I'll explain what I mean by baggage. I'm famous, she's...less famous. People breathe down my neck and watch my every move. People aren't stalking Lydia's every move. And she should be with someone who doesn't get her critique for...what? Existing? What if we're photographed, and people make comments about how she's dressed? I can't put her in a position where she'll be judged for her every move."

"Did you decide that?" Cindy asks. "Or did you let her decide?"

"I decided that," I say. Is that the wrong answer? "I just knew that it was better for everyone, even if it meant we had to break up."

"Let me ask you something, Griffin," she says, leaning a bit closer to me now. I stiffen my back as her eyes pierce into my very cloudy soul.

"When you and Lydia first started dating, do you think she was aware she was going to be thrust into the spotlight because of your fame? That she was willing to risk public scrutiny because she wanted to be with you?"

"I..." She was. In fact, our first time "getting together" wasn't even for love. It was for her to gain respect from her peers. And because she thought she could teach me a lesson since I didn't want to start dating for the very reason I broke up with her. Man, how wild it is that things come full circle like this? And how, after everything, I still don't think that us dating is a good idea. If I did, then maybe I would have tried harder to hold onto her.

"Not a lot of people know this," I begin, rubbing my sweaty palms against my pants, "But when Lydia and I first started publicly dating, it was fake. We did it as a publicity stunt because we met online while playing video games. She told me she was struggling with gaining respect from her colleagues and thought dating me could help with that. Turns out, it did.

Obviously, we didn't want it to be fake for much longer after that, and I told her I was falling in love with her. She felt the same way, but I was still scared of what was going to happen. I didn't fully get over my fear of being in the spotlight, and...when I took a risk, it backfired. I guess that's how we got to where we are now. I know she is open to having her life be under the public eye, but..." I sigh. The feelings buried deep inside me culminate, and I do something I hadn't done in years. I didn't even do it when I broke up with Lydia. I cry.

"I'm sorry," I tell Cindy through my ugly sobs and the snot oozing from my nose. She rushes to hand me the tissue box that I didn't even realize was right in front of me.

"You don't need to feel sorry," she gently informs me. "It is difficult to release these feelings that you've suppressed throughout your entire professional career, really. You decided to play professional hockey because you love the sport, not to gain attention from the public."

"Exactly." I blink over and over when I realize that the reason I feel this way is really that simple. There are plenty of people in the hockey world who embrace fame. They put on a show so everyone can talk about them. But me? I keep my mouth closed and my personal life behind closed doors. People hope that one day I will change because I need to "come to terms" with the fact that I'm famous and that somehow gives people the right to expect something from me. But after this? I'm learning control. And I'm not going to be sorry for how much or how little I'll share.

"I think that helps a lot. Realizing that I don't owe people my life. And maybe try to talk through solutions instead of forcing the ones I love to do something I think will help them when *they* should be making those decisions. I didn't believe in Lydia enough to handle things on her own and selfishly thought this was the best solution."

I don't know how or what I need to do to start the process of winning Lydia's love and trust back, but right now, there's nothing else I want to do except figure out a way to win back the girl of my dreams.

And hope that she'll want to take me back, the still broken, still learning, imperfect person I am.

It's only been fifteen minutes, and there have been at least ten people who have come up to me, asking for an autograph or a picture. And you know what? I wasn't mad about it.

Operation Get Lydia Back takes me to Guildhouse, the esports bar conglomerate where Lydia and I met and made the fake dating pact. Where we played mindless games of *Mario Kart,* and it was the most fun I've had playing a video game. Being back here reminds me of how Lydia had the power to make it feel like we were the only two people in the room. How she caught my eye and later my heart.

But today, I'm not meeting Lydia.

Landon Goh steps into the bar, and I can't tell if he wants to see me or he's ready to beat me up. There's nothing bright about his furrowed brow and downturned frown when he catches my gaze. He storms over and sits across from me, slamming his phone and wallet on the table when he takes them out of his pockets.

"Thank you for meeting me here," I start.

He scoffs. "Whatever. You better not be full of bullshit by trying to win my sister back. Don't think I've fully forgiven you yet for rejecting her after you two somehow met online playing *Hero Seek*."

"Yeah, well, I thought you'd be a little more understanding when you learned I rejected her because I'm kind of a famous hockey player..."

He rolls his eyes. I knew that in my conquest to win Lydia back, I had to win over the most important person in her life. Well, the one I'd already met. I've never met her parents. I hope I'll get to meet them someday. Landon, on the other hand, said to my face that he looked up to me but after I broke his sister's heart the first time, I'd lost a fan. That hurt me more than I thought it would, coming from someone I didn't know.

"It doesn't hurt to ask how she felt," Landon explains. "You need to stop thinking that you know what's best for Lydia."

"I know. That's what got us into this mess in the first place." I make a flamboyant gesture with my arms. I feel like I've been needing to shake it off, like those inflatable flailing arm men that tell you to buy a car. "I'm trying to make things right. To at least have a chance."

Landon stares down at the cocktail I ordered for him and sighs. It baffles me that he's still a college student. He's graduating in a few months, but he's much more mature than some of the players on the team. I'm glad that he obviously loves Lydia and that he'll do anything for her, including potentially attempting to murder professional hockey players who have ruined her life.

"Look, Griffin. I get that you're probably going through a lot. I'm not famous, and I don't think I ever want to be for this very reason. All the scrutiny and everyone breathing down your neck and shit. And a part of me doesn't want that for my sister either. But if you really love her, then I will give you my blessing or whatever to win her back."

I slurp up the remnants of my drink. I honestly did not think that Landon was going to cave this easily. I was about to do something similar to jousting to our deaths if it meant I got his blessing to ask Lydia to take me back.

"Really? I thought you'd make me work for it more, to be honest."

He shrugs. "At the end of the day, it's up to Lydia. All I want is for her to be happy. And right now, she's not."

My heart sinks when I imagine Lydia unhappy. It already breaks my heart, thinking back to seeing her sob on the floor, grasping onto me, hoping I wouldn't let go. I don't know if she'll take me back if I'm honest. She might have found some nice professor who visits her office and they stay late playing *Hero Seek* together.

My head is turned down, fixating on my drink as I dream up awful scenarios. He shocks me when he reaches over and puts a hand over my wrist.

"If there's anyone that can cure her from her unhappiness right now, it's you. As much as it pains me to say this, she still loves you."

I smile. "I still love her too. Now, I just have to prove it. Again." And hope what Lydia's brother says is true. If anyone can cure her from this hurt that she's feeling, it's me. The one who started it but is ready to fix it.

25

Lydia

A MONTH AND A half after the breakup

"Guys," I whine. "We need to make it to the arena ten minutes ago. You need to get registered."

How is it I have a group of college-aged boys to look after, and I'm ready before all of them? Don't stereotypes paint the girl as someone who takes forever to get ready? And yet, I'm the one who is waiting around.

A part of me understands it. We're back in Vegas for the Collegiate Esports Championships. We qualified for a few tournaments after the one we hosted, and if I'm being honest, I didn't think that we could do it. Some schools spend money on scholarships to recruit the best players, and then there's us. The newbies. When we won the Celsius Invitational and took home a whopping ten thousand dollars, I couldn't believe it. We beat out one of the top-ranked colleges and the commentators called it, and I quote, "a twist I never saw coming."

"They are from Silicon Valley," the other commentator quips. "Maybe we should've."

It wasn't by chance that the kids won the tournament. They practice a lot. They're losing sleep because of how much they're playing. I have to ask them if they're still doing well in their classes because if they aren't, they're on probation. And now that there's big shit on the line, like the chance to compete in the Worlds tournament in Seoul and the possibility of being picked up by a pro team, they're going to regret not working hard enough on their classes.

Everything's feeling bittersweet after our home tournament, where I confessed to Landon that this would be it. Whatever happens after this tournament is the end for me. I thought that I was stronger than I actually am. I thought that I could try and push past the negative thoughts that have become associated with video games, but it only hurts me even more. Because Griffin and I aren't together. I want to respect his wishes to focus on himself because his mental health is important too, but what if he's it for me?

All at once, the team flocks to me. Shit, took them long enough. Why does it look like they didn't even do anything to their appearances? What were they doing upstairs this whole time? You know what, I'm not going to ask. When the opening ceremony starts, and they aren't there to see whatever famous streamer makes the opening remarks, they'll be sorry. I'm tempted to leave them behind. They're announcing the Director of the Year at this ceremony, and even though I applied, I don't think I will win.

I eye Landon, the appointed manager of the weekend because I didn't want to subject myself to walking into their hotel rooms to do a wellness check on them. He's the last one to join the group.

"What took so long?" I scowl.

"Sorry," Landon speaks on behalf of the group. "We got...distracted."

"I swear to God if you tell me you got distracted by the fucking Switch in the room..."

'We got a PS5," Dev whispers.

A PS5? What kind of room did they get upgraded to? And why did I get stuck with a Wii? You know what? I take it back. I'm making a mental note to immediately load up Wii Sports when I get back. I need the release, and what better way to do it is to play a game of boxing, or three?

"Don't you have a PS5 at your apartment?"

"Yeah, but you know us, Lids. You put us in a hotel that comes with a console in every room. We're not going to waste the opportunity to play."

I roll my eyes. I can't believe that in a few short weeks, some of these boys are going to be in the workforce. For some big-name tech companies too. Well, I guess with the jobs they'll be working, they can work whatever hours of the day as long as the job gets done. If that means starting at eleven in the morning but jumping back on at eight at night, then so be it.

"Okay, but we still need to check in, and there's a ceremony being held. And we need to go all the way to the Venetian." It may only be two blocks, but two blocks on the Strip almost equates to half a mile.

"Sorry, Lids. I shouldn't have lost track of time." Landon chimes in. I'm elated that my little brother is here, and I think that he makes a good team manager. I wish that he could have done more to help out with esports this season, but he had his internship, and now we're playing the waiting game on whether or not they want him to return. He's the only one who knows about my departure, and I wanted him to be here when I tell the team over dumplings tonight at dinner. I really can't be too hard on him because he is volunteering his own time to help me. That, plus bribing him with free lodging and food pretty much sealed the deal.

"It's fine," I say as my shoulders sag. "Let's just start moving."

We speed walk down Las Vegas Boulevard and past a marquee that, in big letters, says, "Your Western Conference Finals meets again! Knights v. Stingrays, Friday at 7 PM." Behind the big letters are two players in uniform, crossing their arms menacingly. One is a Vegas player, and the other is Griffin. They both look intimidating, with no smiles, like this really was going to be a serious game that filled the stadium. A part of me wished I could reach out and touch his face on the marquee, if I was tall enough. Or had a ladder.

My pace slows, and without thinking, I stop in my tracks to stare up at the marquee.

"Lids," Landon grabs a hold of my arm. He looks up and nods when he realizes what's stopped me from taking another step forward.

"You okay?" he whispers close to my ear.

"I didn't know he'd be here," I say, my voice barely above a whisper. Griffin doesn't owe me anything. I mean, I doubt he knows that I'm here too. He's got a lot going on, obviously. Playing a team that he considers a big rival. I guess it just took me by surprise. That despite whatever powers that be not wanting us to be together, we're still stuck being in the same place at the same time. Again.

"Come on, Lydia," Landon says. "There's so many people in Vegas. There's no chance that you'll run into him."

"I know." But what if I wanted to? Is that really desperate?

I feel my cheeks flush, and tears fall from my face like raindrops. I was getting on the boys for making us late, and now look at me. I'm holding everything up because I can't seem to get over the love of my life, and as much as I tell myself that I don't need to get caught up in a celebrity romance because I've learned that I don't want people talking shit about me behind my back. Seeing Griffin everywhere drives me to the edge, where I feel like I'm trying to balance myself, but I feel like I'm going to fall.

"I really miss him, though," I sob. Landon stands in front of me and wraps his arms around mine. I grip onto him for dear life, and he doesn't complain that I might be crushing him. He just lets me cry it out. On the Strip. While hundreds of people walk by us and stare. I know I'm being weird. That a freaking street performer or someone dressed with nothing but pasties and feathered wings looks like they belong more than I do. But I'm in so much pain that I just need to let it out, and that's what I'm allowing myself to do.

"I know," he says into the top of my head. "No one ever said getting over a breakup was easy."

"I'm conflicted, is all. I want to tell myself that I understand why Griffin did it. But I'm also realizing that unless I'm as famous as Griffin is, there's not a world where we can be together."

"That's not true. There are plenty of famous people who date nonfamous people, and they seem to get through it just fine." He pulls back for a moment. "I'll say this bluntly because I'm your brother and I love you, and you need to hear it. If Griffin really loved you, he'd try to figure out a way to persevere through the media to still be with you. His wanting to take the easy way out only proves to me that he's a coward. And you don't deserve that."

Ouch. But it's the truth. I was going to try and make it work, even if I might be thrown expletives and vitriol for the rest of my life. Because I love him. But if he doesn't want to do the same for me, then maybe we have different priorities.

"I don't," I remind myself. I wipe the snot from my nose and keep walking towards the hotel. "I deserve the best. And I'm going to give that to myself."

We make it to the ballroom, somewhat sweaty and quite uncomfortable. The room's dark and full of students and staff watching the stage as the "guest of honor," a streamer that goes by DeeDeeKay speaks to the crowd about how one day they can be like him and play esports professionally. A lot of references to "sacrifice" gets thrown around, and I forget for a moment that this guy probably dropped out of college to pursue esports full-time. Do I want to be spreading the same kind of message? Not really, but if you gotta dream, then shoot for the stars.

"There's something so special about being a part of the esports community," he continues. "When I was a kid, I loved to play video games, but my parents never believed that it could be my real life. They didn't see esports being the next big thing. Frankly, because they thought staring at a screen all day was going to rot my brain. To me, playing video games was the escape that I needed after a day at school. After a day of being bullied. After another failed test. But somehow, I was able to be quick on my fingers, and after practicing every day, I became one of the top-ranked players in the world.

"There were a lot of times when I felt like giving up, don't get me wrong. I would win a game but then lose the next four. When I was in college, I wanted to drop out because I was doing so well in gaming, and I thought I needed to devote as much time in the day as possible to playing. Trying to convince my parents was...a battle, to say the least." He chuckles, and the audience joins in, maybe because some of them can relate.

"They told me that if I was going to essentially throw away my career—that they thought would be in Electrical Engineering, which is what I was studying—then they weren't going to help me. They said I could fuel my passion with the money I earned. So I dropped out of college and worked to become a professional gamer. My income came from people who paid for subscriptions to my stream and eventually from tournament wins. My parents thankfully came around too and support me now, even though they didn't before."

I peer over at the students sitting next to me, how their gazes fixate on him like he's ethereal. They all aspire to be like this one day, and even if their pathway may be an unconventional one, they know that they have to work hard to get there as anyone would for a job. My mouth tilts up a bit when I realize that even if the last few weeks have been a lot, I'm happy to be back here with these eager students, excited to see where they'll go after they graduate and leave the university.

"A lot of you here might be in the same boat. Thinking about going into this full-time, but wanting to give it up in search of something that might bring more success. Don't give up, guys. Your belief in the success of esports paves the way for people to continue paying attention. Don't let the *what if* bring you down. Remember why you love the game, and find a way to keep going. Because let me tell you, we're just getting started."

The crowd roars in applause and some begin leaping out of their seats, giving this guy a standing ovation for how he was able to touch the hearts and minds of almost everyone in this room. Myself included. Griffin may have given up on us, and I might have wanted to give up on my team, but I need to remind myself that I made it this far, and if I let this go now, someone else will take this opportunity. I can't let them do that. There's still work that I need to do, and if these kids want me to be with them for the long haul, then I will. I'll do it for them.

The tournament producer walks up and thanks the streamer, whose real name is Daniel Kim (middle name not Dae, but everyone does wonder), and segues to the next part of the program, announcing the Director of the Year. Honestly, I had forgotten about this award until I got a reminder email a week ago from the Collegiate Esports Association. My computer flashed with animated fireworks, "We can't wait to welcome you back to Las Vegas for some fun gameplay and exciting awards, including our prestigious Director of the Year award, complete with a trip to the League Worlds Championship in Seoul!" and it perked me up for a moment, before realizing that I probably didn't win. If I do, if somehow I have an application that wows the judging panel, then maybe that's even more reason to stay.

"Now, I have the pleasure of announcing this year's Director of the Year. Many amazing directors submitted their applications to be considered, and as part of the judging panel, I can tell you it was difficult to choose just one person for this award. The Director of the Year is someone who we believe exemplifies what it means to be a leader. Someone who devotes themselves to their team and their success, someone who, like Daniel mentioned, isn't going to just give up when the going gets tough.

They're always working hard to improve their team and figure out ways to make it better. They're championing esports to their school communities, even when people want to question the success of esports as a whole.

This director is someone we believe goes above and beyond for their team and their school. Who has faced a lot of adversity in only a few short months, but we've seen them thrive and succeed. Their esports teams have won several tournaments and are here today to hopefully win one more."

I rub my sweaty palms together. He could be talking about so many people. It can't be me, even if I'm checking off the boxes too.

"When we asked the students what they thought about their director, they said, 'We know that they have gone through a lot. We've seen them at their lowest lows. And even though we were hesitant to give them a chance at first, we can confidently say they have done so much for us and for our esports teams that without them, we don't know what we would do. We don't think we could survive.'

It is my honor to present this year's Collegiate Esports Association Director of the Year to Lydia Goh, Los Gatos University."

I don't blink. I don't move an inch. I'm still as the people in the room roar for me. I turn to Landon as he tries to grab me by my elbow and hoist me up. He gives me a huge bear hug and whispers, "I'm so proud of you."

The team is clapping wildly as Landon and the team move me to the aisle because I'm too stunned to move myself. I stumble before making it down the rows and rows of teams and try to flash my smile to everyone who's now standing and clapping for me. When I walk up to the stage to accept my award, the director steps aside as an invitation to say a few words. Shit, I didn't rehearse anything. I don't even know what I could say beyond a simple "thank you."

"Um, wow." I breathe. "It is so surreal that I am up here right now accepting this award. Um. I'll try to keep this brief because I know we are ready to move into a night of gaming. I just want to say thank you to the LGU esports teams. You all make me so proud with everything you've accomplished this past year. They aren't here, but thank you to the LGU Department of Student Life that gives their time and resources to growing esports. Um...to my parents who have been there for me and supported me when I made this scary career change. Oh!" I look to the row to the rest of the team.

"The biggest shout out to my brother, Landon. These last few weeks have been some of the hardest of my life, but Landon has stood firmly by my side, and I am so happy that he could take time out of his busy schedule to assist me this weekend and see me accept this award. Landon, I love you, and I'm so proud of you and everything you've accomplished the past four years. Thank you to the Collegiate Esports Association, again, for this amazing award and honor. I...it makes me happy to be surrounded by people who love the sport so much. Just keep playing. That's all I have to say. Thank you again."

The crowd erupts in claps again as I walk to take my seat. I sit down, and the team takes their turns congratulating me on my award while I try to calm myself down from the high of walking up and taking the stage. I actually did it. I managed to somehow make a difference in the esports world.

I just wish I could tell the one other person who stood by my side for most of the journey about it as well.

26

Lydia

WE'RE CELEBRATING WITH DUMPLINGS on the table, but there's a weird aura around us.

The students were all so elated when I came back to my seat with my award in my hand, but after some more sitting and listening to announcements for what's to come this weekend, they haven't really been saying much.

Even Landon isn't matching me level-for-level with how excited I should be.

Is it something with the tournament? I mean, the first school that they are going up against tomorrow is well-ranked, but we've beaten them in a tournament before, so I don't believe that it should be intimidating them.

"Guys." I reach over and grab another Xiao Long Bao. "Is it just me, or is there something fishy going on? And don't say it's the shrimp."

No one meets my gaze, and to my dismay, wordlessly reach for the fresh dumplings in steamers covering every little part of our round table.

"Guys!" I try and get them out of their slump. "I just won Director of the Year, and you're acting like we freaking lost the championship. We haven't even played yet. What's going on?"

"We're really happy for you, Lydia," Drew says. "We just…"

"We got you something," Dev interrupts. "And we bought it really early because even if you won or lost, we wanted to just tell you that we appreciate you so much, Lydia. But…well, let me just pull it out to show you."

Dev gives me a manila envelope with my name written in big capital letters on the front. I undo the clasp and open the contents inside. I pull out a piece of paper that reads "Your Suite Confirmation" for the Stingrays-Knights game happening to-morrow.

"We didn't know what was going to happen at the time. We bought it before, you know, the breakup. We just wanted to do something that showed our appreciation for you Lydia. If you don't want to go…"

"Guys." I set down the paper. This must've cost thousands of dollars. I don't want to know how much of their hard-earned money was spent on this suite. And despite the current state of my relationship, the fact that they poured out any amount of money for something that they thought I deserved warms my heart.

"This is very thoughtful of you. Thank you so much."

Noah sits up in his seat. "You're not mad?"

"No!" I exclaim. "Of course not. You guys bought it before everything happened. You couldn't have known that things might change. The fact that you thought about me at all is...it's really touching. I'm blessed with an amazing group of students that care this much about me."

I set the paper down on the cushion next to me. "I'll let you guys in on something. When I was flying down, I was rehearsing with Landon what I was going to say tonight. Because I was going to tell you guys that after this school year, I would be putting in my resignation."

They let out a collective gasp and I hurry to stop them from assuming the worst.

"I'm not going to," I reassure them. "I decided during that speech that I can't give it up. And it's mostly because of you guys. You impressed me so much this past year, being a team completely new to the collegiate esports world and winning against teams who have been doing this since the beginning. And then I won Director of the Year and that solidified it. There's a lot to look forward to, and this is only just the beginning."

Next to me, I hear a huge sniffle and I turn my head to see Landon trying to unsuccessfully hold back tears, that are now falling down his cheeks.

"Landon, are you okay?"

"Fine," he sniffs. "That was really touching, that's all. I'm not crying over it or anything."

"Sap," Blake jokes.

"Stop." Landon rolls his eyes. "I'm just proud of Lydia."

"Did you know?" Dev asks. He and Landon have been close friends since their first year. If anyone's close to being considered as Landon's best friend besides his girlfriend, of course, it's Dev.

"Yeah," Landon nods. "It was during the home tournament." He turns to me. "I never told you this, but I felt really guilty after you told me that you were thinking of giving up because I just kept egging you on about how badly Griffin treated you and how you needed to do whatever you could to escape the memories you built with him. I should have tried harder to convince you to stay. I was just really mad at him. When I got home, I wondered if I should have told you to give it another shot instead."

"It's okay." I pat his arm. "You're allowed to be upset. I mean, you kind of had it out for Griffin since the game where we bumped into him."

"He's a good guy," Landon notes. It makes my ears perk up a little bit. I don't think I've ever heard Landon give compliments to Griffin. He's been warning me about him from the beginning. "Despite the breaking your heart part. Heard he's going to therapy, which is good."

"It is." All the good things they say he's doing online make me happy, even if I'm not a part of it. It makes me realize how important it really is to prioritize your mental health and find that balance. Maybe when everything winds down, when I have some time to not think about school and what's coming next, I'll take a solo trip somewhere to relax. There's plenty of getaway places in California. Quaint beach towns, wineries. Hell, a solo trip to Disneyland sounds like a dream. And I can get onto rides faster thanks to the single-rider line.

"So you're going to go to the game with us tomorrow?" Dev chimes in. I'm feeling weary about it, but after a quick glance at everyone's faces, eager to have me celebrate with them even if it's at a game where my ex will be on the ice, I muster up enough courage to nod and say yes.

There is no shortage of people flocking to the arena to watch this momentous game. And what surprises me the most is that it's not just fans decked out in Vegas jerseys. It's almost an even split between Vegas and San Jose fans. And then there's me, wearing a black puffy jacket and jeans because I still can't believe that I'm here tonight.

The team is all decked in their San Jose gear, and even Landon is sporting his jersey with Griffin's name stitched on the back.

"You know I had this before you two were a thing," he says. "And I don't really have any other gear."

"Fine by me," I shrug. "You're not the one that he broke up with. For all I know, you two can be best friends."

Landon answers a little too quickly after my statement, his voice sounding a little more exaggerated. "You know I wouldn't hurt you like that."

"Yeah, don't worry," I swipe my arm. "I trust you."

We're ushered to the suite, and it brings back memories of that game in San Jose where Landon and I got to sit in the Penthouse lounge. It's very similar here, with plush reclining chairs overlooking the rink and chafing dishes with hot food lining the bar counter. The only difference is this is all for us. We're the only group in here, and when our dedicated concierge comes in to ask what drinks we want, the boy's eyes sparkle, and they're the giddiest I've ever seen them as they ask for a beer. They should be happy that they don't have to pay regular arena prices for drinks. Twenty dollars for a seltzer feels wrong on so many levels.

I sit down and watch as the players skate on the ice and stretch during their warmups. I spot Griffin in an instant. He's sprawled on the ice, grabbing a hold of his leg to stretch out his muscles, and there's a small crowd of people pressed up against the glass, watching his body move on the ice. Fangirls ogling after him, the same way it was before we started dating. The way it'll continue to be. Everyone staring at Griffin in awe and wondering to themselves whatever happened with that Esports Director ex of his.

I'm too far up in the arena for him to catch my stare. He's probably got a lot on his mind. This game, the desire to win, the hope that they'll make it to playoffs. I think about whether

I would go if they do make it. The honest answer is probably not because it would cost an entire paycheck for a ticket to see them. But maybe I'll watch from my television and clap in my seat every time Griffin scores a goal. I'll wish I could be there when they win and that I could see him after the game. I'll wish that he'd hoist me up and grab onto me tightly, laughing in my ear that he actually did it.

"You okay?" Landon asks, taking the seat next to me.

"I'm trying to tell myself that I will be," I answer. "I'm telling myself to give it time. Trusting the process and all that jazz."

"Well, you're looking at him and not crying. That's a good start."

"Yeah," I chuckle. "What's next? Us having a conversation?"

"I mean…if that's what you want. I'm sure I can figure out a way."

I shrug, reaching to take a sip of my drink. "No, that's alright. I'm taking it one step at a time."

The game begins and it's a race back and forth on who is going to score first. Defenses on both sides are putting in the work to protect the goal, and after a scoreless first period, everyone is glued to their seat to see who will take rein first. When the puck drops for the start of the second period, I watch intently as Micah takes control of the puck and tries to skate to the opponent's side to get a good opening to take a shot.

When the other team blocks him from trying to make any sort of move, his head quickly turns to see if there's someone open. Thankfully, Griffin is there, so he gets ready to pass it to him. Griffin skates a little closer so he's better able to take control, but immediately after Micah passes it to him, two Vegas players stampede Micah and Griffin. Micah's body is thrust hard into the glass, and he falls, taking Griffin down in the mix with him. The arena goes bone-chillingly silent. And when neither Micah nor Griffin get up, a scream gets caught in my throat, and my hands rush up to cover my mouth.

"Lydia!" Landon rushes over to wrap his arms around me when I realize I'm shaking. Both of them are still lying there on the ice.

"He's not moving," I sob. "Why isn't he moving?"

"He might need a minute to let the pain pass," Landon tells me. "But he's going to be okay."

"Can we go down and see him?" I ask. I feel so helpless that I'm so far away, watching him in pain and unable to do anything to give him the comfort he probably really wishes for right now.

"Lids, we can't go onto the ice."

Why the fuck not? I want to protest.

Just before I yell another expletive, Griffin gets up and is ushered by someone, who I assume is part of the athletic training team, to the locker room. But before they skate off, he rushes to kneel by Micah's side, who still hasn't moved. I don't know what Griffin is telling him, but his body language tells me that he's scared for his best friend right now. And I am, too. It's been at least five minutes, and Micah hasn't made any effort to get up.

I rush out of the suite and run down to the lower level in hopes that I can get a closer view of the ice. It takes a lot of begging because I don't have a seat assignment down there, but the person keeping guard somehow recognizes me when I lie and say Griffin's my boyfriend and tells me I can pass. I make it to the tunnel, where people are lining up already, and there are medical personnel lifting Micah onto a stretcher. Griffin kneels with the rest of the players on the ice, and when they wheel Micah off, he gets some help from the trainer to skate off, presumably to get checked.

As he takes off his skates and passes through, I yell out his name. People turn their heads to see who's yelling for him and I hear their whispers as they put two and two together.

"That's Lydia Goh."

"Are he and his ex back together?"

"What's she doing here?"

My senses start to feel overwhelmed again. While I thought I could handle strangers talking about me behind my back, the reality is that I don't know if I can get over the anxiety I feel when I think about how people view me.

"Lydia," Griffin breathes as he meets my stare. "What...what are you doing here?"

"I...I'm in the area. It's a long story. Are you okay?"

"Um, yeah, yeah, I'm okay." He nods. "Can you stay?" He turns to the person standing guard near the tunnel. "Can you escort her to the locker room? She's my girlfriend."

The guard gives him a perplexed look but ultimately nods. "Sure. Yes. We can do that."

"Is that okay, Lydia?" Griffin asks me. His eyes are down-turned, like sad puppy dog eyes. I forgot how long it's been since we've seen one another. Griffin has a little bit of stubble across his face and his hair's grown a little longer too. He looks rugged, and it's igniting a flame in me.

"Yeah," I nod. "It's okay. I'll see you in a little bit."

The guard escorts me down through the tunnel and through to the back, where the locker rooms are. It feels weird to be back here, especially when there are still people playing hockey and even more so when everyone on the Stingrays is not on their A-game after watching Micah collapse like that. I can only hope that he won't have to go through any extreme surgery, but seeing that he was on the ice for a long time, there's a likely chance that he won't be playing for the rest of the season.

The guard takes me into a room with a sign on the side that reads "Visitor Locker Room."

"I'm just going to check it's okay for you to head inside. This is kind of a unique situation."

"Sure thing," I nod. I wonder if any player has asked this before. Everyone else is on the bench, watching the game, but when the period's up, there might be players making their way back here.

He comes back out from the locker room and nods for me to come in. I walk in and immediately spot Griffin with his jersey off, wearing nothing else but his shorts and socks.

"I'm just going to be outside. I'll knock when it's time for you to head back into the arena."

"Thank you," Griffin tells him. The door clicks shut, and I walk over to take the seat next to him.

"How are you feeling?" I ask.

"I don't feel hurt or anything. But...I'm worried about Micah."

"Yeah." I look down at his clenched fists on his shorts. "I saw you kneeling over him. Did he say anything when you got closer to him?"

"He was just telling me there was a sharp pain. That he might've torn something. He's out for the rest of the season, for sure. But...after he gets surgery done, I don't know if he'll play again."

Griffin, Micah, and Ross are all older hockey players. They're in their thirties now, and soon, whether they like it or not, they'll have to think about retirement. It sounds like if Micah isn't going to make a full recovery like everyone hopes, then this might be the final hockey game he'll ever play.

"What are you doing here?" he asks. "I...didn't know when I'd see you again."

Were you making plans to?

"I'm here for the Collegiate Esports finals. My kids surprised me with suite-access tickets, but they bought it when we were still together as a way to say thank you and as a reward if I won Director of the Year, which I did. Even though we aren't together, I thought I'd come anyway to watch you play. I can't say I was expecting to see you get injured, though."

"Yeah, sorry about that. It happens. I'm okay, though. I just got the wind knocked out of me for a moment. Needed to get my breathing right again. The athletic trainer just wanted to keep me here for concussion protocol before I can get cleared to go back on the ice. Wait," he eyes my worried face. "Did you just say you won Director of the Year?"

"Yeah," I give him a faint smile. "I did."

He beams when he sees the bit of happiness creep over my face as my thoughts shift slightly to the good that happened before the bad. "That's amazing, Lydia. I...I knew you would all along. Congratulations. I'm so proud of you."

"Thank you," I nod. "I'm really proud of myself too."

Griffin's expression goes solemn again. "It sounds like I might have burst that little bubble of joy you had coming here."

"Not really. Maybe a little bit. I was just scared," I whispered, clasping my hands together. "I've never seen you get injured before. And when you wouldn't get up, it got me all nervous. If what happened to Micah, getting lifted off the ice, happened to you...I can't imagine what I'd do. Go hysterical. More hysterical than I already was, which Landon will tell you was...a lot."

He puts one of his hands over mine. God, his hands are so warm and soft. I missed how safe I felt when he'd hold onto me like this. I invite him in when I pull my hands apart and take one of them to interlace my fingers with his. We look up at one another immediately after, and I see Griffin's face turn soft. All of a sudden, the last few months flood through our minds in a perfect slide show. The memories that we shared, each one a stage in our journey of falling in love.

"Lydia, I..." Griffin's gaze turns down to our hands. "I'm so sorry."

"It's okay," I whisper, leaning closer to rest my face on his arm.

"No, it isn't. You were right. I gave up on us. I just wanted to protect you from strangers who want to spindle lies about us just for their own gain. I took what I thought was the easy way out by letting you go. But I miss you so much."

"I miss you too. And I'm sorry too, for that post. For allowing my job to dictate how I was supposed to feel about the situation, for being upset with you when you were obviously going through a lot. I want to tell you how proud I am of you for taking that leap and going to therapy. When I heard you were doing that, I was really proud of you, even if it meant we needed to be apart."

"Thank you." He kisses the top of my head. "She's great. Cindy, my therapist. I talk to her about you sometimes."

"Oh yeah?" I laugh. "What do you tell her?"

"That there are few people in this world who have changed my life for good, and you're one of them. That I needed to keep working on me because my end game was getting you back. Although, I pictured that a little differently. I was going to try to do it after I got back to San Jose. After this game. Landon gave me a list of all your favorite things to surprise you with. Shrimp rice rolls, passion fruit boba tea, and, of course, a game of *Hero Seek*."

"Landon?" I pull back for a moment. "When did you talk to him?"

"Not that long ago. I had to get permission from him to ask you out again. I don't want to get on his bad side a second time."

I shake my head. Wow, I can't believe there was already a plan in the works for Griffin to try to win me back. I'm a little disappointed, though. I wish he had surprised me with all my favorite things instead of scaring the bejeezus out of me when I watched him fall on the ice.

"I see."

"So," Griffin looks into my eyes. "If you'll have me back, Lids, I want to spend forever loving you. I want to be there for you and all of your accomplishments. And this time, I'm not going to give you up for anything."

I feel tears stream down my face and nod. "Okay," I tell him.

That's all the affirmation he needs because Griffin takes both his hands and places them on either side of my face, pulling me to kiss him. He firmly presses his lips to mine, like he's longed for them for so long, and as I wrap my arms around his neck, he opens his mouth to play with my tongue, and I flick mine against his.

"I love you, Lydia Goh." He says when we break for air.

"I love you too, Griffin Markey."

"Where are you staying tonight?" He asks. "Can I stay with you? Or you can stay with me. I don't care. I just need to make love to you, stat."

I chuckle. "I'm at the Blossom. But shouldn't you wait until the game ends?"

He groans. "Yeah, I guess I should. But we're staying there too, so that works out perfectly. I just need to make up for every minute I've been apart from you."

I clutch onto his bare chest and then slide my fingers down, tracing them along his abdomen. "Don't worry. I'm not going anywhere."

27

Griffin

THE GUARD KNOCKS AT the locker room door, and Lydia and I quickly pull apart. We're both disheveled from gripping onto each other's hair, and my heart skips a beat when I see that I've left marks from my stubble on her face.

Lydia scratches at her neck. "I like the stubble. Are you going to grow it out?"

I shake my head. "It gets too patchy. But I like how it looks like I've made my imprint on you," I say, caressing her cheek.

She rolls her eyes. "It is a little itchy, not going to lie."

The guard opens the door and doesn't turn. Just yells out to us, "Game's over, lovebirds."

"Looks like that's my cue." Lydia stands up, and I follow her to the door. "I'll see you later?"

I give her a quick peck. "Text me your room number? I'll swing by when I'm done here."

"Sure thing. Although, I can't guarantee I'll be in my room. Something tells me I should be pressing my luck tonight. Looks like I'm on a streak."

"I think it's me who's the luckiest guy in the world. I love you."

"Love you, too," she says and gets up to exit the locker room. I peer up at the television in the top corner of the room to see the banner of the final score.

Three to nothing. Makes sense when two of your best players don't play the majority of the game. And after Micah's traumatic injury, who wants to think about anything else?

Slowly, the team begins entering the locker room. Everyone's faces are sullen, devoid of any happiness. I hate that it feels like the universe, or whatever divine being out there, has it out for us. How can we get put through something like this weeks before the playoffs? I want to scream, "But I've been a good person!" Well, I did get my girlfriend back, so I guess out of the entire team, I'm getting the best outcome.

Ross sits down next to me, and when the rest of the team sits down, Coach is the last to enter. No Micah. I hope Coach will address any updates about him. I don't think I'll ever be able to forget seeing him lying down on his back on the ice. His body unable to move, and his face wincing in pain. It's the worst thing that could happen: seeing your teammate hurt. And when it's someone who has been on this wild journey as a pro athlete with you from the very start, your insides ache almost as if you're feeling their pain.

"Hey," I say, nudging Ross. "How was the rest of the game?"

His expression is blank, and he doesn't answer me. I lean over to get a better look at him and see that his eyes are swollen, probably from crying. Somehow, I've held it together, even though I almost broke when we were on the ice together. But I saw Lydia, and I felt like I needed to stay strong for her. Now that she isn't here, I feel like I might also be one step closer to falling apart.

"I'll talk to you after we clean up," he whispers.

"Have you heard any news about Micah?"

He shakes his head, and before I can ask a follow-up question, Coach claps his hands to get our attention.

"Um," he begins. His voice lacks any of the confidence that I'm so used to him carrying. "I know that wasn't our best game. And I know you guys want an update on Stone. So, we'll do that first. Micah was rushed to the hospital, and the last update they gave me was that they took some X-rays and confirmed he had broken his leg. He'll be out for at least six weeks and won't be playing for the rest of the season. Markey," Coach turns to me. "What's up with you? You doing okay?"

"Yeah, Coach," I swallow. "They just checked me for a concussion, and I passed."

"Okay, that's good." Just those words of affirmation, and Coach suddenly has relief written all over his face.

Coach continues to discuss some of the things that he wished we did better about during the game. Stuff that I didn't see happen because my eyes were closed and my lips were kissing Lydia's. I know I should have been paying attention, so I could feel ready for the next game, but the moment Lydia called out for me with worried eyes, there was nothing that mattered more than getting her next to me, and eventually in my arms.

Check and check.

He dismisses everyone and Ross holds his phone out to me.

"Hey, did you get Micah's text?"

I peer over at Ross's phone, where Micah has sent a text to our group.

> Micah: hey when you guys are done @ the arena can you come see me

"He just dropped a pin where he's at, it's just behind the Wynn."

"Um, shit." I hurry to pack my bags. "Yeah, do you want me to call a car?"

"Yeah, can you? And if anyone asks, just tell them we decided to hitch a ride back to the hotel together."

Thankfully, no one pries, and in a few short minutes, a car comes to take us to the hospital, where they're keeping Micah for the night. He tells us what room he's in and we speed walk, carrying all our equipment to his room.

When we get inside, we see Micah lying on the bed in a hospital gown. He's got a cast on his leg and some IVs stuck in his arms. Wheel of Fortune is playing on the television. Beside him are the remnants of the sad hospital food that they gave him. It looks like he's devoured most of it, and weirdly, it makes my stomach grumble. The way I could go for an entire buffet spread right now between the playing and the stress that's bubbled up inside me. I'm starving.

"Hey, man," I put my bag down in the corner and stand next to his bed. Ross joins me at the foot. "How are you doing?"

"Awful," Micah murmurs. "My leg's broken. I was diagnosed with a concussion. I've got needles in my body. I hate hearing the beeping on the monitors telling me I'm still kicking." He turns to me. "How are you, Griff? Did you get tested too?"

"Yeah," I nod. "They ruled out a concussion, thankfully."

"That's good."

"We lost," Ross chimes in. "If that makes you feel any better."

"It doesn't. If Griffin and I weren't out, we could have won."

Out of the three of us, Micah is the most cynical. It's hard seeing him in this state of helplessness, where he's just accepting defeat. "I'm sorry, bud," I tell him. "Even if the guy from Vegas was the one that fucked us."

He sighs. "Well, I've been using this time to think about some things. The future and all that. And I think this is my sign to hang it up."

Ross's eyes almost bulge out of their sockets. "Wait, hang it up? You mean..."

"Yeah, Ross," Micah says. "That was my last game. I've decided I'm gonna retire."

"Micah..." I want to tell him that he's thinking irrationally. That he still has a lot of life in him. He can recover quickly, and after some physical therapy in the off-season, he'll be as good as new. He can't give it all up yet. We went into this big, scary world of the National Hockey League together. We're leaving together.

"You're serious?" I ask him.

"Yeah," he says with a sadness that tells us he wishes it didn't have to be this way. "Maybe if I was in my second or third season, I'd be pushing my body to fully recover. But I'm not. I'm in my thirties. I've been playing hockey for a long time. If I even try to recover, I'm not going to come back and play how I once did. I feel it even now. This was my lowest season for goals scored. It's not worth the heartbreak down the line when I realize I'll never be in my prime again. And if I get injured again, it could be worse. It's better just to leave it like this."

Ross sniffs and wipes the tears from his eyes. Drama queen. But when I feel a drop on my cheek, I realize he's not alone.

"Okay man," he says between hiccups. "If that's what you want, we're here for you. Now and forever, you know that."

"Yeah," Micah smiles. "I do. You guys will always be my support."

"So, what happens next?" The three amigos need to figure out what their next course of action is. There's still hockey that needs to be played, and Micah's going to be watching us from the sidelines. I'm hoping that we'll bring home the Cup. Now it feels like we've got something more to play for. Now, we're doing it for Micah.

"I'll do a lot of physical therapy," Micah says. "Watch from the bench. You guys better win the conference. And then the

Cup. Not gonna lie, Vegas is strong. A bunch of our conference is strong. They can try and predict as much as they want who will take home the Stanley Cup, but if I'm being honest, I don't have a clue. We need to bolster our defense and stop allowing goals through. I can't believe I'm saying this, but we are not as strong as we used to be."

"No, you're right. I feel so fatigued after a game." My line isn't on the ice for the entire game, but in the few stretches of time where I am, I feel like I need to take a breath a lot more often than I used to when I switch off with another player. The uniform is starting to feel a little more heavy on my body, and my knees feel like they want to buckle after every pass or shot. I know that I can't play hockey forever, and my career has an expiration date. But I've never thought about when "the end" will be more than I have tonight, hearing my best friend announce his.

Ross turns his head to me. "Oh no. Are you thinking of retiring too?"

"Not right this minute! But after this season, I would've played hockey for ten seasons. I'm in a relationship, and I can't believe that I'm thinking about shit like settling down and getting married. Starting a family. But I am, and it's kind of exciting. I want to be present for this stuff."

"Um, wait a minute," Micah narrows his eyes at me. "You're in a relationship? Did you get back together with Lydia?"

My nod results in a slap from Ross and a grin from Micah.

"Dude, that's awesome!" Ross yelps. "When? Tonight?"

"Yeah, she came to the game. She's here for a conference. Wish that she didn't see me lying on the ice in pain. That scared her a lot. But if it didn't happen, then she wouldn't have run to the tunnel, and I wouldn't have locked eyes with her and made up with her." Shit, I was meant to see her after the game. I need to text her that I'm getting back to the hotel a bit later because I'm seeing Micah.

Griffin: Visiting Micah @ hospital, sorry forgot to give you a heads up. Hope you're staying awake for me. <3

Lydia: Yes, still awake. @ a slot machine. Played some roulette but wasn't lucky. Of course I'm staying awake for you.

Griffin: Good, because I'm hungry and I'm ready to eat you out.

Lydia: OMG GRIFFIN

I'm ready for you too. Xoxo.

My cheeks flush, and when I look up from my phone, Micah and Ross raise their brows at me. Look, I know that I'm in the so-called "honeymoon phase," and every little thing that Lydia does sets off fireworks in my mind, but after feeling like I've finally found the one, I wish that my friends would too, instead of making fun of me for being so deeply in love.

"Why are you looking at me like that?" I ask, equal parts playful and annoyed. "It's called being in love. Maybe you guys need to try it sometime."

Micah gives me the side eye, and Ross just looks down on the blankets covering Micah's body. If Micah ever finds the woman that can change his life, I'll be impressed. That man barely ever shows any sort of affection. And then there's Ross, who shows too much affection sometimes, but I know he's hung up on his childhood best friend, who can't stand that he completely ghosted her after making it big in the hockey world.

"Sorry," I blurt. "That was mean of me. I'm just...happy."

"We're happy for you, Griffin," Ross says. "Lydia's a great girl. And you've started going to therapy. Right now, it might feel like we're feeling low, but things are going to look up for us soon. I can feel it."

"I can, too," Micah grins softly. "Because we have each other."

My heart feels like it grew three sizes a la The Grinch. "I love you guys," I blurt.

"Love you too," they reply in unison. And in this moment, amongst the beeping and the guessing of letters on the television screen, our invisible bond tightens a little more. And it feels like nothing can break it.

28

Lydia

I SHOULD PROBABLY STOP gambling away all my money.

I've been sitting here for hours now, and after not churning out anything positive on roulette—my bet on the twenty-three trick backfired on me—I've fed too many dollars into this slot machine for it to not make a fun noise telling me "I did it!"

I definitely do not have a problem.

As I see the number of credits dwindle down to a number too low to make another bet, I sigh, defeated, and press the "cash out" button. I can always be thankful that I had a fun time playing the slots and other table games when I came here, never reaching a point where I went bottom up.

But if Griffin's going to be taking this long, I might be nearing that point.

No, he's seeing Micah at the hospital. That's what a good friend should be doing. We've got the rest of our lives to make memories together, so I shouldn't be harping on about not seeing him after only an hour.

I get up from the very comfortable cushioned seat at the slot machine with my ticket for a whopping fifty cents when I almost ram right into the man that just occupied my thoughts.

"Griffin!" I squeal.

"Hey, babe," he grins at me. "Going somewhere?"

"I was just about to head up to my room." Because I spent my slush fund already, very quickly.

"Good," he beams. He bends down and gives me a quick peck.

"How's Micah?"

"He's good. Well, as good as you can be being holed up in a hospital room. He's....accepted that shit happens, and he's made the decision to retire. Tonight was it."

"Oh my god." With all these thoughts of giving up and everyone who's told me that I shouldn't, there's Micah, who just did it. Micah's a quiet guy; he didn't talk much the one time I met him at Griffin's games night, compared to Griffin and Ross. He's played in his fair share of All-Star games, and people always talk about how good of a player he is. If he didn't get injured, then he probably would still play until Griffin or Ross retires. It blows me away that they've been playing for the past ten seasons together. Dedicating yourself to one team for that long is wild. I'd be amazed if LGU had me for ten years. But there might be bigger things on the horizon, and I just haven't found it yet.

"How do you feel about that?" I ask Griffin.

"I'm not enthused that Micah's deciding to retire. I wanted the three of us to retire together. There's an emptiness without him on the ice after playing with him for so long."

"When do you think you'll retire?" I ask Griffin. "I know that's a heavy question." I'm not asking it to try and push him to retire. But I wonder if Griffin has a point where he'll be ready to not play hockey anymore.

"It's funny," he laughs, taking my hand to guide me to a chaise near the elevators. "I was upset at Micah for seeming like a quitter. I could argue with him that if he did enough physical therapy, he'll make a full recovery and play almost as good as he used to. But he doesn't think he can. He'd rather stop playing hockey than come back and do worse. Or get injured again.

But I thought more about it and...I don't know how much time I have left in me. I love hockey. It's my favorite thing in the world." He looks at me, takes a strand of hair covering my face, and pushes it behind my ear to look me straight in the eyes. "But eventually, I'm going to want to think about my future with you."

I bark out a laugh. Wow, this skyrocketed to a level I was not expecting. The most I thought we were going to do was have sex and watch AdultSwim naked until we fell asleep.

"Wait, this isn't a proposal, right?"

"What?" Griffin's eyes go wide. "No. No, I mean, we're in Vegas, so it's not the most far-fetched thing to happen, but I'm somewhat of a romantic. I have big plans for when I propose to you."

I rest my head on his shoulder. The thought of us and this proposed future together makes me feel all giddy inside. I never thought that I'd be so in love with someone, where I'd be thinking about marriage and the future we'll build together.

"Oh yeah?" I peer up at him and raise a brow. "Care to share?"

He tsks, and suddenly, his big arms envelop me from the side, pulling me in so my head rests against his hard chest. The place where I feel safe. The place where I want to be when I wake up in the morning and when I go to sleep at night.

"I can't ruin any surprises," he tells me. "Just know that adventure is out there, Lydia. And I can't wait to embark on the journey with you."

We sit for a beat, still in each other's arms. A fan comes up to Griffin and asks for an autograph. Although Griffin hesitates at first, he softens and gets up to sign a cocktail napkin the guy runs to the bar to grab. Griffin even goes so far as to ask if he would like to take a selfie. The fan's face lights up as he frantically tries to take out his phone from his pocket. His hand shakes when he tries to get a photo of them together, so that's when I muster up some courage to jump in and ask if they would like me to take the photo. The fan excitedly nods and hands me his phone.

"Thank you. Lydia, right?"

I blush. Slightly creepy? Maybe. Am I thinking to myself that it's sweet that a fan recognizes me because I'm on some euphoric high right now? Yes.

I take the photo and hand him back his phone. He thanks us for taking the time to stop and snap a photo with him—we soon find out his name is Everett and he flew from San Jose to watch the game, also wishing for a better outcome, but he's excited to indulge in some crab legs tomorrow to make himself feel better—and goes on his merry way.

Griffin stares down at me once we're alone again. He bends down and whispers into my ear. "Why do you still have your clothes on?"

"Hey!" I point at his chest. "I'm not the one who stopped to take a photo with a fan. I'm proud of you, though. You didn't seem overwhelmed by that at all."

"It's amazing what airing out your anxieties in therapy can do. And realizing you're so in love with someone that it squashes those anxieties. Now," he takes my legs and hoists me up in one fell swoop. I let out a cackling yelp as I grip him like a tree trunk. "About this clothes problem we have..."

Griffin carries me to the elevator, and when the doors close, he sets me down and pins me to the back wall. I jump a little, and go to crane my head over Griffin's body to make sure the door doesn't open, and someone walks in on our rather hot moment.

"Don't worry, I'm listening," he whispers with his hot breath on my neck. He's planting small kisses down from my neck to my breast after each word is muttered.

"Okay." I tilt my head back and let out a loud moan when his hands hurry to push my bra up, and his mouth latches onto my nipple.

"Oh, Griffin," I breathe.

"God," he says, gritting his teeth together. "The way you say my name like that makes me absolutely feral, Lydia. Are we there yet? I want to rip your pants off and eat you out right now."

Shit, with the way he's spilling his feelings like it is, I want him to also. Thankfully, Vegas hotel elevators move quickly to expedite getting guests to high floor levels, and before I spontaneously combust a la orgasm in the elevator, the soothing, sensual voice calling out Griffin's floor number rings out.

"Finally," he whispers and grabs me by the legs to hoist me over his shoulder. I playfully squirm a little at how the feeling makes me feel so light and airy. He takes long strides down the quiet hallway and, while still keeping his arm around my ass, fishes out his keycard from his wallet and taps it on the door.

Griffin's room is on the 68th floor of the Blossom, which is also its top floor. Most of the floor is taken up by a penthouse suite that's about the size of my childhood home, but his room has a beautiful view overlooking the Strip, across from the Bellagio fountains.

The door closes, and he throws me gently onto the King-sized bed. I don't have to do any of the work to take my clothes off. Griffin's doing it all for me. He's unbuttoning my jeans, he's propping me up to take my shirt off, he's unclasping my bra with quick work of his hands.

He's doing everything to take care of me, sprinkling kisses in between each garment leaving my body.

"I've missed you," he tells me, and I see his eyes go glassy. "I've missed you so much. You're it for me. You and all your beautiful curves." He takes a hand and strokes it down my body, from my neck and over my breast, down to trace the curve of my ass and over my thigh.

"I never want to be in a place where I'm so low that I let go of the one person who brings out the best in me. I want to grow old with you, Lydia."

When a tear falls onto my naked body, I start feeling those emotions too. Our relationship feels like it's straight out of a fairytale. I mean, statistically, what are the chances you'll find your soulmate in a video game? It seems more unlikely than swiping right on a dating app. It took a lot of tears and heartache, but I always hoped we'd find our way back to one another. I just had to keep telling myself to not give up.

"I want to grow old with you too." I want future us to be in our reclining chairs, holding hands and watching game shows. "Are you sure you don't want to just get married while we're here? Even the Taco Bell has a chapel!"

His eyes perk up, and he flashes a smirk. "Well, how can you say no to a Taco Bell wedding?" He kisses me tenderly. "Right now, though, I want to take you on a little ride."

He pushes one of my legs up and holds it before he bends over and buries his head down there, taking one, two licks over my folds before he's sucking on my clit.

I take a deep breath in and let it out through my mouth. The only thing I can utter is a satisfying "fuuuck."

"Good?" Griffin whispers as he comes up for air.

The absolute best. There's little that can top it. Being treated like a queen on the brink of coming.

"Amazing. Stellar. Impossible to beat."

He caresses my cheek and lightly pinches at the end. "I haven't even finished yet. I'm still trying to end up inside you."

I lean into his touch. I think Griffin underestimates how much I've longed for this. Come to think of it, maybe he does understand. Because I don't know if I've ever seen Griffin Markey cry. Not when we broke up or at any point we were together. But he shed a tear tonight when looking at me unclothed and thinking about us and our forever.

"Well, then. Carry on."

"You still on birth control?" he asks.

"Yeah," I nod.

"Is it okay if I'm bare?"

"Yeah."

He kisses me on the forehead and slides his briefs down his legs, tossing them behind him. He crawls up over me slowly, tenderly, and in an instant, he's pushed his way into me. His dick fills me up, and my eyes widen when he slowly thrusts in and out.

In.

Out.

In.

"Damn, Lydia." Griffin's chest rapidly rises and falls. "I'm so obsessed with you."

"Yeah?" I whisper. Seems like that's the only word in my vernacular when my mind is fixated on Griffin and his magical dick.

"Yeah, baby." He kisses me tenderly. But I don't let him leave. I bite his bottom lip, and he moans. He thrusts with more force now, and I'm losing my breath, moaning into Griffin's mouth, kissing, tilting my neck back until Griffin enters into me one last time, and he lets a breath out.

He pants over my shoulder, and I wrap my arms around him.

"That was..." great? Better than great. It was like I was cata-pulted into the sky. Like when you feel yourself lift out of your seat when you're coming down on a rollercoaster.

"That sent me to space," I say, giving him a quick peck.

"Too bad we have to come back down," he says.

We go over to the bathroom to clean up, and he moves to turn the shower on.

"Need to rinse off?" he asks.

"I could use a good shower."

He opens the curtain and beckons for me to enter, before he steps in and closes the curtain behind him. I feel the hot water beating on my back and start to wet my hair.

"Here," he says, reaching for the shampoo. "Can I wash your hair?"

I purse my lips. Talk about getting the royal treatment. I grin and turn around so my back is up against Griffin's naked body.

He starts to massage the shampoo into my scalp, and I exhale, leaning my head into his chest so he can cover the rest of my head.

"This is nice," I tell him. "Thanks."

"Anything for my Liddy. And this just gives me an excuse to spend more time with you."

As we continue, taking turns washing each other's hair, scrubbing soap on each other's bodies, Griffin noting to "make sure I get his dick squeaky clean," we end the night back in bed, unclothed. We watch adult cartoons until I feel my eyelids get heavy, and I start to fall asleep on Griffin's chest. He kisses my head and whispers, "I love you so much."

"I love you, too. So much," I mumble, nuzzling my cheek into his body like he's the most comfortable pillow. It's the best way to end our night and to begin our rekindled forever.

Lydia

I'VE LOST COUNT OF how many times I've hit the snooze button on my alarm this morning.

Once, when my first alarm went off at six thirty because I told myself I'd be quick in getting ready for another day of tournaments and networking.

Then again, at six forty-five because Griffin pulls me in, wrapping his arms around my bare chest, and I want to linger for just a moment longer. His morning wood pushes into my lower back, and I feel myself go sopping wet. He knows damn well what he's doing, and I'm trying to remind myself that if I don't get out of bed now, I'm going to be late.

"Do you have to leave?" He whines, still groggy from our late night. "The kids are adults. They can handle themselves."

"They've almost made it to the finals," I laugh. "I want to watch them."

"Okay, fine," he murmurs into my hair. "Can I come?"

I roll my body over so our noses are almost touching. "You want to come?"

"Did you not remember what I said last night?" Griffin gives me a quick kiss. "I don't want to leave your side."

I raise a brow. "Even when I'm going to the bathroom?"

"Okay, I guess there are some times I'll let you fly solo. But today's a travel day, and I can see if I can change my flight to come back with you. When do you fly back home?"

"Tomorrow morning." Just in time for the kids to hunker down and wrap up their classes before finals.

"Okay, that should work perfectly then. I have to be back for practice by tomorrow afternoon, and then I get to spend two weeks in a row playing at home until I'm on the road again."

"Yay," I beam. "Well, if you can get into the tournament, then you're more than welcome to join me. It's fun; a bunch of computers are set up and they have multiple screens up to show the different games going on. Today starts the second round, and if the kids keep winning, we might get to see them in the championship game."

"That's exciting," Griffin says, grinning. "What time do you need to be there?"

I grab my phone from where I left it next to my pillow. Shit, how is it already seven? I swear, time feels like it's going at double speed when Griffin and I are intertwined like a pretzel and peppering kisses every waking minute.

"In an hour. And it's going to take me at least half an hour to walk there."

"I'll order a car for us," he says. He pulls away from me and gestures for me to go get my ass out of bed and to the bathroom. "Go get ready."

When my legs feel too heavy to move from the plush bed, Griffin gets his naked body up, erection still ramrod straight and pulls the curtains back. The sun's bright rays spill into the room, and I blink a few times to get my eyes adjusted to the light.

"God," I grab a pillow to shield my face. "The sun does not need to get in my face like that."

"It absolutely does." Griffin chuckles and grabs me by my hands. Of course, it only takes him a slight tug, and I'm up and at it because my strength is no match for Griffin's. After I sit up, he reaches over to carry me from my waist, and I cling to him like a koala. He sets me down at the entrance of the bathroom and gives me a kiss.

"Go get ready," he reiterates. "I don't want to be late."

"Okay, okay," I roll my eyes. "Bossy, are we?"

"To be honest, I'd much rather have you boss me around." He winks and then gives me a nudge to step into the bathroom.

"Wait," I realize when I look over at the sink, and all I see are Griffin's toiletries, that I didn't sleep in my room last night. "All my things are in my room."

"Oh yeah. I'll go get those for you. Here," he runs out and returns with a Stingrays T-shirt that fits him perfectly but goes down to my thighs. "Do you have your key?"

"Yeah," I go grab my purse that has the keycard sleeve and hand it to Griffin. "My room number's on there. 5412."

"Awesome. Is it okay to grab all your stuff and bring it up here?"

I nod. Griffin tells me that he'll try to be as quick as possible before making his way down to my room. Knowing that there is a high chance that I'm not going to make it in time for any opening remarks or the first few minutes of gameplay, I reach over to text the kids.

> Lydia: Running a little late. Not sure if you guys are in the lobby but if you are, head over to the convention center. I'll be there soon!

We make it to the event right on time, and it only took me running for the first time since I was forced to in high school. Damn, I should've brought pocket deodorant because now my armpits are sweaty, and I'm worried I'm radiating a "wet dog smell."

"Can you sniff me and see if I smell okay?" I ask Griffin.

He shakes his head and laughs. He leans in close to my armpits and takes in a big whiff. "You smell just fine to me."

"Are you sure that I don't reek of sweat?"

He barks out a hearty laugh. "Babe, if you don't smell like me after a game, then you don't reek of sweat."

Of course. I forgot hockey players sweat a lot because of the layers of uniform that they have to wear. I'm already making a mental note to buy noseplugs to ensure I do not need to take a whiff of Griffin's uniform when it comes to doing the laundry.

"Touché," I note. "Sorry, I don't really run all that often."

He pulls me in for a side hug. "It's okay. You're shaking a little bit. Are you cold?"

"No. I think just being here knowing what's on the line is making me a little nervous."

"They're gonna take home the gold." There's no hesitation in Griffin's tone. "I can feel it."

We meet up with the kids, who cheer and whoop when they see us approaching them, holding hands. Dev tries to nudge Griffin and say, "What's up, Daddy?" but before he can get the parental nickname out, Landon does his own elbow to Dev's side, and he lets out a pained whimper.

"Fuck, Lando. You've got some bony elbows."

"I'll take that as a compliment," Landon says, flashing him a wink.

"How's everyone feeling?" I ask. "We made it to the second round!" I say it with so much forced enthusiasm to mask my own nerves that we could lose it all in a matter of minutes.

"Alright," Blake shrugs. "We're playing St. Peter's next, and they're like, second in the nation."

"I'm starting to believe that we might not be cut out for this," Dev chimes in.

"Hey." I turn my head to see that Griffin's the one trying to get everyone's attention. "You guys beat out a bunch of schools to make it this far. Don't start thinking you can't do it now. I don't go into every game I play thinking that I'm going to lose. I always give it my all, no matter what the outcome is. If we lose, then so be it. But my eyes are always on the prize. And so should yours."

Griffin leads the team in a huddle and tells them to put all their hands in the center.

"Los Gatos on three. One, two, three!"

Everyone starts to scream at the top of their lungs. "Los Gatos!"

"Thanks, Coach," I nudge him when the kids start to make their way to their assigned play area.

"Anytime. Hey, when I retire, maybe I can take up being an esports coach. With enough practice, I think I'll be pretty good."

I wrap my arms around his torso and give him a squeeze. "I think you can be good at just about anything."

"I can't look!" I bury my face into Griffin's chest as the crowd is speaking all at once. The kids are playing on the main stage in the final round, and I'm all nerves, zero chill.

Griffin rubs my back and keeps me tucked in close. "You're fine. They're winning."

"That can change at any moment!" I whine. Admittedly, the kids have been doing exceptionally well. They've won the last three games, and one was a huge upset because it was with a top-ranked school. I don't want to believe that our luck only lasts for three games, but when a collective gasp roars from the audience and Griffin pulls me in tighter, whispering that the other team just scored and now we're only up by one, I feel the sudden urge to get up from my seat and run laps around this hotel to ease my anxiety.

"They'll be fine, Lids." Griffin plants a kiss on my head. "They've got two minutes left."

"Just tell me when it's over, okay?"

The announcer's voice booms through the arena. "And just like that, Los Gatos has found themselves on Santa Maria's side, and NightHawk24, aka Blake Forrester, has racked up another kill! Los Gatos leads by two, and with only thirty seconds left, can Santa Maria do it?"

I tilt my head to peek at the screen, and as the seconds tick down from thirty to twenty to ten, the crowd starts counting down like it's New Year's Eve.

Five. Four. Three. Two. One.

"They've done it! Your CEA Champions are first-year esports team, Los Gatos University!"

Spectators are out of their seats, jumping and screaming over how we, a small school from a small town in the South Bay, did it. We freaking won this huge tournament, and I don't know how else to react but cry. Happy tears, obviously.

Griffin hoists me off the ground and twirls me in our small row.

"They did it!" I squeal. "They actually did it."

"Congrats, Miss Director." Griffin presses his lips to mine, and I don't care if people can see. When he pulls back, I rope him back in for another one. "You did it."

"I can't believe it. I never thought this would happen in our first year."

"They didn't give up. They gave it their all every game, and they did it."

I nod. "I'm so proud of them."

"We'll do it again next year, right?" Griffin asks.

And in that moment, I realize that there was a point in time where I thought of giving up, of leaving my team and my passion. But the rush of joy I feel right now, at seeing our school be crowned winners, over myself being chosen as Director of the Year, and at being held by the love of my life...I'm not taking a path where I have to say goodbye to any of it.

I smile into his neck. "You bet we will."

30
Epilogue

Griffin

SOMETIME IN JUNE

"That's a big cup," I murmur.

Ross sharply turns his head at me. "You did what in your cup?"

I roll my eyes. "Very funny, Mater. I see what you're trying to do."

He holds up both his hands. "I have no idea what you're talking about."

The cup we're looking at, obviously, is the Stanley Cup. We won it. It took a while. Seven back-breaking games and moments where I felt like I didn't know if it'd be possible. I let someone pass me and they ended up scoring the winning goal. I let my pride get the best of me and didn't pass it to my teammate and ended up missing a goal.

But, we pulled through. We fucking did it.

I wish we were in San Jose to do so, but instead, we're at Madison Square Garden. And even though there aren't as many Stingrays fans as there are Rangers fans, we're still ogling the cup in awe that we fucking did it.

We celebrate in the locker room, popping bottles of bubbly, each of us taking turns taking photos with the cup. After the season we had, we deserved it. We lost a few players to trades and Micah to injury and, eventually, retirement. He's been on the bench every day since being discharged from the hospital, cheering us on even if he won't be on the ice in a jersey ever again. I can tell he's still taking his time, processing his new reality. Today may be the first time I've seen a cheek-to-cheek grin across his face when the buzzer went off, and we celebrated winning the Stanley Cup.

I walk over to him, standing in the corner of the room, away from the splashes of champagne and cheering from some of the other players.

"We did it," I nudge him in the arm.

"We did. Well, you guys did. I was just cheering you all on from the sidelines."

I give him a gentle shove. "Hey, you're a part of this team just as much as I am, which means you did it. Doesn't matter if you didn't get to play in the game."

"I know," he sighs, taking another swig of bubbly. "I'm always in this loop of thinking that I'll always have a lot in me to keep going. How old is the oldest NHL player? Has he reached forty yet? Before we know it, we're going to be there too."

Besides the rush of winning, I've been thinking a lot about my future. I didn't think I'd ever see a Stanley Cup with my team etched in as a winner. And now that it's happened, what's next? Sure, we'll try to do it all over again, but after next year, I think I'm ready to hang up the jersey. And if Ross wants to join me, he's welcome to. But tonight, I have big plans in the journey to crafting my perfect future, and it's going to begin right after this.

We gather our things and go greet our families, who have stuck around to celebrate with us. After school finished for the year, I asked Lydia if she wanted to meet my parents. She was nervous at first because when Lydia and I first met, I didn't necessarily paint them in a positive light, but that changed after telling her about the moment when I poured out my feelings about her, about them, and we finally had the chance to sit and talk. Besides, something tells me she might be seeing more of my family in the future, anyway.

We step out of the locker room and head up to a suite that they've set aside for us to continue the festivities. I find my cluster of family and immediately, my mom rushes to envelop her arms around me.

"Good job, Griffin," she says in a weepy voice. "I'm so proud of you."

"Thank you, Mom." Her pride made a huge impact on me, especially on the idea that I betrayed my family by moving across the country. I can see now that I made the right decision.

My dad follows suit, then my brothers and their partners, and finally, her.

She beams as she looks up at me, and I swiftly pick her up and twirl her around.

"I'm so proud of you," she whispers in my neck. "You were amazing."

"Thanks, babe." I slam my lips into hers and we quickly brush tongues. The rest, I'll save for later tonight when we don't have an audience.

Everyone splits off to their own celebrations. Ross asks if Lydia and I want to go to some club with him, and as tempting as that sounds, I decline. Right now, the only thing that I want to do is spend time alone with my girl. Ross knows what my plan for tonight is, anyway.

"Well, text me after it's done. I'm sure we'll still be up and at 'em. Then there's more that we can celebrate."

"Sounds like a plan."

I shoot a quick text off to the group chat I created with my family and tell them we're a go to meet at the next destination. I make a mental note to myself that I never want to be in a position like this again. Devoting a majority of my time to trying to win the Stanley Cup while also planning a proposal? Too many emotions are flooding my mind. But I don't think there'd be a better time to ask Lydia to marry me. We've only been officially together for a few months, but my head and my heart are telling me that I need to do it. It was going to happen some-time anyway. Hell, I would've been perfectly fine to elope in

Las Vegas that night we got back together. But something in my mind told me that we should be surrounded by people we love when it happens. And with my parents here and Landon and Lydia's parents landing today, everything is falling into place. Honestly, winning the Cup was merely icing on the cake.

I wait with Lydia as we say goodbye to my parents and keep her thinking that they are on their way back home since it's a bit of a drive to New Jersey. When the car I book drives up, I tell Lydia we're heading back to the hotel so we can change. Thankfully, Lydia hasn't been around Manhattan enough to know that our car isn't going in the direction of the hotel at all.

He drops us off at the entrance of 30 Rockefeller Center. I prefer their observatory to the Empire State Building's. I get out of the car and rush over to open the door for Lydia. When she steps out, she peers her head up to the skyscraper and looks puzzled.

"This isn't our hotel," she notes.

"You're right." I take her hand and lead her to the doors. "I thought we'd check out the view first before going back."

A worker greets us and takes us to the elevator that shoots right up to the observation deck. Before the doors open, I grab a hold of Lydia's hand and our fingers interlace. We turn a corner and when Lydia sees the carpeted path, lit by small candles floating in the water, she stops in her place and gasps.

"Griffin," she utters with tears already streaming down her face.

I chuckle and grab onto her hand again. "Come on."

I walk her down the carpet to a beautiful floral archway that I had someone come in to make once the observation deck closed. If you have the money, you can wiggle your way into shutting down the deck for sole access. And I may have bartered with a potential guest appearance on one of NBC's shows to sweeten the deal.

We reach the end and I turn to face Lydia, taking in a deep breath before I potentially fumble one of the most important questions I'm ever going to ask her.

"Lydia," I begin. "I still can't believe that we met playing a video game online. When I talked to you for the first time through my headset, I didn't know if I'd ever meet the woman whose voice and personality had such an effect on me from the start. I know that I'm not perfect. In fact, I'm kind of broken. But you are the best thing that has ever happened to me. You've taught me so much, and I am so inspired by you and your strength. And," this is where the tears begin to flow from my eyes as well, "I want to spend the rest of our lives together. I've never been so sure of anything in my entire life."

I bend down to one knee and pull out a ring box to show her, what I found out, was the ring of her dreams. A simple rose gold band with a large solitaire diamond in the middle.

"Lydia Goh, will you marry me?"

Her trembling nod and shaky "yes" are all the indications I need. I use my shaky hands to place the ring on her finger. I pull her in and plant my lips on hers, moving to kiss her tears away, exploring her mouth.

I press my forehead to hers. "I love you."

"I love you too, Griffin Markey." She wipes her tears off her face. "I can't wait to love you for the rest of my life."

"Me too, babe, me too."

We'd finally met our match. Now comes the rest of the adventure.

Many Thanks

Writing these are always one of the most fun parts of being an author, because I just get to spill out all of my feelings at the end of the book if you decide to read these or not.

First and foremost, I'd like to thank everyone who had a hand in putting the concept of Match Game in my mind, whether you know it or not. To Connor, my first and favorite gaming partner. I still remember the day Mom and Dad bought us our first console, the Wii, and we bought so many games to wear that little console down until it didn't work anymore. It's been fun watching you grow up and become the hard-working, determined, and INQUISTIVE (iykyk) person you are, and I'm so proud of you, little brother.

To Mario, my forever roomie and partner in life, I'll always be your player 2 (whether you want me to be or not.) Thanks for somehow getting me interested in Magic the Gathering and D&D even though we have too many Magic cards in our house. Even though we now share a home and two wonderful cats together, I still keep the fond memories of us playing co-op

Stardew and Animal Crossing while we were long distance in my mind and heart.

To Tim, Max, and Lizzie, aka the Furtnurt crew, playing hours of that game with you during the pandemmy was some of the best nights of my life. (& to Tim, thanks for always being there for me whether you're five miles away or thousands.)

To Carlos, whose love of sports and games inspired me to get back into hockey. Here's to the Sharks making it to the playoffs again one day. And to the San Jose Sharks, we'll always be rooting for you.

To Kels (@myblogisgreat) thank you for creating such a beautiful cover for Match Game. Whenever your work appears on my feed, I always get so excited. You're so talented and I'm so happy with how the cover came out for this.

To Sarah, Laura, and Cassidy: thank you for all the work you did into polishing Match Game to it's glory. To all my author friends and the indie author community, thank you for all your support in sharing my work. We're a mighty bunch. To Shaye and Lindsey at Good Girls PR, thank you for all the work you've done getting Match Game in the hands of readers. It's been amazing to work with you and to have so many people hear and love Match Game as I've been working on it. To Adriana Herrera, who may or may not read this book (I'd cry if she somehow found this book in her hands, or any of my books for that matter.) but inspired me to finally write a hockey romance. It was what she said at Steamy Lit Con in 2023 that stuck with me so much that I needed to do something about it. Yes, we do need more diverse hockey romances. And I hope that mine will make someone out there excited to read about a Mixed-Asian player in hockey. We're a small percentage, but we're mighty. Here's to more sport romances in the future with Asian leads, and hopefully, more Asians making their way onto the sports scene.

To everyone who's been here and shouted out my work this year, thank you again. 2024 was a huge year for me with the release of my debut novel, and I am so floored by the response I've been receiving for all the work I've done. It has been a rollercoaster to say the least, and some days I find myself in a rut, but you all get me going. Here's to putting out more books and trying new things every day.

Coming Soon from Brittany Arreguin

Sin City Player – a mafia romance by Bri Wong coming December 2024

Fielded Dreams – a baseball brother's best friend story coming soon

Get Lucky – The Vegas Series #2/Kayley's Story (2025)

Resleeved – San Jose Stingrays #2/Micah's Story (2025)

About the Author

Brittany Arreguin is a Mixed-Asian romance author based in the San Francisco Bay Area. She is a Full-Time Events Coordinator and loves to read and write romance novels in her spare time. She lives with her husband and cats, Princess Peach & Boo. Her debut novel, Waking Up in Vegas, released in January 2024.

instagram.com/brittanyarreguinwrites

amazon.com/author/brittanyarreguin

www.ingramcontent.com/pod-product-compliance
Lightning Source LLC
Chambersburg PA
CBHW051131130726

47988CB00005B/1790